Courting Murder

Courting Murder

by
Bill Hopkins

Southeast Missouri State University Press • 2012

Courting Murder
by Bill Hopkins

Softcover: $15.00
ISBN: 978-0-9830504-38

First published in 2012 by Southeast Missouri State University Press
One University Plaza, MS 2650
Cape Girardeau, MO 63701
http://www6.semo.edu/universitypress

Cover art: Photograph, "Kentucky Floods 2010," courtesy of National
Resources Conservation Service—Kentucky, May 2010

Cover design: Liz Lester Design

Disclaimer: *Courting Murder* is a work of fiction. The characters, events,
and dialogue herein are fictional and are not intended to represent, re-
fer to, or disparage any known person or entity, living or dead. Certain
physical characteristics and other descriptive details in this book may
have been embellished for the sake of storytelling.

Acknowledgements

My first readers Sara leNeve McDaniel Snipes (RIP), Candy Harvey, Jill Mabli, and Ruthie Deck Burkman; Guppies (Sisters in Crime group); fellow writers who patiently gave me incredible amounts of their time (especially Hank Phillippi Ryan, Alan Orloff, Leslie Budewitz, Serena Stier, Grace Topping, Jess Lourey, Deborah Sharp, and Allan E. Ansorge); Charles and Marian Hutchings; Lois Jackson of the USDA for permission to use the cover photograph, Patricia B. Smith (editor extraordinaire), Susan Swartwout, and the thousands of people who've told me stories since I was a child.

None of this would've been possible without my wife, Sharon Woods Hopkins, who is my toughest editor, most honest critic, and who's one super-excellent writer.

Chapter One
Monday morning

Grumpy was too happy a word to describe how Rosswell Carew felt. Despite the early hour, summer heat was already leaching into his pores. He missed his booze. All he wanted was some quiet time alone to feel sorry for himself for being so damned sober, but now he had to pretend to be nice to the nosy, dimwitted park ranger blocking the entrance to his refuge of choice, Foggy Top State Park.

"Hey, Judge Carew."

Rosswell stopped and eased out of his Volkswagen. He'd parked next to the rock gazebo that served as the guard hut to chat with the ranger. Rosswell's mother bought the car brand-new, right after he was born, and named it Vicky, after her college roommate. He didn't quite know why he still drove the old car; it just felt comfortable and familiar.

Next to the park's entrance, a farmer harvested a first cutting of hay. The tractor's chugging and the smell of the freshly cut timothy grass created a bucolic scene. Norman Rockwell could have painted what Rosswell beheld.

What a glorious morning it would be if only I didn't have to talk to this guy.

The ranger scratched his mustache, as scrawny as Rosswell's. "You're up with the chickens." The round-faced man, stuffed into a tan and green uniform, pointed to the early morning sun. In spite of the heat and humidity, the air hugging the ground lay clear, not hazy. Yet things at a distance appeared wavy, as if stuck in a mirage.

Pushing his trifocal glasses up onto his sweaty nose, Rosswell shoved his brain into gear. He couldn't remember the ranger's name, although he'd met and talked with him before. The ranger was related to someone Rosswell knew, but he couldn't remember who it was. The judge's memory was slipping.

"If the sun's shining, then it's time to get up," Rosswell said. "I don't waste daylight. I've got deadlines for the things I want to do."

Earlier in the year, a diagnosis of leukemia had finally convinced Rosswell to cherish his time. The possible death sentence transformed hours into precious coins he planned to spend wisely. If he was going to die, the last part of his life would be the best part. Although he didn't advertise it, he felt the chemo treatments had affected his brain and sometimes left him weak. Needless to say, his brain was essential, like the hands of an artisan. A judge's brain could turn to evil or good, the same as a technician's hands could commit sin or virtue. Rosswell had pledged himself to do good. Among other things, there was little chance he'd spend his last days in jail.

Although Rosswell had nothing resembling a picnic basket in his car, the ranger asked, "Are you having a breakfast picnic?"

If only his Ranger Rick uniform had a nametag. Wait. I've got it. Harry. That was the guy's name. Rosswell had remembered it. Sometimes he forgot names, but when a name came back to him, he was always right.

"Harry, I had breakfast at four o'clock this morning." The ranger's last name surfaced in Rosswell's brain: Hillyard. Harry Hillyard. He'd captured the name from all those brain waves scrabbling around inside his head.

"Hermie, Judge. My name's Hermie Hillsman."

"Sorry." *Damn. My perfect record of recalling names ruined in an instant.*

"No big deal. You meet a lot of people." Hermie picked up a clipboard. "It's hard to remember everyone's name."

"Thanks for understanding," Rosswell said. "I appreciate it, Hermie."

Hermie scanned the papers on his clipboard, making Rosswell wonder if his name was on some terrorist watch list. He looked up at the judge. "You don't have court this morning?"

Rosswell decided Hermie was probably an undercover agent for a citizens' watchdog group, whose goal was making sure that judges didn't goof off.

"I'm starting my two-week vacation today."

"I see."

Among other things, it was Hermie's job to track the visitors to the park. Rosswell had heard that the ranger sometimes nursed a bottle more than he watched the traffic. Rosswell noted burst blood vessels tracking across Hermie's lined face, confirming his love of America's favorite addiction. Rosswell couldn't fault him for being a boozehound. Pot calling the kettle black and all that.

Hermie's Smokey Bear hat perched askew on his head, and he'd tied his green tie in a lumpy version of a Windsor knot. Rosswell thought that if Hermie opened his bloodshot eyes any wider, he'd bleed to death. The Coke bottle he clutched was covered with Spanish writing. Rosswell recognized the real Coca-Cola, probably bought in the Hispanic food section at Walmart. The Mexican version of the popular soft drink was made with sugar, not corn syrup. Hermie obviously craved a real sugar and caffeine high. A faint odor of alcohol floated from his wide mouth. Maybe the soda was spiked. Rum goes better with sugared Coke.

Hermie asked, "What brings you here this early?"

"Mushrooms."

Rosswell expected Hermie to accuse him of being a hippie searching for hallucinogens.

"Mushrooms?" Hermie repeated, his distaste for them evidenced by his scowl. "What kind of mushrooms?"

"Non-poisonous."

"Yes, of course," Hermie said, although Rosswell knew he meant, "I don't know what you're talking about."

Rosswell pulled a Missouri Department of Conservation handbook from his back pocket. "I'm fully prepared. I know what I'm searching for." He waved *Safe Mushroom Hunting* in front of Hermie's face. The ranger swayed a bit, trying to follow the book, as Rosswell made sure Hermie could see the cover. The publication illustrated every mushroom growing in the state.

Hermie said, "You could poison yourself."

"I'm not going to eat them."

Jawing with a minor bureaucrat at the gate of a state park didn't improve Rosswell's mood. This was taking far too long. Being friendly was one thing. Being nosy was another.

Another puzzled look from Hermie. Then, "Oh, right. You know it's illegal to pick them in a state park. You wouldn't break the law now, would you? Being a judge and all." Hermie moved his hat around, as if screwing it onto his head. "Why are you hunting them?"

"Let me explain. You're absolutely right, Hermie, but I'm not going to pick them. I'm going to take photos of them." Rosswell flourished his Nikon. "I've studied all kinds of plants and animals. You do that before you take pictures of them."

"You have to study to take pictures?"

"Right," Rosswell said. "If you want something done right, then you must draw up a plan before you attack."

"My wife's a good photographer. She's teaching our boy to take pictures. He's twelve next week."

"That's great," Rosswell said. "The world needs good photographers to record all its beauty." Since he believed his own words, he spoke them with sincerity.

"Uh, yeah," Hermie said. "Don't do nothing illegal."

"I'm pretty sure it's legal to snap the little critters. That's what I'm here for."

"Critters? Mushrooms ain't critters."

"You're right again, Hermie. I was using the word 'critter' as a generic term for the concept of 'thing'."

"Yeah. I see." Hermie, who clearly did not see, chewed on this before adjusting his hat again. "You're not going to take pictures of poisonous mushrooms?"

A rumble of thunder many miles to the west startled Rosswell. There was no ozone stink from a lightning bolt. The storm was not yet close enough.

"I agree," Rosswell said. "I shouldn't discriminate against poison mushrooms."

Hermie grinned. "Be careful up there. It rained nearly three inches last night and it could rain again this morning. The river's running bank full." He pointed to the gray clouds now heading toward them, growing darker by the moment. Hermie didn't miss a thing.

Brief yet intense thunderstorms often marched through this part of the country during the summer, dumping torrents of water in a short time. The supercell storms sometimes not only produced excessive amounts of water but often whipped up tornadoes. Rosswell could feel the barometric pressure dropping, a sure sign of a storm brewing. Something nasty crawled around inside his head, fixing to stomp his brain. Migraine headaches accompanied by auras were a couple of delightful things he often experienced before major storms.

Rosswell assured him, "If it rains, I won't drive through any standing water. I don't want to get swept downstream."

Hermie pointed again to the west where cumulonimbus clouds massed. "Don't drown." He straightened his tie. "Turn around."

"There's another saying."

"Another saying?"

He offered Hermie something else to chew on. "There are no old, bold mushroom hunters."

There was a peace symbol where the VW logo had once been on the tongue-shaped hood of the Super Beetle Cabriolet. Rosswell touched it for luck, hopped back in, and then drove his convertible, top down, into the park. With a hard right and a drive up a hill, he pulled into Picnic Area 3. He was alone at his favorite picnic site. Attendance at the park had plummeted the last few years. First, the park was located off a gravel road, which intersected with a rarely used and paved county road. Second, water parks, swimming pools, electronic games, cable television, cell phones, the Internet, McDonald's and whatever, had outranked sitting around in the open staring at trees, eating stale sandwiches, and drinking lukewarm sweet tea.

The picnic area roosted on a low and isolated hill. It was surrounded by thick woods and bisected by a small stream that ran into a river. Mimosa trees sprouted their spiky pink flowers around the clearing. Rosswell caressed and smelled one of the blooms. The hill beyond the picnic area tapered down into the river, which produced a soothing sound that only running water makes. Rosswell decided he'd take a nap by the river when he took a break from snapping pictures later on. The view afforded him a horizon to horizon panorama of valleys, ridges, creeks, and other hills. It was nowhere as spectacular as the Rocky Mountains or even the Smoky Mountains, but it was home and it was beautiful.

As Hermie had pointed out, there had been a tremendous thunderstorm last night with plenty of rain. The drenching had freshened up the place. Although it was early in the summer, the heat was already stifling and the humidity was rank. Perfect weather for mushrooms sprouting. The air smelled of vigorous growth. Rosswell was stalking the Chanterelle, a small golden mushroom that lived in the semi-darkness surrounding the park's stands of decades old white oak trees. He knew Chanterelles were most likely to grow around the bases of such trees.

When he ambled around a bend and approached a white oak festooned with mistletoe in its upper branches, his super-sensitive nose shifted into overdrive. The odor was familiar, but not pleasant. Definitely not sweet. It was the beginnings of the worst smell in the world, a smell he knew, thanks to Uncle Sam awarding him a free tour of the Middle East. A smell that clung to your clothes, hair, skin, and the insides of your mouth and nostrils long after you'd left its source. Stuff cottage cheese, lettuce, meat, and milk in a garbage can. Let the crud fester in a sunny room in a closed-up house during the hottest days of summer. After a week, pry off the lid and suck in a deep breath. That wouldn't even be close to what he now smelled. The assault on Rosswell's olfactory system blossomed into a nuclear bombardment. The migraine ballooned from a minor irritant to a full-blown head banger.

Rosswell gagged. If he'd brought Vicks VapoRub, it would've melted in the heat before he could swab his nostrils to block the odor. As much as it offended his sense of smell, he drew several deep breaths to keep from puking. When that seemed on the verge of failing, he breathed through his mouth.

Pushing himself towards the nauseating odor grew harder and harder. It commanded all his willpower to move forward. He really wanted to run like a hornet had stung his ass, but he pressed on. Something up ahead had mushroomed into a major stinkfest. All around him lay nothing but what seemed to be normal woodsy stuff, until he heard the buzzing of a million insects. Swiveling towards the sound, he watched a flurry of dark flying things rising and falling, great masses of bugs hovering over mounds of something. The swarm sang of death and decay.

He inched closer.

About thirty feet away, two bloated figures lay on the bank of the stream, now running full nearly to overflowing due to the previous night's rain. Perhaps it was a double drowning. No, people didn't drown and then crawl up on the bank. Maybe a murder-suicide. Or maybe garden variety natural deaths. No. He doubted that two people had died natural deaths while lying next to each other. There was only one explanation for what he saw. He was looking at two murdered humans.

He scanned the area again. No one else around.

Rosswell snatched up his cellphone. Two words: NO SERVICE.

He galloped back to his car and drove the convertible out of the site, stopping to pull a big log across the road. That should forestall any more accidental discoveries of the grisly scene. People don't move logs off roads. It involved manual labor.

Back at the front gate, Hermie said, "Done already, Judge? That was quick." The faint odor of alcohol had grown stronger.

Two bars popped up on Rosswell's phone. "Hermie, don't let anyone else into the park." Speed dial rushed the call. A slug or two of Jack Daniel's sounded good to Rosswell. He pondered for a millisecond about asking Hermie if he had any booze to spare and share. No, that would get the rumor mill pumping full steam. In addition, he'd been sober for five years, three weeks, and two days. Since he hadn't worn his watch, he wasn't sure of the number of hours. Rosswell checked the time on his phone. Add fourteen hours and thirty-seven minutes to the time of sobriety.

On the other end, the phone rang. No answer and no voicemail. It simply kept ringing.

"How come I can't let anyone in?" Hermie shined his badge with a shirt cuff. "The park's open and I have to let people in." He'd undoubtedly heard rumors about the judge who did and said strange things. Especially after Rosswell had a snootful. "I can't tell people they're barred from the park. The taxpayers expect their park to be open."

"That's a court order. No one comes in this park. And you stop and detain anyone who tries to leave. That's a court order, too."

"Court order? Stop and detain?"

"Something bad's happened."

Rosswell's call ended. He pressed redial.

Hermie's eyes brightened. Apparently, the thought that he might stop and detain someone under a court order from a judge put visions of a headline-worthy arrest in his brain. "Stop and detain. I got it. Stop and detain."

Rosswell could tell that Hermie liked the sound of the phrase. The ranger straightened his spine, jutted his chin and belly forward, pulled his shoulders back, and dropped his hands to his side. He saluted Rosswell, whose gut rumbled a warning that Hermie couldn't be trusted to guard a crime scene.

"Frizz," Rosswell said when he eventually got an answer, "I'm here with Hermie Hillsman at the front gate out at Foggy Top. There're two bodies in Picnic Area 3."

Hermie belched and stiffened even more, whipping his head left and right to inspect the area around him. The news sobered him. His frown made Rosswell glad the ranger didn't have a gun, else he may have shot an innocent picnicker on sight if the picnicker didn't want to be stopped and detained.

"*Bodies?*" Sheriff Charles "Frizz" Dodson yelled into the phone at his end of the conversation. "Rosswell, don't you touch a damned thing. I'll be right there."

Frizz seemed particularly cranky. He hung up before Rosswell could tell him goodbye. That was no way to talk to a judge. And what the hell did he think Rosswell would touch? His cellphone felt hot, as if Frizz's blast had heated up its innards.

Hermie said, "There are two bodies up there?"

"Correct."

"Are they fresh?"

Rosswell sniffed but at this distance couldn't smell anything nasty. "Not very."

"How long have they been dead?"

"Hermie," Rosswell said, ignoring his question, "do you have video surveillance here?" He waved his hand around, pointing to various locations in the gazebo.

"You mean like a movie camera?"

The heat made sweat pour down Rosswell's face and neck. "Yeah, like a movie camera." His patience evaporated as the sweat increased. The thickening clouds in the sky had no effect on the high temperature, but they made his head hurt. The migraine made Rosswell long for clear blue skies.

Hermie shined his badge with his shirtsleeve again while he surveyed the park for people. "The state barely has enough money to keep this place open, much less put up movie camera surveillance." After turning a complete circle, he said, "I'll keep my eyes peeled."

"When was the last time you saw anyone come in here?"

"Today?"

Rosswell's estimation of Hermie's intelligence lowered by the second.

"Hermie, any time. Today. Yesterday. Whenever."

"Must've been yesterday sometime. Or maybe the day before. No cars."

Hermie could've been passed out and missed a parade. The killer could've driven right past him and he'd have never noticed.

Hermie said, "I saw a couple of people in a canoe, paddling down Cloudy River."

He referred to the quarter-mile-wide river, now running high with last night's rain. Cloudy River lived up to its name during most of the year, running muddy and murky.

"Did you see anyone drive up to Picnic Area 3? Or any hikers? Did you see anybody on foot?"

"No, I didn't see anyone doing any of that." Hermie stopped, then tapped a finger on his forehead, evidently to demonstrate that he was thinking. "Wait a minute."

When he didn't continue, Rosswell scratched his mustache and said, "What is it?"

"A couple of weeks ago, there was a car up there. Maybe two cars. Some guy drove a car up and then drove a different car down. And then he drove the first car down. Or maybe it was a woman. Then there was that fraternity party from out at the university. One girl took her clothes off and all the boys cheered. Rough looking characters. The next day some Methodists had a church picnic up there. They sang a lot of hymns. Then there was a couple of guys who looked like homeless bums. About a week ago, teachers from the school brought some seventh graders out to look at caterpillars or snakes or something."

"Thanks," Rosswell said. A lot of good all that would do. Anybody coming up here that long ago couldn't have had anything to do with a recent murder. "One last thing. Can you smell the bodies?"

Hermie sniffed, like a beagle searching for a scent. "No. Sorry."

Maybe that meant the bodies weren't as ripe as Rosswell had first thought. Yet, with the heat, decomposition would've been rapid. The murders could've taken place yesterday or even earlier that morning.

Rosswell said, "Don't be sorry." Pinching his nose again didn't improve the smell in his nostrils. "You're not missing anything."

"Judge, I'll do my duty."

"This is a crime scene, Hermie. Do your best. I'm counting on you."

When Rosswell turned to leave, Hermie saluted him again.

Rosswell drove back to the death scene and left Vicky to go stand guard by the log. After several minutes, he grabbed his camera, forcing himself back to the grisly site, careful not to approach closer than thirty or so feet to the bodies.

The corpses, he noticed on closer examination, were laid neatly next to each other, but not touching. Race, white. Probably. He guessed one male, the other female, each probably under forty. Both were about the same size. The male was dressed in blue jeans and a long sleeved red shirt. Rosswell found the long sleeves odd, considering the heat. The female wore a yellow sundress and, if his eyes weren't deceiving him, red high heels. *Who the hell wears high heels and a dress to go out in the woods?* The male, on Rosswell's left, had both arms pointing down at 45 degree angles. The woman had her left arm pointing up at a 180 degree angle from her body, her right arm down at a 180 degree angle.

The scene was strange, so Rosswell inspected the bodies again.

There was something odd about their placement. It would come to him if he thought long enough. He didn't see it.

The longer he stood there, the worse the smell became. *Aren't you supposed to get used to a smell if you hang around sniffing it for a while?* Deep breaths were alleged to help, but the deeper he breathed, the more his mouth tasted like a full garbage can sitting in the sun on the shores of the Dead Sea.

If he'd known one or both of the victims in life, he couldn't recognize either of them now.

How had they died? With the bloating, he could tell little. Gazing at a bloated, dead human being was something he hadn't done since his time in the military. He hadn't missed doing it. Or much else about the military. Combat trauma made him view dead people in a skewed light.

Rosswell didn't venture any nearer to the corpses. Death he could stand. Listening to the sheriff bitch about him screwing up a crime scene he couldn't stand.

The scene worked a number on him. Acid reflux, his ever-present friend in times of stress, roared around his gut and seared his throat, joining his migraine for a happy dance on his whole body. Naturally, his allergies felt obliged to join in the assault on his health, inundating him with sneezing fits and burning eyes.

He returned to the barricade on the road and tugged the log off. This time when he moved it, he dislodged a mess of white wormy things. Termites. The formic acid stink of alarmed termites joined the other nasty odors. He saw something else besides wood and termites. A ring, a man's ring by its size and appearance, fell out of the log. He scooped it up, and examined the skull and crossbones emblazoned on its onyx face and the writing inscribed inside the band.

When he heard a cacophony of sirens, he dropped the ring in his pocket.

Chapter Two
Monday morning, continued

Rosswell leaned against his little convertible, still parked by the log, waiting for the squadron of Bollinger County's finest. Vicky's Monarch Orange Pearl paint job shone like a beacon for the cops to follow.

The heat, while unbearable, kept the wind down. Without a breeze blowing his way, he hoped he could manage the smell from the bodies, which grew stronger. Tree frogs, crickets, and some other critters screeched in rhythm. Unpleasant background noise to a ghastly tableau. Rosswell's keen hearing made the scene worse instead of better.

Sheriff Frizz Dodson arrived first, his spotless silver sedan sporting a shiny tag reading: Bollinger County SD #1. Rosswell jumped to the side to avoid Frizz's splatters when the car fishtailed and slopped through a mud puddle. The sheriff's sedan suffered glop slung all over the formerly shiny body. Rosswell remained untouched.

"Judge Carew, why were you up here in the first place?" Frizz yelled out the window before the car lurched to a stop, throwing more goop everywhere. Rosswell wondered why the hell Frizz couldn't stay on the dry parts of the road instead of aiming for every mud hole. Frizz hopped out. When the tall man grimaced, his bright, straight teeth made him look like he had a mouthful of sixty-four pearly whites instead of thirty-two.

Rosswell, shaking his head over the mud bath on the patrol car, pushed his glasses up onto his nose and ambled over to greet the sheriff. "Hunting mushrooms." Rosswell hooked a quizzical look onto his face. The gesture made him appear innocent and trusting. No one could disbelieve him.

"That's a load of horse puckey." Frizz yanked his hat from his head, and the mass of curly black hair on his oversized head that gave rise to his nickname popped out, soaked with sweat. He forked a huge handkerchief from his back pocket, scrubbed his smooth, unlined face, and then buffed the inside of the hat. "You're standing at a murder scene."

"I just murdered two people and thought you should know."

"Stop with the sarcasm." Frizz sniffed. "What a god-awful stink."

"You started it."

"The stink?"

"No," Rosswell said. "The sarcasm. I'm sorry if I inconvenienced you."

"Did you get my voicemail?"

Rosswell checked his phone. "No."

"I was having a nice breakfast conversation with my wife over some personal issues."

Rosswell said, "A couple of people out here had some personal issues."

"So you say." Frizz scratched his nose, the scent of death no doubt insulting his olfactory nerves. "Picking mushrooms on state property is illegal."

"I'm the judge, remember? I've read a statute or two in my time." Rosswell strode back to his car, snatched his camera off the passenger seat, and thrust it towards the sheriff. "I didn't say I was picking anything. I was taking pictures, not searching for supper."

Rosswell clicked through a preview of the sixty or so photos of mushrooms that he'd taken other places, careful not to show Frizz any of the pictures of the bodies. Some of the mushroom snaps showed poisonous ones. Every time Rosswell clicked on an *Amanita* or a False Morel, he'd say, "If I'd eaten one of those, we wouldn't be having this conversation."

Frizz clamped a hand on Rosswell's arm, signaling him to stop the slide show. "You got plenty of film?" Frizz apparently wasn't impressed with Rosswell's mushroom pictures.

"It's a digital camera. Film died at the end of the twentieth century."

"Yeah," Frizz said. "I knew that. What I meant was, can you take a lot more pictures?"

"A couple of thousand." Rosswell was prepared. Eighty gigabytes worth of memory cards nestled in the camera bag. "That's an under-estimation."

"Then start shooting. Everything. And when you finish, go back and take more. Every possible angle."

Rosswell nodded but said nothing. It would only irritate Frizz if he knew that Rosswell had already snapped a few photos of the bodies.

Frizz's request meant that he needed Rosswell to assist him, didn't it? And why shouldn't Rosswell be a sleuth? His leukemia, in remission now, wouldn't kill him for a long time. Maybe not for another year. Maybe even longer. The only thing standing between Rosswell and his desire to be a detective was common sense. In truth, Frizz didn't need Rosswell anymore than a goat needs a watch, but he wasn't going to admit that to Frizz.

Rosswell grinned. He reached up to smooth his red power tie, then realized he wasn't wearing his customary suit, but a sweaty tee shirt and dirty blue jeans. Catching a whiff of himself, he realized that his body odor hovered just this side of repellent.

Rosswell said, "You're deputizing me?"

If they caught the bad guy, Rosswell would be a witness, not the judge. This freed him to help in the investigation. Anticipating a Sherlock Holmes role, Rosswell raised his right hand, palm towards Frizz. During Medieval times, people did that to show that they were peaceable and carried no sword. Waiting for the swearing in, Rosswell blinked several times and sneezed twice. *Fricking allergies.*

"No," Frizz said. "I'm only drafting you to take pictures." The big man replaced his hat. "For free. You're an unpaid consultant. Put your hand down and get to work."

"You need help. The Harley riders are due on Thursday. Maybe some will be here tomorrow or Wednesday. You have three deputies. There's one city cop and he's an idiot."

"I can handle it, don't worry."

"This is a double homicide. You'll need all the help you can get."

Frizz said, "I've got all the help I can get."

"But not all the help that you need."

Frizz's face turned red. "Rosswell, you're the judge. I'm the cop."

"After all, I did find the bodies." Rosswell sneezed. "And I'm a wit-ness here, not a judge. A judge can't hold court when he's the witness."

The argument over whether Rosswell would be an official detective or an amateur sleuth moved into the hold position when a Road Rescue Ambulance equipped to the max with hundred-decibel sirens and supernova lights howled towards the two men. Late last year, Homeland Security had awarded the wicked vehicle to Bollinger County. If terrorists ever targeted the Ozarks, Bollinger County stood ready in uptown style. At least in the ambulance department.

Neal Borland, the medical examiner, lumbered out of the ambulance when it stopped. Red and blue lights swirling, its sirens ripped apart the quiet of the death scene. Two EMTs, one male, the other female, opened the rear door, jumped to the ground, and pulled on clear rubber gloves.

"Dr. Borland," Rosswell yelled, "can you cut off the sirens? You're scaring the squirrels and the deer with that racket." The traffic in this part of the county was nonexistent, leaving no need for sirens, lights, and speeding.

"Standard operating procedure." Freckles blanketed Neal's large face, hairless except for pale red eyebrows, two shades lighter than his unkempt hair, which, as always, stuck out in disarray atop his square head. "Saves time when we're in emergency mode." He motioned to one of the EMTs who cut off the siren. "Besides, it's a Federal regulation."

"Oh?" Rosswell said. "Was there traffic?" Maybe Neal was trying to deafen people so he could garner more patients for his medical practice. The medical examiner position didn't pay much.

"Where are the bodies?" Neal asked, not even favoring Rosswell with a glance.

Frizz pointed to the corpses, then glared at Rosswell, with a look that he understood meant *Shut your trap*.

Neal, wiping sweat off his large face, trundled to the bodies while Rosswell snapped pictures. The EMTs blocked his view in a couple of shots, and he told them to move.

"Any ID?" Neal asked. The smell must not have bothered him since he made no expression of disgust nor did he slather the inside of his nostrils with Vicks.

"Didn't check," Rosswell said.

"I wasn't talking to you, Ross."

"It's *Rosswell*. I don't have an abbreviation for that name. It's a family name. From way back." Rosswell sent a silent prayer up, requesting forgiveness for his anal reaction to Neal's barb while they were at a death scene. Coming to his own defense, Rosswell knew his Scottish forebears would be horrified to hear Neal kicking around the sacred surname.

"Frizz," Neal said, "you got any idea who these bodies are?"

"These bodies," Rosswell said, "are people."

"Not a clue." Frizz rubbed his face with his handkerchief. "I didn't search them. I was waiting for you." Frizz inched toward the bodies. "Besides, they're unrecognizable."

"Got that straight." Neal bent close to what Rosswell presumed was the male corpse and waved the bugs away. The dark swarm of critters buzzed angrily. Maybe they'd bite Neal. "Throat slit." He clumped around to the other body and knelt beside it. "I can't see any wounds, but with the way this corpse is puffed up, there's no way to tell for sure."

Puffed up? Is that a medical term I'm not familiar with? What's the next goody Neal would come up with? Smelling like rotten crap? Green as goose grease?

The relationship between Neal and Rosswell wasn't doused with honey. The friction partially resulted from Rosswell's penchant for moving court proceedings at a steady pace. Neal's testimony tended to consist of explaining how a split hair could be further split seventeen different ways.

Rosswell asked Neal, "How about doing an autopsy?" That suffocated any rapport that may've been left.

Neal, without averting his gaze from the face of the dead woman, said, "Judge, what's your official capacity here?"

"I asked him to take pictures," Frizz said. "He's got his camera."

"Yes, you need a camera to take pictures." Neal eyed the Nikon. "I'll need a print of all your shots."

"My prices are quite reasonable," Rosswell said. "I do insist on the money up front. My bookkeeping isn't set up for time payments."

Neal said to Frizz, "Did you call him out here?"

"Nope."

"I discovered the bodies," Rosswell said. "I called Frizz out here. Then he deputized me."

Frizz said, "I did no such thing."

"Frizz, you drafted me to do detective work for free, which made me a deputy."

Neal stood, brushed his pants off, and turned to Rosswell. "You were out here with a camera and just happened to discover two bodies?" His eyebrows shot up in what Rosswell took to be a sign of disbelief. "What a happy coincidence."

"If you must know, I was searching for mushrooms. I didn't get far before I found those two."

Neal said, "You always have a very smooth explanation."

"You got that from *The Maltese Falcon*, didn't you? I love that movie."

"Never saw it." Neal stopped brushing his pants. "It's illegal to pick mushrooms in a state park."

Rosswell said, "No crap?" Neal frequently generated a one-man cluster. Rosswell again pegged the times Neal testified in court, often wandering into strange territory. Many times Rosswell had told him, "Dr. Borland, if someone asks you what time it is, don't answer by telling us how to build a watch."

Neal said, "In my experience, the best suspect in a murder case is the guy who saw the victim last or the guy who finds the body."

"I don't recognize that," Rosswell said. "What movie is that from?"

Neal said, "It's not movie dialog. It's fact."

A streak of lightning knifed across the sky. Another bolt crashed into one of the big oak trees where Rosswell had been searching. The explosion reverberated in the hills for what seemed several minutes and would ring in his ears for what seemed hours. The tree split from top to bottom, yet didn't fall apart. Daylight shone in places along the oak's naked wound. Tree bark flew everywhere, a chunk of it missing Rosswell's head by a millimeter. Thunder boomed and rattled without let up. A rip in the dark sky poured out a deluge worthy of Noah. Mud from the river's bank fell off in clumps into the torrent. The rain, thick and fast, blinded everyone as they lunged for cover. Frizz scrambled for the patrol car. Neal and the EMTs bolted for the ambulance.

Rosswell headed for his convertible. He struggled to fasten the purple convertible top in place, pinching his fingers several times before he succeeded. He'd kept the car in pristine condition from the time he was sixteen. After his mother died, he couldn't bear to sell it. Fortunately, there was only about a half-inch of water in Vicky the Volkswagen by the time he secured the top. He loved Vicky, even though she was a machine. Tina loved tooling around in the old car. If Vicky was ruined, Tina would cry and Rosswell would be ready for the grim reaper to come fetch him. Worse than that, Rosswell would be consigned to driving his boring black 1994 GMC pickup truck.

Thirty minutes later the rain slowed to a drizzle.

The noise of the river, now flooding higher than Rosswell had ever seen it, grew louder even as the storm abated. A horrendous volume of upstream water chugged downstream. Rushing past the picnic area, the murky water tore out large trees and ate up the banks. Small trees tumbled down through the water, now darker than he'd ever seen it.

Frizz jumped from his patrol car and slogged to where the bodies had been discovered. Neal followed Frizz. Rosswell followed Neal. The EMTs stayed in the ambulance.

"Damn," Frizz said when they reached the spot.

"Oh, shit," Neal said.

"Holy crap!" Rosswell said.

After the storm, Rosswell's acid reflux and allergies soared to epic proportions, yet his headache had disappeared.

Along with the bodies.

Chapter Three
The killer

The killers planned Eddie Joe Deckard's murder on a cloudless, starry night, under a full moon. Torturing and blackmailing him hadn't achieved the result they wanted. Execution was the only way.

"Do you really think we could pull it off?" the killer asked Babe as they sat in the dark woods at the edge of the broad bank leading to the river. Unlike a lot of streams around there, the bank wasn't gravel but earth, all the way to the water's edge. The trees stopped and the bank sloped gently for several more feet until the shore met the water. The scent of honeysuckle and rose verbena pervaded the air. Whippoorwills called to their mates.

A beautiful place. A place for lovers. A place for murder.

"It's spooky out here. Why'd we have to come here?"

As usual, Babe had a problem answering a direct question. The bitter taste of anger flooded the killer's throat and mouth. "I asked you, do you think we could do it and not get caught?" Repetition shouldn't have been necessary for the bitch. Her listening abilities were excellent. This wouldn't turn out good unless she paid attention as she did in her real life. Lawyers listen and pay attention. The killer had spent a lot of time lying flat, working out all the details, and the killer wanted her to listen.

Babe said nothing. She rose and, in the same motion, brushed away the dead leaves, grass, sticks, and small rocks—the stuff that clings to a woman's butt when she sits on the ground in the woods. She made no move to leave but continued standing, still breathing hard, still looking around, and wringing her hands.

The killer watched the show of nerves as long as was bearable. "God damn it, I asked you a question and I want an answer." The killer knew Babe had been beat down so much in her life that the only way to get a response was to beat her down some more. She'd done a superb job of hiding that from the public, but the killer had discovered it and used it against her. Besides, the killer liked beating her down.

Babe plopped down beside the killer and collected a new bunch of stuff on her butt. "If I didn't think . . . believe . . . we could do it, then I wouldn't be here, would I?"

Just like a woman. The killer knew about being a woman. "Would you listen to the question? Read my lips." Why can't women answer a direct question? "Do you think we can do it and not get caught?"

Now Babe pouted. "I can't see your lips all that good. It's dark. Or hadn't you noticed? Spookier than all get out."

"It's not that dark. There's a full moon and lots of starlight." The killer clenched fists and pounded Babe's arms. "Do you think we can get away with it?" That got her attention.

"Stop it," Babe whimpered. She rubbed her arms but didn't return the killer's blows. "Mighty testy tonight."

The killer stayed silent. Sometimes, after getting Babe's attention, the killer had to give her time to think.

"All right," Babe said. She started with the labored breathing and worrywart stuff again. "Yes, I think we could get away with it. If we're careful and nothing screws up the plan, we can escape without them noticing and live happily ever after. A fairy princess story for sure." Babe laughed and laughed. "Now, that's pretty funny. A fairy princess story. We're sure a couple of freaking fairies." Babe laughed again but the high-pitched whinny wasn't pretty.

"Good." The killer moved a hand between Babe's legs. "We'd fit good in a fairy princess story."

"And if the plan does get screwed up? What if someone gets on to us? Then what do we do?"

"After the first execution, the second one gets easier." The killer continued caressing Babe, the feel of her shooting waves of pleasure. "Someone gets in our way, we kill them. Simple."

"Something else." The touching didn't stop Babe's talking.

"And what would that be?" The killer spoke in a coy, shy, altogether fake voice. The fingers of the other hand moved, exploring the place where the stuff had collected on Babe. Her earlobe tasted salty when the killer chewed on it.

"Why," Babe said, stifling a moan of pleasure, "did we have to come out here? I hate being in the dark. Outside in the dark."

"Is that your silly little fret? I never noticed you hating the dark."

The killer used both hands now, rubbing front and back. Even that didn't stop Babe from talking. Her moans of pleasure sounded better than her whiny voice.

Between deep breaths, Babe said, "Outside in the dark, reminds me of things. Things that didn't go too well. He liked the dark. I mean things still have a way of—"

"Shut up." The killer stopped exploring, taking her face in both hands. Babe appeared to rock on the edge of an abyss. The killer had to stop her from throwing herself over. "Keep your mouth shut tight."

"I'm shut," Babe mumbled through clenched teeth.

"I'm not real sure you need to dwell on those things." The killer stuck one hand down Babe's pants and the other hand on the back of her neck. "Those things are over and done, and we'll stamp finished on it. Look at it this way—maybe those things will help you when we carry out the plan. You have to search for silver liners in black clouds."

"Linings."

The killer paid no heed. "Yes, think of those things that way. It will help you."

Babe choked back a sob. "They keep playing over and over in my head. Those things replay like a YouTube video stuck in repeat mode. They play in my mind where I see scenes of him—"

"Stop."

Babe stopped. Then summoning a trace of tenderness, the killer spoke, gently explaining the necessity of this death. "You know why we have to do this. It's the only logical and rational thing to do. We went over all the reasons before. No one but us will punish that bastard. He violated both of us and no one cares." Babe scooted close to the killer. "We came out here because here's where it's going to happen."

"Here?" Babe's voice cracked. "I didn't know that was part of the plan. Here?"

"I've checked it out. There are no houses for miles, the road isn't used much, and it's a nice place. In fact, except for the camping area, no one is allowed here after sundown. We're trespassing." The killer smiled and cooed at Babe. "There are trees, rocks, birds, streams, plants, and animals. This is nature at its best. A nice place."

"A nice place?" The wonder at the label for the place was plain in Babe's voice. "All that's here is a bunch of dirt. Dirt and dirty stuff. Woods are junky places full of green crap. Towns are nice places."

"Now that's where you've gone wrong. This is a nice place, a perfect place for the death. Spring is the time of rebirth, a time for new resolutions." The killer gestured at the words, although it's doubtful that Babe could see the hands moving. Gesturing helped the talk flow. "We should begin the new year in the spring, not the dead of winter. It seems more like a new year when new things are budding and new animal babies are being born. This is a good time to bring to life resolutions about death. Don't you think?"

"What are you talking about?"

The killer reminded her that the question was what she thought about springtime. Hitting her again seemed a possibility.

Babe said, "I think often."

"You should be more romantic. Thinking too much means not enough action. Thinking is simply thinking. Action is romantic."

"Thinking is my job," said Babe. "When will we do it?"

"The execution?" The killer felt Babe move her head, and silence fell for a few moments. "We'll have to seize the first chance we get. It could be days, weeks. I don't know." The killer shook a finger at her, much like a parent scolding a kid who'd raided the cookie jar. "We have to be prepared when opportunity rings the doorbell. We have to be ready at all times."

"How will we do it?" Babe said.

"Who? What? Where? When? How? What are you? A journalist?"

"If I'm in on this, I need to know how. The plan. How can we have a plan if we don't have details? You keep springing new details on me and then you won't tell me other details. I've got to know."

"A gun would be nice."

"And bring the neighbors running? That's stupid."

"I told you," the killer said, "this place is isolated. Even if one of these ridge runners hears a gunshot, he'll think it's one of his kinfolks shooting deer before the poachers kill them off." Not only did the killer have to grab Babe's attention, it was work keeping it from wandering.

Babe said, "There's more than one way to shoot an old dog."

The killer laughed. Babe said something funny? What a miracle!

"He's a son of a bitch," the killer said. "A dog shooting is exactly what we're going to have. A gun right between the mutt's ears would turn the deadly trick." The killer's target practice had been regular and effective. The shots wouldn't miss.

Babe said, "I'd like a gun."

"You would. A gun is just like you." Babe was a woman who loved guns.

"Or a knife. That would be quiet. Quiet and effective."

"Do you have a gun?"

"No," Babe said.

"Also just like you not to have a gun," the killer said, once again pointing out the obvious. She claimed to love guns yet didn't have one. "Then how about a knife? You're right that a knife would be quiet. You have a knife? And I don't mean a butcher knife. A butcher knife is meant for dead meat. We need a knife meant for live meat."

"A knife." Babe snapped her fingers so hard it sounded like the pop of a firecracker. "Yes, a knife would be quiet and quick."

"Got one?"

"Everybody's got a knife, and I don't mean a butcher knife. You can never tell when a knife might come in handier than a thumb on a monkey. There's a knife in the office."

The killer had a better idea. "No, I've got it. A hangman's noose. A nice noose for an execution in this nice place."

"A noose it is." Babe kicked at a sweet smelling golden currant shrub. "It might take longer. Choking takes longer. But it would be quiet and it would work. I'd enjoy watching that dish of crap choke to death." She crushed several of the shrub's yellow flowers in her hands. "But what do we do with the body? Bury it here?"

"That's the last thing we want to do."

Babe said, "Then what?"

The killer listened to a bullfrog belching love songs for a few seconds before answering.

"If we dump the body in the middle of everything, where we talked about before, they'll never suspect us. They'll never suspect us."

"Why? That makes no sense. I'm not sure I understand this part. How would it help us to dump a body on the courthouse square?"

"We're smart, outlandishly smart," the killer said. "They'll think whoever did it was stupid to dump the scum there. Distraction is our insurance. We'll be magicians, pointing one way with the right hand while the left hand does the deed. It's so simple, it's subtle."

To emphasize the feeling of ingenuity for figuring out this part of the plan, the killer kissed her. Deep. She tasted sweet.

Babe said, "The hammer strikes, the anvil remains."

"What the hell does that mean? You're just full of witty sayings, aren't you?"

"But if we dug a grave here, no one would ever find it."

"Right. No one would find it. No one, that is, until one of these hillbillies goes coon hunting. The dog would lose it when he got near the body. I'm not getting my ass in a squeeze from some tie hacker's mixed breed coonhound sniffing a corpse."

"I see," Babe said. "I think I see." She tilted her head back to stare at the sky, now full of clouds. "I'm not sure I see. If someone finds the body here, they'd suspect us but if they find it in the middle of everything, they won't suspect us? I don't get it."

"Trust me, it'll work. Isn't this a nice place? Such a nice place."

"A nice place for a murder. My Taser will make it even nicer."

"Stun him first. I like that." The killer laughed. "But God damn it twice. We've talked about that. It's not murder, it's an execution."

"It's the excitement. I forgot."

"I'm sorry you have to be outside in the dark. Perhaps I can make it up to you."

Without standing, the killer took off every stitch of clothes, not bothering to knock away the stuff of the forest floor, which now clung to bare skin. Then the killer removed Babe's clothing. A hand, then the mouth went to Babe's favorite place. And the killer did other things, glorious things, to Babe. And Babe returned the favors.

They touched each other everywhere. Then the killer made it up to Babe. No maybe there.

On the sunny, appointed day, the killer drove Eddie Joe Deckard into the country.

When they reached the chosen spot, the killer said to Eddie Joe, "Let's go for a walk." The killer hiked away from the victim.

"Where are we going?" Eddie Joe said. "I've got a lot to take care of. I don't have much time."

"That's for sure," the killer said in a soft voice. With assurance, the killer said to Eddie Joe, "This won't take long," then led him around the bend to the spot where death would come to buy another soul. It was the nice place. A stream, trees, wildflowers, and a picnic table under a roof.

A scenic lane, beneath the crest of a forested ridge and far from where anyone could see or hear them, fit the plan. Safe ground.

The killer said to Eddie Joe, "I've got something to show you." Then smiled.

"Show me? I thought you said you wanted to talk."

"Show you, talk to you, whatever. Don't be so literal."

Eddie Joe said, "Don't be so mysterious."

The killer pointed. "Sit there."

"There?" Eddie Joe asked, also pointing. "What's that Caddy doing in the middle of nowhere?"

"Please take the driver's seat. I'll explain."

Eddie Joe sat, stroked, and praised. "Nice. Super nice. You've done good and I always believed you could do it." He sat. The stroking and praising stopped. "This is yours, isn't it?"

"It's not mine. It belongs to a friend."

"A friend? Then what do I want to see it for? Is this what we drove all the way out here to see? This car's not even yours and we came all the way out here to see this—"

"No, this isn't what we came for. We didn't come for me to talk or to show, we came for me to do."

On cue, Babe walked from behind a clump of cedar trees.

"Hey," Babe greeted Eddie Joe. "Good to see you again."

"Hey," Eddie Joe said. He frowned, but started to leave the car. "Nice to see you again, too."

Babe, ignoring Eddie Joe's outstretched hand, pushed him in the chest, forcing him into a sitting position behind the steering wheel once more. She was a strong woman who worked out every day, and he wasn't a big man. Good thing.

"Don't bother, my friend," said Babe, "because you'll never stand for anything again."

"What's going on here?" Eddie Joe studied the killer, who didn't explain Babe's words and deeds. Eddie Joe repeated his question to the killer. "What's going on here?"

"You probably have a good idea now, don't you? Can't you guess what's about to happen?"

"The hell I can." This time directed to Babe, Eddie Joe said, "What's going on here?"

"Since you're so dense, I'll tell you what's going on here." Babe shoved Eddie Joe again. "You're dead."

"Dead? Dead!" Eddie Joe shrieked. "What do you mean dead?"

"It's a simple concept," Babe said. "A simple word. Dead, as in not alive. You dragged me outside in the dark and made me wish I was dead. You used my body like you owned it."

"You liked it," Eddie Joe said. Babe kicked him in the balls.

The killer said to Eddie Joe, "I've taken all the filthy trash off you I'm ever going to take. You've betrayed me for the last time. Played around on me."

"Trash?" Eddie Joe said, gasping with pain. "Filthy trash? What the hell does that mean? And how in the hell did I betray you, for Christ's sake? What are you talking about?"

"You had your fun with me when I was too little to resist. You did the same thing to Babe. You're scum and you've betrayed me for the last time, you son of a bitch. You like to play around."

"Betray?" Babe said to the killer. "Played around?" Puzzlement at the killer's unexpected words danced plainly on Babe's face. She said to the killer, "I thought it was only you and me. How could this scum betray you?" She snapped her fingers. "You played around with Eddie. You're a liar. You're a cheat!"

The killer said, "I've had lots of sex with lots of people. I like sex."

Surprise spluttered to the surface of Eddie Joe's fear and confusion. "You," he said to the killer, "and . . . this?" He pointed to Babe. "What shit." Eddie Joe's fear sweat stank.

Babe turned her anger from the killer and said to Eddie Joe, "You liked me a lot when I couldn't resist."

"Shut your pie holes," the killer said to both of them, then to Eddie Joe, "When you have as many secrets as you do, you can't keep track of all of them. And you have one hell of a lot of secrets."

Eddie Joe said, "You're not making sense." A yellow jacket buzzed around his face, attracted by his perspiration.

The killer said, "You never did know what I was talking about, did you?"

Eddie Joe said, "I don't know what you're talking about now."

"Neither do I," said Babe.

The killer ignored Babe. "That doesn't matter anymore," speaking to Eddie Joe. "You're dead now and welcome to it."

Excitement roiled inside the killer. There's a taste of anticipation that comes before sex and killing. Savoring the taste, the killer stroked Eddie Joe's stubbly cheeks. Eddie Joe had forgotten to shave.

"That does it. I'm leaving," Eddie Joe said and stood on the ground. Babe kicked her shoes off and tagged Eddie Joe with her Taser. Then she pinned him in a full nelson. Babe may've been stringy, but she was tough for a woman. And a stun gun softens up everybody.

Eddie Joe tore at Babe, managing only to seize air with his hands now formed into claws.

"Where is it?" the killer said.

"It's on the floor," said Babe. "Get it."

The killer snagged the knife off the car's floor and held it up where all three of them could see it.

"Jesus! Jesus! Jesus!" Eddie Joe said when the thing appeared. Then silence. Maybe a real silent prayer.

"That's right," the killer said. "You'd better pray. This is your last chance. But I don't think it'll do you any good." The killer spit on Eddie Joe. "Jesus doesn't recognize you and the Devil hears no prayers, only resignations. You're going to hell."

Not loosening her hold on Eddie Joe, Babe said, "Give it to me."

The killer clutched the knife with the ferocity of a miser's hand in rigor mortis grasping an earthly treasure.

"No," the killer said, drawing the knife back. "It was my idea, I'll do it." Showing teeth and curling lips upward, the killer mimicked a smile. "You," the killer said to Babe, "hold this filthy trash and I'll do it."

Eddie Joe said, "Stop! Don't do this. I don't deserve killing. My God, what did I do wrong?"

"Don't listen," Babe said.

"You," the killer said to Eddie Joe, "are filthy and I'm through taking filthy trash off you."

"What . . . what?" Eddie Joe said.

The killer said, "Don't act like you don't know what you did."

"Stop lecturing. Do it," said Babe. "I can't pin this sucker forever. Do it."

Eddie Joe said, "Jesus! Jesus! Jesus!"

The killer said, "Forever."

Eddie Joe said, "My God. Please don't. Please don't. Please don't." Not very memorable for famous last words, but it was all he could manage.

Babe said, "Do it. Do it. Do it."

The killer said, "With pleasure," and, leering, sliced Eddie Joe's throat.

Babe unpinned Eddie Joe.

His fluttering hands clutched his nonworking throat after trying speech and finding it impossible. Damn near popping from sockets and spurting tears, his eyes bugged out cartoon-style. Eddie Joe's forehead beaded sweat, which collected and ran in streams down his face, which grew whiter. The streams of sweat ran further down his neck, which grew redder. The sweat did little to pinken the red goo.

Coppery and bright, the aroma of blood cascaded around the three of them. The killer sucked in the smell with deep breaths. Eddie Joe bubbled and sputtered, unable to catch a single good breath.

The dying man scratched at his scudding heart, gripping under an aching rib cage. He fought to hold the wildly pounding muscle in his burning chest.

As death shambled toward him, Eddie Joe bared his teeth as if growling at the stranger, the old man hulking down the road, the final visitor, coming, coming, coming. If not with speed, then surely with certainty. The final visitor for the final appointment for this flopping thing growing greasy with blood.

Eddie Joe's breathing sounded gritty, as if death had poured a bucket of finely ground sand into his flaming lungs. He thrashed, escalating into convulsions. At one point, he fell on a small log, hugged it, and jerked his arms and stomped his feet. A fat and purple thing that was his tongue jutted from between his white teeth stained with red. He pulled at that fat thing, ripped at his mouth wet with blood and spittle, and then tore at a throat that had given up.

There was no air.

There was no life to be had. As the killer had planned, the condemned man tumbled into the Great Void, tripped by the old bastard Death who never ever loses. Never.

The killer spoke the words breaking the hush after the execution. "Our friend here got some of his precious blood on the Caddy. Messy, isn't it?"

"What the hell did you expect? Murder is messy."

"I told you not to call it that."

"It's that excitement thing," Babe said. "Sorry. I forgot."

"Shit for brains is what's sloshing inside your skull. Don't forget again." The killer then ogled the body. "Messy, but worth it. Executions are bloody messy, aren't they?" The killer clapped. And laughed. And it felt good.

"Right," Babe said through the not-funny laughter. "An execution can sure be messy."

The killer cut off the laugh attack to direct Babe, "Clean it up."

"Wait one minute," Babe said, holding both palms facing out and up. "What was that talk about betrayal? About playing around? What did that mean?"

"Crazy talk. People talk crazy when they're about to be executed."

"You were making it with Eddie Joe after you told me you were through with him."

The killer spit on Babe. "You want me?"

Babe trembled. "I need you."

"Then stop with the accusations. We're in it up to our breathers.

We can't afford your asshole allegations about me and someone who no longer walks the land of the living now, don't you agree?"

Babe agreed. "What about this?" Babe held up the knife. Filthy stinking stuff from Eddie Joe's throat dripped from the point of the knife onto a patch of clover. Buzzing insects circled the knife, sensing food.

"Pitch it."

Babe didn't pitch it. She handed it to the killer and said, "Don't be careless with evidence."

"I'm going to change clothes and go back to work. If we don't stay in our daily routine, someone could notice. Someone might notice my bloody clothes even if I did stick to my routine."

"Everybody thinks I'm gone."

"Don't screw up."

Babe said, "You've got fancy moves, but you've got cheese for brains."

"Must've got them from you. Whore."

Babe said, "I hate you. You were still doing favors for Eddie Joe. You liked it, didn't you? You lied to me when you said you were through with him."

The killer didn't speak.

Babe stood, yet made no other movement. After a moment she launched herself, knocking the killer to the ground. The killer fell backwards, a rock slamming into backbone. The pain in the spine caused a momentary blackout. Babe punched the killer in the gut. That brought the killer around, although breathing was impossible for a few seconds. A damned girl punch. A man would've beaten the killer's face until all sensation was gone. Babe had found her Taser, which headed for the killer's face. The killer shoved a hand into her face and pushed her away. When she fell, her Taser disappeared into the brush. She jumped up and kicked the killer's butt, landing a couple of blows on each cheek. The killer rolled away. Babe staggered backward when a kick she'd aimed missed. There was no way the killer could get up. Rolling toward her feet, knocking her to the ground, the killer screamed. Babe lay panting in the dirt with the killer straddling her.

Babe said, "Won't be long before you join Eddie Joe and me in hell. We'll be waiting."

The knife was within reach. The killer grabbed it and stabbed her in the heart.

"To quote me, 'After the first execution, the second one gets easier'."

34

No more Eddie Joe. No more Babe. The killer would learn to get along without them. Shit happens. People bleed. People die.

The killer arranged their bodies. No one would ever notice the ingenious pattern used. Some Fast Orange would clean the killer's hands. "You always need clean hands for any kind of work."

The killer cradled the knife. The second part of the plan, the part Babe knew nothing about, the part that just sprang into the killer's mind, needed a knife. The killer let out a howl of victory and a laugh of triumph.

Something crashed in the woods behind the scene. Whatever it was snapped dead branches that had fallen to the ground. The killer thought a deer must've been scared.

Lightning flashed and thunder rumbled. Black clouds rolled across the sky.

The killer's tongue flicked in and out, catching the first drops of rain.

"It's nice of Mother Nature to clean this mess up."

Chapter Four
Monday morning, continued

Rosswell stumbled into the sheriff's station in Marble Hill, his eyesight haloed by lightning, hearing thrumming from thunder, and clothes dripping rainwater. Frizz and Neal followed him.

Tina Parkmore sat at a desk behind a long plywood counter, varnished and shiny, that served to keep the public in its place.

For Tina's sake, Rosswell hoped the drenching rain had washed away his stink. He didn't want to offend her. He always found a reason to talk with her. The perky dispatcher, in Rosswell's mind, looked the same as when she'd reigned as the head cheerleader in high school ten years ago.

Slender and tall, the strawberry blonde's job was to handle all the phone calls and radio traffic, as well as to give information to the public. Her green eyes saw everything, her delicate ears heard everything. She wore the hint of a perfume scented like lilacs. Her mouth never opened unless she said something worth hearing.

Her two-tone brown sheriff's department uniform wasn't as sexy as her cheerleader outfit. Rosswell knew that because he'd seen her wearing it on occasion lately. In private.

"Rosswell?" Tina Parkmore queried when he sloshed through the door, then she noticed the other men. "I mean, Judge Carew." Their relationship was no secret; although during work hours, they tried to keep it professional. "What's wrong?"

Frizz didn't wait for Rosswell to answer Tina. "Two people were murdered up at Foggy Top."

"Who?" she asked, swiveling her chair around to face the sheriff. She was interrupted by the radio. An officer was trying to find the owner of a flock of chickens whose hen house had been flattened by the storm. Tina transmitted the owner's address, then turned to Rosswell. "Anyone I know?"

Neal said, "Go ahead, tell her, Judge."

Rosswell wanted to say *Thanks, Neal, for making me look like a stupid jerk in front of Tina.* Instead, all he could come up with was, "No thanks. That's the sheriff's job."

Frizz pointed at Rosswell. "You're so all-fired ready to be part of this fiasco. Go ahead and tell her." He shook his hat and water flew across the room.

The three males, their machismo deflated, hung their heads, each of them reminding Rosswell of an embarrassed lion trying to regain his pride. The single bright spot in this sorry picture was Tina, who grew more beautiful every day.

Tina said, "If it's a secret, then never mind." She turned her attention to a stack of papers on her desk.

Rosswell cleared his throat. No one else was in the place but the four of them. "We don't know who it was."

"Ah," she said. "Neal has to identify the bodies? Is that the secret?"

Neal said, "We lost the bodies."

Tina's eyes widened. The phone rang and she answered it. Rosswell listened to a conversation about a stray cat digging in some old lady's garden, preparing a place to poop. "We'll check into it," Tina said and then hung up. She again turned to Rosswell. "How did you lose the bodies?"

"We had the bodies," he said. "From a preliminary examination, we think they were murdered. When the big storm came, it washed them down the bank into the river. They must've floated away down Cloudy River."

"Ah," Tina said again. "The bodies flushed away during the storm? What are y'all going to do now?"

Again pointing at Rosswell, Frizz said, "Judge Carew is not going to do anything. I'm calling out the search and rescue volunteers." He smoothed the wet brim of his hat. "I guess that they're really just going to be the search volunteers. Going after corpses. No live people, so there won't be any rescue."

Neal said, "We'd best be finding them today."

Frizz said, "Or there's hell to pay this weekend."

From Thursday until Sunday, the Harley Spring Ride—Hogfest—would inundate Marble Hill with a couple of hundred hog lovers. The courthouse would be closed Thursday, Friday, and Saturday to keep citizens from using the toilets and generally messing up the place. Foggy Top State Park would be crammed full of campers. The small town's streets would be packed with folks attending the street fair that accompanied the deluge of riders. Saturday night would be a full moon.

They had to find the bodies and solve the murders quickly. Today.

Tina began calling out the volunteers.

Without bothering to close the door, Neal and Frizz conferred in the sheriff's office, a place the sheriff called "headquarters." Rosswell relinquished the Nikon to Tina so she could download the pictures of the crime scene to the sheriff's computer.

"Nice mushrooms," she said, winking at Rosswell. He hoped Neal and Frizz didn't catch her flirt. She whispered, "I wrote you a letter."

Before he could answer, the volunteers began drifting in. Tina finished the download and handed the camera to Rosswell.

He said to her, "More later."

"Yes." She winked again.

Beep. A MISSED CALL message popped up on Rosswell's phone. It was a call from Frizz early that morning. *Beep.* A VOICEMAIL notice. Rosswell clicked to play. "I'm finishing up at home and then I'll call Neal," Frizz said. "Stay right there at the park."

"Great service," Rosswell muttered.

Frizz appeared and instructed the assembled searchers. Most were local farmers and ranchers, with a healthy dose of teenage boys driving four wheelers. All of them were high on testosterone, searching for adventure.

Rosswell hoofed it across the courthouse square to Merc's Diner, hoping to find a certified genius, the town drunk, and his personal snitch, embodied in one person. Ollie Groton. Several of Ollie's jail stays could be credited to Rosswell, but Ollie never took it personally. A judge needs a snitch to keep himself informed on the activities of the criminal classes. Ollie promised Rosswell that he'd spill the secrets he found and Rosswell promised Ollie he wouldn't ask where the secrets came from. Information was handy when sentencing a perpetrator. Clearly, Rosswell wasn't supposed to have a snitch, but no one need ever know.

The restaurant coffee shop, operating in a refurbished hotel, served as the headquarters for the local gossip mill. Folks traipsed back and forth, carrying tales like ants carrying sugar. The interior of the cedar-sided building was as crusty and ancient as most of its customers. The rumor was that the booths were built from the wood of barns torn down before the Civil War. Merc Leadbetter kept the place immaculate, although no matter what he did in the way of cleaning, he couldn't hide the floors worn slick or the graffiti carved into the booths. Such things, according to Merc, "gave the place character."

For gainful employment, Ollie had built a healthy business installing, maintaining, and repairing computers. When not busy at his job, he sat eating, drinking coffee, and sopping up the local chatter at Merc's. He soaked up tidbits of information like a dry sponge thrown into a rainstorm. Ollie was the gossip's gossip.

Some of the less charitable folks in the county said that "Merc's" actually meant "mercury," which described the taste of the tuna sandwiches. If there was mercury in Merc's tuna, then Ollie's brain was as full of it as an old-time thermometer.

Ollie kept his entire body shaved and boasted a star-shaped tattoo on his bald head. The purple tat beaconed his location in the coffee shop, especially since he'd given his skull its daily sheen of Vaseline. He sat alone. Rosswell slid into his booth.

Ollie said, "You look like shit."

"You have a purple tattoo on your bald head and you say I look like shit?"

Ollie squeaked, a high-pitched sound a mouse might make after the bar of a trap slammed across its spine.

"I feel like crap," Rosswell said, rubbing his face. He could still smell the corpses. He suspected that he smelled like them also. "I need to stand in a shower for a couple of hours." His eyes were more bloodshot than usual.

Without asking him, the waitress brought his standing order, a 20-ounce cup of the strongest coffee this side of New Orleans. He snagged the sugar jar and shook it, working the lumps loose, stirring ferociously.

Ollie said, "The coffee danged near melted the spoon."

"The way I like it." The coffee was blacker than midnight on a cloudy night at new moon and thick enough to need two hands for stirring. Rosswell heaped in sugar until the jar ran empty and the liquid became syrupy. The brew smelled sweeter than an angel. He dipped his forefinger in the boiling sludge, then touched it to his tongue.

The waitress tapped her pencil on her order pad. "Anything else?"

Rosswell said, "No, thanks." He waited for her to leave before he spoke to Ollie. Without so much as a *You're welcome*, she sauntered off. Her manners ranked right down there with Ollie's. Rosswell would've crossed her off his Christmas card list, but he didn't send Christmas cards.

A large man stomped through the front door and barreled for the waitress. He spoke to her and, although Rosswell couldn't hear what he said, the man didn't sound happy. The waitress replied and the man grabbed her arm. Merc stormed from the kitchen and yelled at the man, "Get the hell out of here. She's busy."

The waitress said, "It's nothing, Merc. He's okay."

The man left without another word.

Rosswell said to Ollie, "What the holy crap was that all about? Is that guy stalking her?"

Ollie pointed to Rosswell's cup. "That stuff will kill you." When Ollie didn't want to talk about something, he changed the subject. Rosswell knew better than to try working any information out of his snitch. It had to come voluntarily or not at all.

"Wrong." Roswell stirred and stirred. "Cancer will get me before this stuff gets a chance."

"Judge Carew, you're mighty cheerful today." Ollie's nose twitched. Another mouse-like attribute. "Have you had a bad day?"

They weren't within earshot of anyone. "We had a little problem this morning." The coffee needed more sugar, which Rosswell filched from the adjoining table.

Ollie's eyes searched the area around them. Rosswell scanned as well. Nearby, but out of earshot, were ten to twelve other patrons. A real estate agent, whose name—was it Nadine?—escaped Rosswell, talked to a young man and woman that Rosswell supposed might be buying a house from her. Across from her at another table, Gerald Somebody, a farmer, sat chowing down with his pimply son. Some tourists were scattered inside the place. Three giggling teenage girls sat in one corner drinking Cokes.

Rosswell assured himself that no one was paying any attention to him and Ollie. Apparently, Ollie had decided no one was listening either. The patrons at Merc's had long ago stopped going goggle-eyed when Ollie and Rosswell sat together. Strange people attract their own kind. That's probably what the patrons thought when they spied the two of them together.

Ollie rubbed the tattoo on his head, then wiped his hands on a paper napkin. "You mean losing the bodies out at Foggy Top?"

Rosswell wondered if he did that head rubbing thing for good luck. Or wisdom. Or maybe his noggin just itched.

Rosswell stirred the sludge and then took a tiny sip. Pouring in a touch more sugar made it better. A dash of salt made it perfect. He took a big swallow. It burned all the way down. The caffeine and sugar began to work their magic. The buzz he needed revved up his brain.

"How do you hear about stuff so quick?" he asked Ollie.

"Why did you want to talk if you didn't think I knew something?" Ollie countered.

Rosswell gave Ollie his heartless glower. Sometimes it was hard for Rosswell to look at Ollie. Ugly? The best that Rosswell could say about Ollie was that he resembled a giant, hairless rat. Ollie didn't succumb to the heartless glower. Rosswell figured his lack of caffeine diminished its effect.

"Ollie, are you going to tell me or do we have to dance all day?"

Ollie whispered, "You want to know how I know all that stuff?"

"Yes," Rosswell said, also in a whisper. "That's what I asked you."

No one paid them any attention, yet if two grown men kept whispering to each other, they'd eventually raise eyebrows.

"We have an agreement that I don't have to divulge my sources."

Rosswell leaned close to Ollie. "Make an exception."

Ollie nodded, pointing his head toward the waitress. "Her."

Rosswell took a gander over at the mousy woman Ollie pointed out. Mabel Yolanda Smothers. She wouldn't bother the Miss America people much, what with her bad skin and stringy hair.

"I think," Ollie said, still whispering, "she's my daughter."

"Cut the crap."

"I'm not shitting you." Ollie wasn't whispering now, but his voice was still low, as was Rosswell's.

"Why," Rosswell said, "do you think that sweet girl would be any kin to you? You don't know?"

"Her momma and I were. . . ." Ollie stared down at his own beverage.

"Were what?"

He looked up at Rosswell. "Close."

"Does Mabel know that you think you're her daddy?"

"She knows everything. I told her that I'm proud of her. She takes after her momma. She's never been in jail."

"That's an accomplishment to be proud of."

A low hum came from Ollie, which Rosswell took as a squeak precursor.

"Smothers," Rosswell said. "Her momma's the nurse, Benita Smothers?"

Ollie swigged a long drink of ice water. "I'm pretty sure."

"You're pretty sure Benita is her mother or that she's your kid?"

"Maybe."

Rosswell really wanted to discuss the disappearing bodies, not Ollie's possible contribution to the gene pool of Bollinger County, but he had no choice. "That doesn't tell me why you think Mabel Yolanda Smothers is your daughter." Ollie had a way of roping a conversation and pulling it his way. If Rosswell didn't like it, Ollie clammed up.

"Her momma told me."

"Right," Rosswell said, giving up. Trying to pry information out of Ollie was like catching flies blindfolded. Rosswell inspected Mabel as casually as he could. "Did Mabel tell you about the bodies?"

"Yeah, I already said that."

"She told you because you're her daddy?"

"You're on track."

"How did she find out?"

"I told Mabel I was her daddy."

Rosswell removed his glasses, covered his face with his hands, and breathed deeply. All the times he'd been in Merc's, the thought that Mabel was possibly related to a hairless human rat had never crossed his busy mind. How many more relatives did Ollie have scratching around here? Rosswell didn't want that conversation with him now.

Rosswell replaced his glasses. "No, I mean about the bodies. How did she know about the bodies?"

"No secrets in Bollinger County." Ollie started with the rodent grinning. "If you think you know someone else's secret, then you head to Merc's and spill your guts."

"And the reason you never told me before that Mabel's your daugter?"

"It didn't seem important before. She's never had any really good info until now."

"I need your help."

Ollie grinned more but said nothing.

"Frizz is swamped. He can't handle the investigation by himself, whether he wanted to admit it or not."

I know everyone in the county and remember most of their names. Some of their names. Some of the time. I'm essential. My mushroom hunting can be shunted aside for however long it takes. My docket is clear. I'm on vacation.

Rosswell said, "I need to help Frizz. Two bodies. That's never happened before in Bollinger County."

Ollie shook his head. "No way. I'm not in the mood to piss off the sheriff."

Rosswell gritted his teeth. Ollie had been drifting around for the last few months in one of his periodic bouts of sobriety. He knew more about esoteric stuff than Rosswell did. Ollie made the trivia sites on the Internet look like something that stupid third graders had cobbled together. Add to that he knew how to work computers and Rosswell didn't, and you then had a guy who could be useful to Rosswell for the investigation. Useful? Try essential.

"Ollie, I can pay you."

"I'm making lots of money off my computer consulting business, thank you very much."

Someone, Rosswell couldn't tell who, dropped a load of dishes, the crash reverberating through the restaurant. Merc yelled. A couple of customers laughed.

Rosswell said, "Think of the intellectual challenge." Ollie held a Mensa membership. Mensans were noted puzzle aficionados. There was no way he could pass up an intellectual challenge. "It would be a great intellectual challenge. You could help me find the guy who killed two people."

"The only intellectual challenge I currently have and the only one I need is my study of the Book of Revelation. I'm writing a complete study about the prophecies."

"You don't care that two people got murdered?"

Ollie stared at Rosswell for a long time without saying a word. Had Rosswell offended Ollie? After a couple of minutes, Ollie said, "None of my business."

"There's nothing I can say to convince you to help me?"

"Not a thing." He half squeaked and gurgled a mousy half laugh. "But we'll still be friends." Now he was fishing for something.

"I'm not going to apologize for throwing you in jail. You deserved it. That's irrelevant to this conversation."

After Ollie was released from jail the first time Rosswell imprisoned him, they'd met accidentally at Merc's. When they realized they both shared the trait of being nosy bastards, a common bond formed.

"I've got to eat and then go see some of my clients." Ollie pointed to his tuna sandwich, potato chips, and pickle. "You'll have to excuse me." The pickle juice had moistened the potato chips, leaving them soggy. Rosswell hated the smell of dill pickles. The thought of eating potato chips soaked in dill pickle juice nauseated him.

Rosswell swallowed the last of the sludge, then rose and grabbed both checks. "Thanks for talking to me." He drew a dollar from his wallet and laid it on the table for Mabel. Remembering who her father might be, Rosswell added a five. Sympathy may as well be worth a couple of dollars.

Rosswell turned and headed for the cash register where Mabel asked, "Is everything all right?"

Not really. There are some wars going on and diseases that can't be cured and poverty grows worse. And it appears that a man almost hurt you right in front of your father. That's what Rosswell thought but didn't say. He said, "Fine. Everything's fine," all the while wondering if there were a minimally invasive way for him to kill Ollie. A way that wouldn't get him caught.

Rosswell opened his billfold and discovered that the last money he had now lay on the table as Mabel's tip. He fished in his pocket, hoping to grab some change and froze.

"Mabel, I'll be right back."

Rosswell moseyed over to Ollie's booth, leaned close to his face, and whispered, "*Virtus junxit mors non separabit.*"

Ollie jolted sideways like Rosswell had broken a watermelon on his head. "Sit down." Ollie had nearly choked on a potato chip.

"Thanks." Rosswell sat.

"Where did you hear that?"

"I didn't hear it anywhere." Rosswell inventoried the room. Only one or two people were watching Ollie and Rosswell. Rosswell took a paper napkin from the dispenser, drew the ring from his pocket, and then cradled it in his lap. After wrapping it carefully, Rosswell brought the ring up and slid it towards Ollie. "I read it."

Ollie did his own glance around the room. When he was apparently satisfied that no one was staring, he opened the napkin and read. Ollie choked again, spitting bits of potato chip on the table. Mabel, who'd been waiting on the table next to the pair, whirled around, probably wondering if she needed to perform the Heimlich maneuver. Ollie drank water, then quickly rewrapped the ring, and Mabel turned back to her work.

"Where did you get this?"

"At the crime scene."

"What makes you think it has anything to do with the murder?"

"I don't know if it does or not."

Ollie slid the ring back to Rosswell.

"Keep it," Rosswell said. "For now. I may need it back."

"When do we start?"

"Right now, but what about your clients?"

"I can catch up with them later."

The two men arrowed for the death place.

Chapter Five
Monday afternoon

"Nothing but mud." Ollie poked his foot into the stinking muck of Picnic Area 3. There were three sewage treatment plants upstream. "If there was any DNA evidence or . . . well . . . any evidence at all, it's been washed away." He stared at a single set of tire tracks, turned over a couple of rocks, booted three or four big sticks out of the way. "Nothing. No evidence. No clues."

"I know that." Every cloud had fled to wherever it is that clouds go, and the sun boiled the pair. The weather forecast had predicted that the heat wave could last another ten days. A sparkling rock looked interesting. Rosswell picked it up and felt the rough surface of the quartz. "There are still things we could learn."

"You're on track." Ollie lowered his head and fixed his gaze on Rosswell's eyes. Ollie's gray eyes always set alarm bells jingling in Rosswell's brain. In truth, Ollie scared Rosswell. "Judge, what were you doing here in the first place? You just happened to stumble upon two corpses by accident?"

"I was searching for mushrooms." Rosswell had set himself up for what he knew was coming next. The running jab was beginning to wear his patience thinner than a muslin dress on a fat woman. *All right, Ollie, get it over with. Hit me with it.*

Ollie said, "Mushrooms?"

"Yes."

Wasn't Ollie going to tell Rosswell that it was illegal to pick mushrooms in a state park? He didn't. Instead, he asked, "When did you start searching for mushrooms?" No surprise showed in his voice. He was used to Rosswell's oddities.

"Since I bought my camera, earlier this year. It was a Valentine's Day present to myself."

"You're taking pictures of mushrooms?" His demeanor hadn't changed, indicating that he didn't think taking pictures of mushrooms was all that strange.

"I'm taking pictures of lots of things. When I finish my mushroom collection, I'll take pictures of frogs or wild flowers or fish or rocks. Something. I print the pictures and keep them in an album. A real world album, not something online."

"How about people?"

"Holy crap. I can't believe I forgot about the pictures on my camera." Rosswell avoided Ollie's eyes while he slunk to the car, doing his best to keep his hands from slapping himself silly. When he returned with his camera, they reviewed the 738 photos Rosswell had taken of the bodies earlier in the day. Ollie snatched the Nikon from Rosswell and again studied each shot without a word. Not even a squeak. Ollie paced and stepped, moving around like an actor trying to find his marks on the stage. Often, he'd hold the camera at ground level. Other times, he inspected the surrounding area and compared it to what he saw in the camera.

Ollie straightened to his full height after finishing his analysis. "These people," he tapped the viewer on the camera, "knew the murderer."

"The corpses knew their killer?"

"What I said. They're the only people on your camera."

Rosswell clicked through the pictures, also studying them. "How do you know that?"

Ollie crossed his arms and leaned over Rosswell. "There was one wound on the man." Ollie with his 6'6" six frame tried to intimidate Rosswell, who stretched to reach 5'5". "I think it was a man. You have to get up close and personal to slit someone's throat. It's highly unlikely that the murderer was hiding in the bushes waiting for these people to walk by. The two victims and the murderer or murderers probably came out here in the same vehicle. The man's throat was slit. That's what killed him."

"That's what Neal thought. Someone sliced the guy's throat open.

Neal didn't get a good look at the woman. There was some blood right where we're standing." Rosswell dug at the ground with his foot. "They were probably killed before last night's rain, so most of the blood had washed away by the time I arrived."

Ollie circled the scene and studied the ground. Then he circled the other way. "The other one, the female, didn't have her throat slashed. She wouldn't have stuck around after the guy bought it if she wasn't in on it, unless she was under some kind of duress."

"You get that from looking at the ground?"

"No. Looking at the pictures. The murderer slashes the guy's throat. The woman is watching. She's in on it. Or drugged. The murderer kills her second. Why, I don't know. Maybe they had a fight. Who knows?"

Kneeling, Rosswell wadded up a ball of mud and smelled it. It smelled like a wadded up ball of mud. Nothing special. He wouldn't taste it if the fate of the universe depended on it. It felt squishy, full of leaves, sticks, and who knew what else. From knee level, he again surveyed the whole area. A bald eagle flew loops high in the air. Rosswell hoped the bird wouldn't mistake Ollie's bald head for a tasty purple treat.

Ollie's reasoning made sense. Rosswell stood and rephrased Ollie's conclusion. "The female helped the guy kill the other guy. That means there were at least three people out here. Could be more, but definitely three."

"You're making assumptions."

Across the river, Rosswell watched an armadillo clawing into a mound of dirt, apparently searching for tasty grubs. Armadillos were supposed to be nocturnal. Had the scent of death awakened the critter?

"What assumptions?" Rosswell said, turning his attention back to Ollie. "Name me one."

"You think the third person was a man."

Rosswell thought about that. Ollie, damn it, was right. "The female helped the male or female suspect kill the male. Is that fair?"

"Fair and clear."

"Maybe we need to be looking for a big woman? The dead woman wasn't all that big. It would've taken a big woman to help the dead woman hold the guy so they could slice his throat."

"Not if he was drugged. Or perhaps shot."

"You just pointed out that his throat was slit."

"Maybe his throat was slit." Ollie sounded like he was about to bray that fricking squeak of his. "Do you have the autopsy reports? No, you don't. You lost the body. Bodies."

Rosswell thought about that too. He recalled why he consulted Ollie often. Ollie was pissy, yes, but the rodent could think. Although now Ollie could be running down the wrong track.

Rosswell said, "What if the guy and the other person killed the woman first? Maybe one of them shot her. Then the third person, the mastermind, was a big guy who slashed the dead man's throat. That could've happened."

"I doubt that. If the killer shot the woman, then why didn't he or she shoot the man? Why waste all that energy to slash the man's throat?"

"The murderer wanted to send a message."

"Judge, let's not get mired down in all that unadulterated bullshit pop psychology."

"Let me get this straight. We're looking for at least one person, male or female, that could be big enough to kill the guy with the help of the dead woman?"

"That's a good place to start."

"And the man could've been shot before his throat was slit. Or maybe drugged before."

"Judge, now you're thinking like a detective."

"But there could be another, fourth person, another murderer. The two bodies I found and two other people to kill them."

"Or a fifth."

"Maybe not. Even Hermie Hillsman would've noticed a killing party that big."

"Think outside the box."

Rosswell scratched his mustache. "Let's not even get ourselves in a box. Keep an open mind."

"Keeping an open mind here." The Vaseline on Ollie's bald head glistened in the afternoon sun. His hand reached for his head, but he stopped before he could follow through with a head rub.

Rosswell said, "What if there were only two people involved?"

Ollie squinted into the sun. "You're not making sense." He closed his eyes.

"What if one of the dead ones surprised the other two? The mastermind had to kill them both."

"She wasn't planning on coming out here." Ollie's eyes flew open. "The dead woman was decked out for a cocktail party. She wasn't dressed for the picnic area of a state park out in the boonies."

"The guy lured her out here, tried to rape her, she resisted, he shot

49

her, and the other person came along, didn't like what he or she saw, and then sliced the guy's throat. Makes perfect sense."

"You're not only thinking outside the box, you're thinking outside your brain."

"I'll bet," Rosswell said, "the dead female was surprised. Her throat wasn't slit and there wasn't much blood around her. The killer could've just shot her without warning."

"UNSUB."

It still had to be close to a hundred degrees. Rosswell stunk, the place stunk, and he was hungry, tired, and irritated. Every insect within a mile must've pledged itself to torment him with its biting and buzzing. The last thing he needed was more of Ollie's games. "What kind of word is that?"

"You're being intentionally dense."

"Dense?" Ollie started to squeak but Rosswell shot up a hand and wiggled his fingers. "Don't do that again for the rest of the day. Tell me. That's all, just tell me."

"UNSUB is an FBI acronym for unknown subject. That's why we'll call this person the UNSUB."

"No, let's not call anyone that. I hate acronyms. And sometimes synonyms. And I'm not real fond of antonyms."

"Okay."

Ollie and Rosswell searched Picnic Area 3 again. Rosswell crouched while Ollie lay face down, giving himself a worm's eye view. Nothing. Ollie rose muddy. They both walked backward, looking down around their feet as they shuffled. They also walked forward, staring at the area around their feet. Nothing.

"Damn," Rosswell said after two hours of finding nothing. "This detective business is tiring."

Ollie grabbed him by the shoulders. Ollie's tight grip hurt Rosswell. There's something unsettling in being grabbed by a big guy you've thrown in jail. Rosswell made no move. What Ollie thought at that moment wasn't clear to Rosswell. What the large snitch wanted that caused him to grab Rosswell was a mystery. The fact that Ollie had never beaten him up before was comforting. Not much. But a little.

"You," Ollie said, "need to learn something."

"What?"

"We've just started." Ollie dropped his arms. "If you're giving up, then take me back to town."

"No."

50

The thought that a third murder or perhaps a good thumping was in the works raced across Rosswell's mind like a scared jack rabbit with a wolf on his tail. A detective slaughtered by his snitch was bad karma.

Ollie pulled out the heavy silver ring Rosswell had given him at Merc's. "Either take me back to town and keep your ring and your whining to yourself, or show me where you found this." He held out the ring. Rosswell considered it but didn't take the ring.

"What's that Latin phrase mean?"

"*Virtus junxit mors non separabit.*" Ollie said it with a sepulchral tone, as if he were pronouncing doom on someone. "'Virtue has united and death shall not separate.' Or, maybe, 'Whom virtue unites, death will not separate.' It depends on your translation."

"Sounds like something out of a wedding ceremony."

"Nope. Masonic."

"Ollie, what in the hell are you talking about?"

"You didn't see the rest of the inscription." He pointed to three letters on the opposite side of the inside of the ring. "EJD."

"Somebody's initials?"

"Could be. Or it could be the abbreviation for a motto."

"We need to find a Mason who has those initials."

"Or," Ollie said, "someone who knows if that's an abbreviation for a motto."

Rosswell, by then tired as a lost dog, pushed himself to walk to where he'd found the ring. Exhaustion hulked down the road towards him like an 18 wheeler on the interstate. The log, following the rules of nature, had sailed down the river along with the bodies. "It was under a log which is probably floating in the Gulf of Mexico by now."

"Did someone hide the ring in the log?"

"Got me."

Ollie said, "You're withholding a clue you found at a crime scene."

"I'll show it to Frizz." Rosswell took the ring from Ollie. "Eventually," Rosswell added. Every time he touched the thing, it felt heavier. "Let me get this straight. This belonged to a Mason?" Rosswell stuffed the ring into his pocket.

"Got me."

"That's my line." Rosswell tapped his head with a forefinger. "I've got an idea."

"Listening here."

The only thing to listen to now was a gentle breeze, not what Rosswell admitted to himself was the lukewarm air he spouted. "We need to find the bodies." *That was brilliant.*

"Do you expect us to do what the twenty people Frizz called out can't do?"

"Twenty-six."

"Whatever. Wait. Something." Ollie held up his hand and shut his eyes. "Something," he repeated. Rosswell began to speak, but Ollie shushed him with a wave of his hand. Bowing his head, Ollie covered his ears with his hands, and then covered his eyes. Was he praying for divine guidance? Was he going into some kind of mystical fit? Was Rosswell's smell bothering him? Ollie had strange—strange to Rosswell's way of thinking—ideas about the "worlds we cannot see" (Ollie's words), although Rosswell doubted that Ollie thought those worlds were going to solve a double murder.

"Judge," he said, his eyes still closed, "we've missed the mother of all clues. Maybe. Anyway, I guess we should both turn in our Junior G Men badges, we're so dense."

"What are you talking about?"

Ollie opened his eyes and pointed. "Tires."

"Damnation." Rosswell whipped out his cell phone. No bars. "Ollie, don't move."

Rosswell touched the peace symbol on his car, then jumped in, and raced down the hill to Hermie's gazebo.

When he got there, Hermie sprinted to his car. "Judge, this morning after y'all left—"

"Okay, Hermie. Thanks."

Rosswell punched in the speed dial and said, "Come on, come on, come on," until he heard her answer.

Chapter Six
Monday afternoon, continued

"Tina, I need your help." He'd called on her personal cell number. No sense in calling on the official line, the one recorded for all posterity. If he did that, there would be evidence he was playing detective.

Tina said in a soft voice, "I hope you need my help." She gave a little growl. She didn't sound like an official dispatcher for a sheriff's department. "I've been thinking about that."

"No," Rosswell said. "I mean your help legally. As a cop, I mean."

Static buzzed in the heartbeat of silence that followed. Then, "What kind of help?"

"You went to the academy and learned all that forensic stuff, didn't you?"

"Yes, but I had to do that for my job as dispatcher." Rosswell heard the radio crackling in the background. Someone was looking for somebody. He heard Tina rustling papers, then tell someone where somebody was. "I'm not a cop," she eventually said to Rosswell. "Not in the strict sense of the word. I'm a deputy, but not one who goes out on the street." Her tone of voice deepened, grew more tense. "You're worrying me. What do you need?"

"Do you know how to pour a mold of tire tracks?"

"Sure."

"Then come out here to the death scene and do it."

He heard Frizz in the background say something to Tina. Why

wasn't he with the search party? She said, "Sheriff, I'll be right with you." Then to Rosswell she said, "Let me talk this over with Frizz. I'll get back with you. We're hugely busy." The line went dead.

Hermie tapped Rosswell's shoulder. "Judge, I was trying to tell you. There was a car out here earlier that drove up to where the bodies were found."

"I know. I called the sheriff to tell him." In truth, he'd called the dispatcher on her private line. Same thing as calling the sheriff. Almost.

"The car came in about an hour before you and Ollie got here. It didn't stay long."

Rosswell moved closer to Hermie to ask a question. "You let them go through?"

The beginnings of a pout started on Hermie's face. "Y'all didn't put up any yellow tape or crime scene signs around the area. The sheriff didn't declare it off-limits. That's a rule, you know." He focused on his shoes, hiding his hangdog look. "How was I supposed to know that people couldn't go up there?" Despite Hermie averting his face, Rosswell could smell America's favorite drug on his breath.

"No one's blaming you for anything." What Rosswell really wanted to ask him was where he was hiding with his bottle when the car came in. Frizz should've given Hermie instructions on what to watch for before the crew packed up and headed for town that morning. Here was another reason the sheriff needed Rosswell on his team. Rosswell wouldn't have forgotten a detail like that.

Hermie didn't raise his head. "Silver."

"What?"

"It was a silver car."

"What kind?"

"Pretty new. Had a chicken claw. Maybe a Malibu." Hermie swiveled his head to stare at a large oak tree with squirrels running up and down its trunk.

Rosswell said, "Chicken claw?"

Hermie let fire an alcoholic belch. "Yeah, one of those things." He made motions with his fingers that Rosswell couldn't follow.

This interview ranks up there with the Titanic.

Rosswell said, "You mean the make of car?"

"Maybe not a Malibu," Hermie said. "Could've been a Lexus or a Kia or an Infiniti. Maybe a Taurus. They all look alike." Still inspecting the tree, he expelled a huge sigh. "No imagination anymore. I could spot your orange car a mile off, but today everyone else has

to drive a car that looks like every other car and a dull color to boot."
Hermie shook his head and his jowls flapped. "Back in my day, we had
cars that were colorful, and you could tell a Ford from a Chevy or a
Plymouth. I remember when my dad's car—"

"Did it have Missouri tags?"

"Yes, he always bought Missouri tags. He lived in Missouri."

"I mean the car that drove out of here." Rosswell ground his teeth.

Hermie answered immediately. "I don't know, but it was silver."

"The license plate was silver?"

"No, the car was silver. I just told you that." Hermie's explanation
was growing harder to follow.

Rosswell said, "Where were you when the car came into the park?"

"See . . . I . . . I was checking on a few things back yonder." He
waved an arm in the direction of the woods. "I didn't actually watch
them come in."

"Them? Did you see the car leave?"

"Oh, yes, sir, I was right here." He pointed to the gazebo. "I saw
the car leave all right."

"Them. You said them. How many people were in the car?"

Hermie closed his eyes and then rubbed his eyelids. Maybe that's
what he did to make answers appear in his head. "One." His eyes
popped open. They were still as bloodshot as they were that morning.

"Did you see who was driving the car?"

"You got that straight. Couldn't miss that."

"Tell me."

Hermie said, "Big. The driver was big."

"Woman or man?"

"I couldn't tell."

"Race?"

"No, they were driving pretty slow."

"I mean was the driver white, black, brown, what?"

"Oh. I couldn't tell. I guess white."

Rosswell said, "There was no one else in the car besides the driver?"

"Not that I could tell."

That narrowed it down to maybe several hundred suspects: A big
person, maybe white, driving a silver car that looked like a Chevy or
Plymouth or Ford or some other brand with tags from somewhere,
maybe Missouri. Rosswell pondered how many actual cars there were
in the area that fit that description. And how many people fit that
description. No maybe about it. There were several hundred suspects
on his suspect list but none on the really good suspect list.

Hermie said, "Besides that silver car, I saw a Cadillac with a big driver."

"You know for certain that this car was a Cadillac?"

"Oh, yeah. A big Cadillac. A big driver."

Rosswell said, "Was it silver?"

"No. White."

"How about the driver? Male? Female? White? Black? Asian?"

"Couldn't tell. The windows were those smoky ones you can't see through. I thought those were illegal."

In his effort to be helpful, Hermie kept losing Rosswell with his roundabout way of speaking. "How did you know the driver was big if you couldn't see the driver?"

"Shadows. The driver was big."

Hermie's too drunk to make sense. How could he have seen shadows in a car with dark windows?

"I don't guess you got a tag number."

"No. Sorry."

"Hermie, did the white Cadillac leave before or after the silver car?" Surely, there weren't a lot of white Cadillacs in Bollinger County. Hermie may've given a good lead and not even realized it. Rosswell silently ticked off the owners of white Cadillacs he could recall. Ambrosia Forcade, a lawyer he suspected of withholding client funds. "Turtles" Rasmussen, a man who owned lots of real estate with no visible means of support; Rosswell couldn't recall his real first name. Susan Bitti, owner of a successful furniture store. Trisha Reynaud, president of Marble Hill National Bank. None of them was a particularly big person.

"The Caddy left first, I'm pretty sure."

Tina Parkmore pulled up behind Rosswell and honked her horn, scaring the hell out of him.

"Hey, Hermie! Hey, Judge!" She'd driven her silver Nissan Sentra with Missouri tags to the park. Fortunately, she wasn't big. Rosswell mentally crossed her off the really good suspect list.

Rosswell patted the hood of Tina's ride and asked Hermie, "Was this the silver car you saw?"

"Oh, no. I'd have recognized Miss Tina."

"I hope so." She flipped her hair and threw her head back in what the old-time movies called a coquettish gesture. "I come out here a lot to sunbathe."

Hermie grinned. Fond memories, Rosswell supposed, of watching Tina sunbathe.

"Judge, why wouldn't Hermie recognize me?"

Rosswell explained, as kindly as he could, what Hermie had said about suspicious cars that had left the park not that long ago.

"Ah." She extracted a plastic tub from the back seat of the car. "I've got plenty of Plaster of Paris."

Hermie said, "Paris?"

Rosswell said, "For the tire impression?"

Tina said, "True enough."

They left Hermie scratching his head, and each drove to the crime scene.

Ollie's eyes grew wide when he saw the dispatcher. "You talked Frizz into letting Tina come up here?"

Tina tugged on Rosswell's sleeve. "We need to talk."

They walked out of Ollie's earshot.

Tina grabbed Rosswell's elbow. They had their backs to Ollie. "Why do you have him with you?"

"He's my research assistant."

"So you say." She leaned closer, put her forefinger on his lips. "I thought I was your research assistant."

"You are." Was his face as red as it felt? "Ollie does a different kind of research."

"How many times have you thrown him in jail?"

He grasped both of her hands. "Don't you believe in rehabilitation?"

Tina released herself and pushed away. "Frizz said that I could take the tire tracks for you, but that's it. He doesn't know about Ollie helping you. He'll be pissed."

"Meaning?"

"Rosswell, he doesn't want you involved in this, much less Ollie. Right now he's swamped with coordinating the search team. This weekend he's got traffic problems all over the county with the Hogfest coming. In fact, there's a bunch of Harleys already here. You can't get involved."

"I am involved." Gesturing toward the crime scene, he said, "I found the bodies. I'm the main witness."

"Just be involved for this one thing, okay?" When he didn't say anything, Tina said, "Please? Just this one thing? The tire track? Promise?"

"Damn it, Tina, two people were murdered. They were human beings with lives that they wanted to live. Frizz needs my help."

The beginnings of a pout started on Tina's face. That morning, Rosswell had made Hermie pout, and now he was making the sweet Tina pout.

"Tina. . . ." Words mixed up in his brain. He wanted to please her but he also had a duty to the legal system. Yes, he was a judge and not a cop. But he needed to help preserve law and order. *What better way to do his duty than to catch the murderers of the two people? Murderers? Did I say murderers? I'm assuming again.* "Tina, I can't promise you anything." He didn't like the expression on her face. Pouting, glaring, the whole nine yards, plus a couple of other yards. "Except that I love you."

"I love you, too, but that's not what this is about."

"Let's do this. Take the tire impression and we'll talk to Frizz when we get back to town."

"Deal."

They rejoined Ollie. Tina whipped out a tape measure and laid it alongside the tire track. "Wow. Three feet of good track. Where's your camera?"

Rosswell grabbed the Nikon. "Reporting for duty."

"I need a million pictures taken from every possible angle. From way down low to as high up as you can reach. Left side, right side, all around the town. I need a lot of ninety degree angle shots to make sure there's no distortion. And keep that tape measure in every shot. Every picture may wind up in a courtroom in front of a jury."

Ollie whistled. "Damn, you're good, Miss Tina."

Rosswell patted Ollie's shoulder, causing him to flinch. "When Tina Parkmore speaks, you best listen."

"I'm talking right now." She bent down by the tire track. "See this jagged edge?"

Ollie and Rosswell peered over her shoulder. A whiff of her perfume improved the scene. Nibbling Tina's ear crossed Rosswell's mind as a good idea, until he realized that Ollie wouldn't appreciate the subtlety of such a gesture.

She used the tape measure to point. "The tires are wearing unevenly. That's what's making the lightning zigzag in the track." She stood, glancing backward and forward. "My best guess is that this tire track is going forward. Here's the direction of travel." She indicated with her toe. "It's a 16-inch tire." She handed the tape measure to Rosswell. "That's my best guess. I'll know more when I run the crown depth and the tread pattern."

Rosswell filled Ollie in on the description of the silver car, such as it was, that Hermie had given.

Ollie stuffed his hands in his pockets. "In other words, we have to track down every midsized silver car with 16-inch tires that has one tire wearing unevenly in a lightning-shaped zigzag."

Tina gave the two a thumbs up. "True enough."

Rosswell said, "That narrows it down to only a couple of hundred or so."

Ollie said, "I can do that."

She pointed to the camera. "Does that thing do video?"

Rosswell said, "Yep."

"I need video," Tina said. "And when you find the car and the big driver, all you have is a car with a big driver, not a suspect. Get to it, Rosswell."

Rosswell glanced up the hill and caught a double glint of light. Binoculars.

Some hunter checking out good hunting sites for the fall deer season.

Chapter Seven
Monday night

After a leisurely supper with Tina, who'd afterwards begged off to go home and clean up, Rosswell returned to his home in Marble Hill around dusk. He checked the mailbox, located where the end of the brick walkway met the street. The heat of the day radiated from the tin roof of the old house, the rising warm air riffling the leaves of the trees surrounding the place. He lived alone, snug as a clam in his white clapboard Victorian. The paint job he'd given the two-story house four years ago was still holding up. He'd owned the place since the day he was sworn into the bar.

He flicked on every light on the ground floor. Being alone was bad. Being alone in the dark was worse. A hot wind had arisen, making the ancient house creak and groan. Another storm brewed in the western sky. The swing on the wide porch, painted the traditional Dixie Gray, squeaked in the wind.

He'd called Tina after he found her letter in the mailbox. "Hey. Are you busy?"

She had a way of talking to him and exhaling at the same time, imitating Marilyn Monroe or Jayne Mansfield or one of the other old-time movie sirens. "Of course I'm busy. I'm always busy. You wouldn't want a lazy girl, would you?"

"I guess you're too busy to come over here?"

"Never."

He sweated, the heat in his body rising steadily. "Are you pure as the driven snow?"

"I used to be Snow White, but I drifted," she said in her best Mae West imitation. "I'll be there in a bit."

He set the letter on a kitchen shelf. Rosswell planned to open it when he worked up his courage. Tina, he'd convinced himself, was fixing to dump him, regardless of how she'd just talked to him. He hoped he'd survive until she arrived. Tina sometimes told him that he exhibited a depressed nature. Yes, he admitted to himself. He did look on the dark side at times. This was one of those times. Women didn't write real snail mail letters nowadays unless they were fixing to dump you.

True to his nature, waiting for Tina gave him time to think about the doom he'd faced before she came into his life. Doom, he thought, is best confronted in the cold examination room of a doctor's office.

He sat in a doctor's office last winter, pondering that it was winter outside and it felt like winter inside. Why do American guardians of the thermostats for public places keep them set at 5 degrees cooler than comfortable? When he blew out his breath to see if it condensed, it didn't. He fidgeted, the crinkly paper on the examining table bunching under his butt. Thankfully, he had his clothes on, making the paper crunching less uncomfortable.

Waiting for the doctor, his acid reflux stomped and roared, adding to his misery. The gastric distress hadn't led him to seek medical help. Symptoms that had earlier forced Rosswell to the clinic were fatigue, bruising for no apparent reason, a wound that wouldn't heal, fullness when he hadn't eaten, and his bones hurt. Those weren't symptoms of acid reflux and he knew it. Test after test followed.

His inspection of the grotesque wall posters depicting the human skeletal, muscular, and circulatory systems was interrupted. Without a knock or other notification that his privacy was being violated, the door opened and the doctor marched in, carrying a thick folder. Rosswell studied his nametag. Hakim Al Serafi. He'd never met the doctor before.

"The news is not good," Al Serafi said, his accent faintly British. No chitchat here. Rosswell admired that. He hadn't come for tea and crumpets. Today, he'd come to learn the results of the series of painful tests he'd endured.

Rosswell said, "Tell me."

For all the emotion he displayed, Al Serafi's Arabic features could've been chiseled from desert obsidian. "Leukemia." He took a fountain pen from a pocket in his white lab coat and wrote on Rosswell's chart, studying the paper with a face adorned by heavy, black eyebrows and a goatee of the same color and density. Then he began talking, his midnight dark eyes never leaving Rosswell's face.

On hearing the scary word spoken over him like an evil benediction, Rosswell's brain shut down, missing most of the technical gibberish the doctor spouted.

Rosswell's brain also kicked into a cherry-picking tour of his mind, a process that usually happened when he tried to sleep. Awake, sitting in front of a physician who rattled off symptoms, treatment options, stages of the disease, *ad nauseam*, he envisioned himself on a merry-go-round, waiting for an insane clown to knock him upside the head when his turn came. There were no brass rings in his future, only knocks in the head. Maybe one solid knock.

Throughout his life, Rosswell had committed important things to memory. Every World Series winner since 1950. The constellations visible from Honolulu at the winter solstice. The smells of eighty-three different substances he'd identified blindfolded in a psychology class at Mizzou, a record that had yet to be broken. He also remembered a quote from *Moby Dick* where Ishmael said:

Who ain't a slave? Tell me that. Well, then, however the old sea-captains may order me about—however they may thump and punch me about, I have the satisfaction of knowing that it is all right; that everybody else is one way or other served in much the same way—either in a physical or metaphysical point of view, that is; and so the universal thump is passed round, and all hands should rub each other's shoulder-blades, and be content.

The universal thump headed his way. Flying at supersonic speed. No, not faster than the speed of sound. Faster than light speed, it aimed for him. Unswerving. Unstoppable.

Unbidden, the memory of Rosswell's first true love, long dead, surfaced in his brain. Especially the memory of Feliciana's eyes. They'd been gray. No, not gray. Silver. He recalled a snippet of a poem or a song about drowning in the eyes of a lover. He could've done that in

Feliciana's eyes. How many times had he stroked her face during love-making, smelling the heat of her body, and felt himself drowning in those glorious eyes? The times couldn't be numbered.

On a bitterly cold and foggy night, he'd gotten drunk. Feliciana was the designated driver. On their way home, a grain truck ran a stop sign and smashed into the driver's side—her side—of the car. Feliciana died instantly. Last night, as he'd done a thousand nights before, he woke to the sound of metal grinding into metal with the shriek of a banshee. Rosswell hadn't killed her. But he felt like he was a murderer. After the wreck, he indulged himself with a year of intoxication, until he awoke one morning in a pool of vomit. He struggled onto the wagon and hadn't fallen off since.

Al Serafi droned on until Rosswell shot his hand, palm out, towards the doctor's face. "Stop." A rude gesture, to be sure. Rosswell couldn't blame himself for being rude during the delivery of a death sentence. "Don't say another word."

Al Serafi blinked. "Yes, I will stop."

"Get to the bottom line."

"Bottom line?" Al Serafi was clearly unfamiliar with the idiom. "What line is that?"

"How long do I have to live?"

Al Serafi flipped open a pair of tiny reading glasses and consulted the chart. "This is the best guess." He flipped pages. "Yes." Flipped more pages. "Yes. Yes." More pages. "Yes."

"Can you give me your best guess today?"

Al Serafi stopped flipping.

"Yes. You're an otherwise healthy man, thirty eight years of age. Average weight for a male of one dot six five meters." Al Serafi stopped, appearing to be counting on his fingers. "That's five feet and five. The only other major health problems you have are poor vision and reflux. I'd mostly say a year to five years, unless you find a bone marrow donor. There are procedures now that make this marrow business almost as easy as donating blood. Your lifespan may be possible for indefinite then. There is also the experimental gene therapy that turns your own blood cells into the little assassins who hunt down and destroy the cancer cells."

"What a bunch of crap."

If Al Serafi was offended, he gave no indication. "There are many social agencies to help in these matters." He handed Rosswell a pamphlet. "You perhaps must talk with someone."

"Social agencies?" That sounded like a place to get social diseases. Talk with someone? Who could Rosswell talk to? He had no lover, no wife, no child, no brother, no sister, no father, and no mother. Who was his closest relative? He couldn't remember. How about a friend? He couldn't imagine discussing something like his impending death with Frizz. That friendship was professional, not personal. Judges in small towns don't make friends easily. Everyone always wants something from you, especially free legal advice. That made him standoffish.

Rosswell faced a stark fact that cold winter's day: He was alone in the world.

He said, "I pay tax dollars to a bureaucrat who will help me feel good about dying?" The paper under his butt scrunched and crackled with his movements, growing more agitated by the second. "I don't need a social worker. I don't need a bureaucrat."

"Bureaucrat?" The physician sounded puzzled.

"Hell, Dr. Akim, I'm a bureaucrat. I wouldn't want to talk to me if I were dying of some nasty disease."

"It is Hakim Al Serafi."

Rosswell studied the name tag again. "Sorry." He teetered on more confusion. "I'm trying to put all this together."

"You are not limited to bureaucrats. Do you have some religious counselor you can talk with?"

"Religious counselor?"

"You can talk with some religious counselor to help you understand that your pathway may take you to death."

"Pathway? I don't have any religious people in my life. Maybe I need some." Scooting around on the cold examining table hurt even though he was clothed. "Where did you go to medical school?"

Al Serafi withdrew a stethoscope from his coat and hung it around his neck. "St. Bartholomew's and Royal London School of Medicine & Dentistry."

"I'm impressed."

"Judge Carew, my credentials have nothing to do with your prognosis."

Rosswell warmed to the man. The guy didn't have the bull crap aura most doctors did. Most physicians expected their patients to fawn on every word that fell from their mouths without question. Even in court, when a medical doctor testified, Rosswell sensed an underlying superiority that most physicians assumed over laypeople.

"Dr. Al Serafi, I'm trying to put your diagnosis into a box so I can examine it."

"That is understandable."

"Will you be here if I need to talk with you?"

"I'm on loan from St. Mark's in Cape Girardeau." He slipped the tiny eyeglasses into a shirt pocket. "They have not enough hands here, but I am only temporary. I go back to Cape soon."

"Telling people news like this is hard."

Al Serafi's cellphone beeped. "Not as hard as getting it." Without removing his eyes from Rosswell, he reached down and cut off his phone.

Rosswell was the same person he'd been when he walked in the clinic, although now the powerful words of doom had been spoken, sealing his fate. Until that second, he'd not noticed the strong smell of rubbing alcohol in the room. *Even that can set off a drunk like me.* From his pocket, he drew a couple of Rolaids, hoping the chalky mint taste would distract his cravings. The taste didn't alleviate anything.

"Doctor Al Serafi, I refuse to give in to the monster living in my body. I'm going to kill it. I want to start chemo or whatever you need me to do immediately."

"I like your attitude."

Feliciana had kept her black hair cut short. Nonetheless, Rosswell had loved running his fingers through the tight curls on her head. That action had aroused him, and it often made her moan with pleasure.

Now, no more Feliciana to comfort him.

It was time to leave, go home, and search the attic for Malachi, the teddy bear he'd slept with until he was ten years old.

But that day he didn't go home to the attic. Instead he dragged himself to the sheriff's station, searching for Frizz. He wasn't there. Tina was there.

"What's wrong?" she said the instant she saw him.

Rosswell told her. Later that night she invited herself to share his bed.

Waiting for Tina now, Rosswell rummaged in the pantry. Behind a ten-pound bag of grits, he discovered a bottle of booze he'd stashed there months ago. Scotch. His favorite kind of liquor. He fetched it down and rested it, still swathed in a brown paper bag, on the Benchwright dining table. There the elixir waited, sitting on a table that resembled an Industrial Revolution worktable that had set him back a thousand bucks. If Rosswell gave in and the doctor found out, Al Serafi would scold him for drinking. Tough crap. It was his body, not Al Serafi's.

Rosswell pulled a heavy chair out from the table and sat. He hunkered there, unmoving, staring at the bottle for a long time, the booze just out of reach. He clicked on an antique-style radio to provide companionship. He had a decision to make. A decision about the bottle.

A newscaster on the radio rattled on.

". . . United Nations sent a strongly worded letter advising . . ."

". . . prices stabilized after plunging . . ."

". . . largest contract ever for a first baseman . . ."

Maybe one more shot of booze for old-time's sake. Or maybe a couple. Maybe the whole bottle. Maybe he should get drunk as a jackass on Sunday, then explain to Tina that he was an alcoholic and would always remain an alcoholic. She needed to search for someone better. He'd cuddle up with his bottle and remain blissfully unconscious until he died. No teddy bear needed.

"What a load of crap!" Had he said that aloud? Yes, he had. He slapped himself for self-induced stupidity. *Suffering from leukemia? Check. Alcoholic? Check.* That didn't relieve him of responsibility. The pity party blew up, and he steered himself toward what he needed to be doing—solving a murder.

He cut off the radio and began talking to himself. Talking to himself, he'd learned, helped him solve problems. Rosswell stared at the distressed wooden floor. Walking to the kitchen island, he rubbed his hand over the bluish-gray granite of the island, noting that the depth of the shiny top seemed to change when he changed position. When the angle of his eyes changed, the light reflected a different color in the granite, giving the illusion of depth.

He reasoned with himself.

"There was a murder. Two people. One woman. One man."

Rubbing the tabletop with his hands soon coated it with a glistening sheen of palm sweat. He folded his hands together and made a steeple with his forefingers. He placed the steeple on his lips and gazed again, almost in a hypnotic trance, at the floor.

The odor of Pine Sol and Comet permeated the air in his tidy house. His gaze rose to a six-foot sword mounted on the kitchen wall. What better place for a cutting instrument than in the kitchen? Its blade shone from the reflected light of the buzzing fluorescent light.

"There are no witnesses. I don't know if the murderer was a man or a woman. I don't know if there was more than one murderer."

The cross guard of the sword held a curlicue snake on each side. A pommel in the shape of a monster's head topped the grip, decorated with the scales of justice. Below the cross guard, the sword's blade gleamed, sharp and deadly.

He paced around the table, nearly tripping over a chair, forcing himself to understand that maybe he knew more about the murder than his conscious mind allowed him to know. After all, he was first on the scene after the killer left.

"What was at that place before the flood?"

He closed his eyes. He stepped through the recollection of the crime scene with excruciating slowness. Bloated bodies. Rocks. Dirt. Trees. River. He got his camera and reviewed the photos on it.

"What am I not seeing?"

Rosswell returned to the table and sat. He stared beyond the bottle to a black and white print of an ancient Scottish battle scene on the wall until the picture became unfocused.

His thoughts ambled to the sword. For the last seven years, he'd tried to convince himself that it was a centuries old relic from his Scots ancestors. In truth, it was a replica he'd bought in a junk store for $169.47, after haggling the toothless woman who owned the place down from two hundred dollars.

"The murderer killed two people and laid them side by side. Why?"

His heartbeat slowed, his breathing slowed, and his vision blurred even more.

"Side by side. They lay side by side. Arms, legs, head, torso. What position, exactly, were they lying in?"

His mind hovered in a meditative state.

"What did I look at that I did not see?"

He recited the mantra several more times.

His cellphone chirped an irritating three-tone chime. A text message.

"Crap," he said, the spell broken by the electronic interference. Only Tina, Frizz, and Neal were privy to the cell number. No one else, not even Ollie, had the number. This late at night, there had to be some emergency. He'd probably have to issue a search warrant. Or maybe Tina wasn't coming over. Wouldn't she call instead of texting?

He stared at his phone. The screen showed the texter's identification: UNKNOWN. The message was clear: *2 DWN UR NXT*.

"Real funny, Neal." He turned the phone off. "You're a real asshole."

His exercise in meditative thinking resulted in zero. The next choice, he knew, was booze or wait for Tina. He reached for the bottle, feeling the weight of the liquor, caressing the smoothness of the glass, touching the highs and lows of the embossed label. Rosswell drew the bottle from the paper bag and lifted it up to the light and marveled at the pure color. The imagined taste of the amber liquid, burning down his throat in blessed relief, blossomed in his mouth.

He checked his watch. Nearly 10:00 PM. Too late to get drunk. And if he did get drunk, Tina would find him. She would leave him if she found him drunk.

Roswell stood. He yawned, stretched, and aimed his exhausted body for the bedroom. What better place to wait for Tina than in bed?

A gunshot shattered his kitchen window, fragmenting the bottle. Tiny shards of glass and a pungent spray covered the table. The noise deafened him momentarily, quickly replaced by ringing in his ears. Who the hell was shooting at him?

Although the scene lasted but a few seconds, in his mind it stretched out like a bad dream that lasted hours. For another second, Rosswell stood frozen. His brain kicked his butt into gear with the knowledge that the next slug would burst through his brain, rendering it useless. He would be dead. He dove for the floor.

Rosswell collected the presence of mind to scrabble to the switch, reach a shaking arm upward, and cut the lights in the kitchen. Once the room was plunged into darkness, he tore the sword from the wall, and sprinted down the hallway, flipping off every light. When he gained the living room, he turned off all the lights. Thus far, there'd been one gunshot. He clutched the sword and waited by the front door.

Breathing so hard he felt like his lungs had inflated to twice their normal size, he used one hand to reach for his cellphone. Patting himself down twice, he realized he'd left the damned thing in the kitchen. He groped for and found his landline phone. His sweaty hand closed around the handset and pressed it to his ear. It was dead. From the living room window, he spotted the phone company's pedestal next to the street. It held the copper snaking to the house. The pedestal had been knocked over, wires strewn everywhere.

Someone rushed through the front door. "Rosswell!"

Rosswell heard a noise outside, at the back of his house. He grasped the sword, hefting it above his head in a warrior's stance and whirled around to see who might be coming in the back door, all the while realizing that bringing a sword to a gun fight wasn't a good idea.

Rosswell yelled, "Come on, you son of a bitch. Bring it on."

Vowing to slice and dice anybody who came after him, he danced around the living room, slashing at the air with the sword. No one would dare attack him when he had that sword.

Another gunshot exploded. Then another. Each shot produced a strobe-light flash.

Before the blackness reached out and grabbed him, he turned around and glimpsed Tina in the living room, standing just inside the front doorway, reaching for him before she crashed to the floor.

Chapter Eight
Monday night into Tuesday morning

"Judge, can you hear me?"

Rosswell squinted through one eye. What he saw through the haze didn't encourage him. Neal leaned over him, their faces nearly touching. Rosswell moaned, expecting the sword to plunge through his heart at any moment. Neal's hair brushed Rosswell's cheek, causing a glacial shudder down his spine. Death hovered close. Instead of the sword, maybe Neal had found Rosswell's .38 and was fixing to shoot him.

The smell surrounding Rosswell conjured a memory of a fireworks display. Was he at a Fourth of July celebration? The taste in his mouth felt as if he'd been chewing pennies. There was another smell. An unpleasant smell. Blood.

There could be only one rational conclusion about what was happening. "I've died and gone to hell."

"No, you're not dead," Neal said. "Keep your mouth shut."

"If I'm not dead, why do I have to keep my mouth shut?" He groaned. "I'm hurt bad."

"Keep your mouth shut."

It hurt him to talk, but Rosswell had to know. "Why the hell did you shoot me?" And, he wondered to himself, *Are you going to shoot me again?* "You destroyed a fifth of Glenfiddich 18-year-old single malt Scotch." He hated giving Neal any ideas, such as that he'd been considering drinking the whole bottle. "Tell me before I die why you shot me."

"Ross, shut up."

"My name. . . ." He found it difficult to think. "It's not Ross. It's. . . ."

"You haven't been shot, so shut up," Neal ordered.

Rosswell's insides burned. Someone must've stuck a red-hot poker through him. Neal was lying. He'd either been shot or was having one hell of an acid reflux attack. No one had ever shot him when he'd served with the Marines in Iraq. He had to wait until he returned to the safety of his hometown before he caught a round.

"Rosswell," a second voice said, "open your other eye."

That surprised Rosswell. He thought both eyes were open. With difficulty, he opened his other eye. The view, although still blurry, cleared with an agonizing slowness. His glasses were still on his face. How was that possible?

"Who are you?" Rosswell asked. "Are you Neal's accomplice?"

"It's Frizz. Your neighbor called 911 when he heard the first gunshot."

"Neal shot me."

"No, Neal didn't shoot you."

"Who shot me?" Rosswell's throat grew dry and his voice croaked.

Frizz said, "Neal and I were driving around, talking about the murders. We were practically in front of your house when we got the call."

Rosswell said, "You were planning my murder?"

Neal still worked on Rosswell, doing something Rosswell couldn't see. "Don't talk, Ross."

"Can you see me?" Frizz asked. He held up three fingers. "How many fingers am I holding up?"

"Is that your foot?"

"No, Judge, it's my hand."

"For Christ's sake," Neal said. "Don't ask him any more questions. He's too stupid."

Rosswell felt Neal's hands on him. That wasn't a good sign. Neal's hands felt like a glob of rubbery worms crawling over his flesh. In the distance, Rosswell heard the electronic warbling of a siren. There must've been a fire somewhere.

"Where am I?" Rosswell twisted his head from side to side.

Neal said, "You're in your house. You cut yourself with your sword."

"You shot me," Rosswell said. "Don't lie to me, you son of a bitch."

Neal said, "I've stabilized you and we're waiting for the ambulance."

Rosswell said, "The . . . what?"

Frizz said, "You must've slipped and cut your arm with your sword. An ambulance is taking you to the hospital."

Then the real horror of the situation walloped into Rosswell's gut. He wrenched his head around, looking left and right, up and down. "Where's Tina?"

Neal and Frizz glanced at each other for a millisecond, but Rosswell wasn't so far gone that he didn't catch it.

His hands rubbed across the floor, finding a sticky puddle. His blood. And Tina's blood. Mixed. It had to be. There was too much blood to come from one wound.

Rosswell said. "Is she all right?"

Rosswell smelled booze. Scotch, to be exact. Had he passed out at a party?

"The EMTs are coming," Neal said.

"Are they going to pronounce me dead?" he said.

The EMTs sprinted into the house and Rosswell passed out again.

###

In his stupor, Rosswell heard a blonde woman tell him, "Do anything you want." He lifted a hand. She said, "Don't mess with the makeup." She poured herself a large single malt Scotch.

"Take your clothes off," he heard himself say.

The blonde said, "Take them off slow or fast?"

Was it Tina talking to him? The woman's face filled with fog. He tried to answer, but couldn't speak.

The blonde changed into a dark-complexioned child with black hair. A little girl. Rosswell screamed at her to run away, but she didn't move.

The blonde reappeared and slipped a dirty spoon to the little girl. The little girl turned around once and showed Rosswell the spoon, now clean. He spun the girl around and discovered that she clutched the spoon, dirty again, behind her back. The back of the girl's head was bloody, blown away.

Rosswell screamed again. "Get the hell out of here. Don't you understand plain English?" He screamed and screamed.

The child lost all color, transfiguring into a ghost. Then Rosswell's father appeared, standing over him with a whip, ready to thrash him. Rosswell glimpsed his mother, hovering behind his father, crying. Rosswell reached around his father, laboring to touch his mother and convince her that everything was all right. He would make sure that nothing hurt her ever again.

Everyone vanished. A curtain fell in his brain and everything faded to black.

Rosswell awoke sweating from the nightmare. He found a tube stuck in his right arm and his left arm patched with a mile's worth of bandages. The windows had the slatted blinds open. Sunlight poured through the clean glass onto his bed and made a striped pattern on his crisp white covers. A nurse, a gray-haired Sumo wrestler of a woman, as broad as she was tall, fussed with the inverted plastic bag hooked to a tube dripping liquid into his veins. He was certain it held a painkiller of some kind, although his arm still felt as if a thousand bees took turns stinging him. Nonetheless, he felt himself floating on a down comforter a mile thick. His mouth felt like it was stuffed with cotton balls. Everything hurt except the parts he couldn't feel.

He lay on death's cold doorstep. The welcome mat invited him to leave the land of the living and enter the country of the dead.

The nurse squinted. "You awake, honey?" she said in a soft angel's voice that didn't match her balloon of a body. If she spoke in an angel's voice, maybe he'd already passed. "You must've been dreaming. You were groaning and making a lot of noise. Mumbling about something."

The exceptionally good dope dribbling into him made her voice sound heavenly. He spotted a crucifix hanging around her neck. When he turned on his side, a lightning bolt shot through his arm. Maybe the dope wasn't as good as he'd first thought.

He said, "Am I dead?"

"No." She rearranged his pillow. "Far from it. You're in St. Luke's Hospital."

"Then, yes, sweetie. I'm awake."

She giggled. The laughter and voice sounded familiar. "You're going to be fine." The nurse straightened the bed sheets while he tried to determine if he knew her. The sheets felt starched and smelled faintly of Clorox. Where had he seen her? Woozy as he was, she still reminded him of someone.

"When can I get out of here?"

"Maybe today. Definitely tomorrow." She looked over her shoulder, out the door, then back at Rosswell. "I'm not supposed to tell you things like that. Wait for the doctor."

"Tell me something else." He tried lifting his left arm. The pain telegraphed spears to the far reaches of his body. "Will I have a cast?"

"No," the chubby angel said. "You'll have a bandage for a while but no cast. The doc will be in later to explain everything to you."

"I need a priest."

The nurse shuffled to an alcove by the sink and called up Rosswell's chart on the room's computer workstation. "Says here when they asked your religious preference early this morning, you said, 'Occasional'." She clicked some keys. "You want me to change that to Catholic?"

"No." Rosswell closed his eyes. "Not yet."

"Just let me know if you change your mind."

"Nurse, hand me my glasses, please." After he put them on, he struggled with putting a name to her face. "What's your name?" He was sure that he knew the woman, but the dope and the pain kept him from recognizing her.

"Benita Smothers." She shuffled to the bed and patted the arm without the bandage. "Mabel—she's my daughter—waits on you down at Merc's."

Even with a fogged brain, he was astounded. Ollie's love interest was Rosswell's nurse. If she could put up with Ollie, then she had to be a saint. Comfort washed over Rosswell until a jolt of fear creased his spine with icicles straight from hell.

"Listen, Benita, what happened to Tina? Tina Parkmore. What happened to her?"

"The sheriff is waiting out in the hall. I'll get him."

That sounded bad. Tina was dead. Benita wasn't supposed to tell anyone. Frizz would break the news to him.

Rosswell said, "About that priest, can you call one for me?" Without Tina, someone would have to pump him full of a good reason to keep on living.

"Sure, Mr. Carew." Benita seemed delighted to be of service. "I'll do that for you."

"Am I going to die?" He turned his head so he wouldn't have to watch her when she answered.

"Yes." Rosswell turned back to gawk at her. Once more, Benita smiled and giggled, sounding like Mabel. "We all must die. It's the rule." She leaned over him and gently closed her hand on his arm. "But you're not going to die from that cut. You have a lot of veins and arteries in your arm. The doc says the blade didn't do that much damage and never hit anything major."

"It hit something or I wouldn't hurt."

"You could've bled to death if it had hit something major. It didn't hit anything vital."

"It's all vital to me. I'm quite attached to my whole body. And I still need a priest."

"Mr. Carew?"

"Yes?"

"Do you mind if I call you by your first name?"

"No."

"I'll call my brother, the priest over at Sacred Heart. He's in the hospital right now visiting people. He's one of our chaplains." She patted Rosswell's arm again. "You're going to be fine, Ross."

He closed his eyes and whimpered.

Chapter Nine
Tuesday morning, continued

"Rosswell?" Frizz sauntered up to the open doorway, pausing in the hallway to rap his knuckles on the doorjamb. "May I come in?"

"Tina?" The dope stopped working. Rosswell's heart galloped around his ribcage and sweat trickled down his chest. He reached the crescendo of an adrenaline high. His body reeked of fear. Frizz could not be the bearer of good news.

"It's bad." Frizz walked to the edge of the bed. The sheriff must have missed his sleep for the last two days, judging by the lines on his face and the bags under his bloodshot eyes. He removed his hat and rubbed the inside of it with his handkerchief.

After Rosswell belched an acidy belch, he closed his eyes. "When's the funeral?" Visions of Feliciana's funeral invaded his brain, soon to be joined by the reality of Tina's final services.

Frizz dabbed at his eyes, then stuffed the handkerchief into his back pocket. "Funeral?" He put his hat on and stared at Rosswell. "Are you doped up?"

"I'm going to her funeral, I don't care if you have to push me in this hospital bed, I'm going."

"There's no funeral, Rosswell."

If he said that to calm Rosswell, it wasn't working. "What're you saying?" Had it been so bad that they'd already cremated Tina? "Has she already been buried? Did you cremate her and spread her ashes?"

"Listen to me." Frizz sat on the edge of the bed. "You hurt your arm. Nothing that a tetanus shot, antibiotics, painkillers, and bandages won't help. Tina got shot. That's bad. But you're both alive. She's here in the hospital, too."

"Oh, Jesus."

"I'm not a doctor, but her wound wasn't serious." Frizz smiled. "In fact, she got off easier than you. A bullet grazed her arm and it doesn't look as bad as your wound. You need to be more careful with that sword." He lost his smile. "We need to talk."

"Talk." Rosswell slugged the pillow with the fist of his good arm. "I'm not going anywhere."

"I don't have any idea who broke into your house and shot Tina."

"I do." Rosswell waited a couple of seconds to build suspense. "I know." Frizz would have to listen to him now.

"Who?"

He enjoyed knowing something Frizz didn't about this case. "I got a text message right before the gunfire started. It said—"

"*2 DWN UR NXT.*"

Rosswell clenched his jaw until it quivered. "You searched my cell-phone?"

"It was an emergency."

"Damn it, Frizz."

"The person or persons who killed those people at the park are after you. That's my working hypothesis."

"I've irritated a lot of people." Rosswell knew where this conversation was headed and didn't like the signposts to the destination. "It could've been one of a thousand people who're pissed off at me."

"No. What do you think *2 DWN* meant? It's an explicit reference to the two bodies at the park. Two down."

Rosswell stayed silent, unwilling to acknowledge the elephant in the room.

Frizz said, "You were out there investigating and you dragged Tina into it. Whoever was after you was after her, too."

"You don't know that. It was just coincidence that she came to my house when she did. Wrong place at the wrong time."

"Tina got shot because she was helping you do something that you shouldn't have been doing."

The elephant took a big dump, right on Rosswell's head. "You think I'd put Tina in harm's way?"

"All I know is what happened."

"Judge Carew?" A priest called his name at the hospital room door. It hadn't taken long for him to arrive. "I'm Father Michael David Smothers." He could've passed for the twin brother of a young Pope John Paul II, except that his hair was shockingly white and his skin was lighter—no, grayer—than the late Pope's. "They call me Father Mike."

Rosswell envied the man's black pupils and clear eyes. No bloodshot there. Dressed in his black priest's outfit, he carried an aura of power about him.

Frizz shook hands with Father Mike. "I'll leave y'all alone. Rosswell, you're off the case. Period. End of story. Even if."

Rosswell took off his eyeglasses to rub his face, which felt gritty. Holding the glasses with the hand of his wounded arm didn't work. He dropped the trifocals.

After Frizz left, Rosswell said, "I met you at your church picnic last year."

Father Mike winked at Rosswell. "You're the one who ate three helpings of chicken and dumplings." The priest hadn't moved from the doorway even though Rosswell had motioned him in.

"Your memory is excellent. They were a tad salty or I'd have eaten four helpings." The pain in his arm increased, causing him to grimace. "Can I make a confession?"

The priest came in, pushed the door shut, and walked to the bedside. "Are you a Catholic?" He spoke in a soft voice.

"No." Rosswell squinted to focus on the priest's face. "I need to confess because I put the woman I love in a dangerous situation. She could've died. Would you hand me my glasses, please?"

Father Mike's ready smile—what Rosswell could see of it—and his patience impressed the judge. The priest searched for a moment until he discovered the trifocals on the floor and handed them to Rosswell. Once he had put on his glasses, the priest came into clearer view.

"Judge Carew, is your death imminent?"

"No." Able to see now, Rosswell studied the man's face more closely. "It's a superficial wound. I'm going home today. Or in the morning at the latest."

"I can't hear your confession, but I'll be glad to talk to you. Let's start with what Benita said. You have other problems?"

"Leukemia. I'm in remission, but if I don't get a bone marrow donor or go through some kind of experimental treatment, I'm a goner."

Father Mike moved the bedside table out of the way to stand closer to him. "You say you put someone in a dangerous situation. But did you do serious harm to someone?" He'd no doubt heard about Tina getting shot.

"Benita said there was a rule about death." Rosswell felt like he was in grade school again with a grownup hovering over him while he worked on a problem at his desk. This must be what it was like to attend Catholic school. "She said all of us are going to die. I'm going to die."

"Yes." Father Mike pulled a quarter from his suit coat pocket, flipping it end over end in one hand like a magician practicing a coin trick.

Outside the window, a pigeon landed on the ledge. The gray bird, boasting an opulent white chest, ogled Rosswell, sharing a soft coo. It strutted up and down, making a clicking sound as it pecked the window a couple of times, then flew off.

Rosswell drank from his water glass. "I know I'm going to die." He removed the eyeglasses and rubbed his face some more. Before speaking again, he put his glasses back on. "I hope it won't be soon."

The priest drew up a chair next to the bed and sat. He flipped the quarter in the air where it disappeared, folded his hands together, and contemplated Rosswell before he answered. "What else is on your mind?"

"What am I supposed to say?"

"Explain the things that are bothering you, and I'll listen until you finish. It's all confidential."

Rosswell commenced, starting with the cigarette he smoked behind the barn when he was six, the money he'd stolen from his mother's purse when he was eight, the sex he'd had when he was fourteen, and on and on in lurid detail, including Feliciana's death and putting Tina in harm's way.

Rosswell said, "All of those are bad things, but then there's the big one." Up until now, his list of sins probably sounded like myriad other confessions Father Mike had heard.

The priest, his face impassive, retrieved his quarter, seemingly grabbing it from thin air. "Tell me." The quarter turned into a dime, then a nickel. Rosswell wondered if he did that in the confessional.

"I was in the military in the Middle East." Rosswell punched the pillow behind him, trying to make himself more comfortable. The pain meds continued dripping, helping the hurt in his arm, although the dope wasn't strong enough to make him lose control of his faculties. "On patrol, I rounded a corner where I discovered a little girl hunkered in a red chair with a bomb strapped to her." Clearing his throat and wiping his eyes bought him a little time before he reached the big one. "She grabbed for a wire on the bomb and I shot her."

Rosswell fell silent. The priest asked for no details, but also fell silent, marching the quarter through his fingers at a slow pace.

Rosswell said, "What kind of monster puts a bomb on a little girl?"

"The kind," Father Mike answered, "whose mind I can't understand."

Rosswell removed his eyeglasses again. "I knew if she set that bomb off, she'd kill twenty people." He wiped his face, hoping that his hands could erase the hideous memory. "I had to choose between shooting her or letting her murder twenty other people. That's why I killed her." Rosswell stared at the eyeglasses in his hand. "The bomb people said it was a fake."

"God knows what was in your mind."

"There wasn't any choice. If it's a sin, then I'm sorry." He replaced his eyeglasses and scratched his thin mustache. "Killing another human being is never right." He fell back on the bed. "I'm through."

Father Mike shifted the quarter to his other hand and flipped it through his fingers for a few seconds before he continued. "God will have mercy on you."

Rosswell hoped the priest would have solutions. Father Mike not only had no solutions, he gave Rosswell a cliché for comfort. The old saying that nothing in life is free is wrong. Just the opposite. If it's free, it's nothing.

Rosswell said, "I lost Feliciana because I was drunk and made her drive. I don't want to lose Tina by doing something wrong."

"God knows that." Father Mike drew a small gold crucifix on a silver chain from his pocket. "I'd like you to have this. It's a crucifix blessed by the Pope."

"Would you put it around my neck?" It felt warm against Rosswell's bare skin.

Father Mike's cellphone beeped. He lifted it out of the holster on his belt, read the screen, and said, "Oops, that's my reminder. I've got an appointment in fifteen minutes."

The priest left before Rosswell could tell him that if Tina died, Rosswell would make sure he himself was right behind her.

Chapter Ten
Tuesday morning, continued

Frizz was right. Rosswell had accepted that he had no reason to be involved in a murder investigation. True, he'd found the bodies. It was also true that Frizz now had the impression of a tire track that may or may not be from a suspicious car, thanks to Rosswell. And Tina.

What Rosswell needed to do was relax, lie in the clean-smelling hospital bed, enjoy the dope, heal, and let the cops do all the worrying. Then, when he left the hospital today or tomorrow, he'd kick back and enjoy the rest of his vacation. Sipping coffee at Merc's and listening to Ollie sounded pleasant to his drug-addled brain. Ultra sweet coffee and Ollie droning on would be the cure. Sitting around all day, working on a caffeine sugar high and chatting, staring out the windows at Merc's, watching Marble Hill plod along. The perfect daydream.

The only worry he nurtured was whether he and Tina would be killed by whoever invaded his house.

That terrifying possibility stabbed him out of his stupor.

Outside the hospital, a distinctive sound signaled that a Harley had exploded to life, its two-piston engine popping. Rosswell knew about the Harley's unique sound. A hog's crankshaft has only one pin, and both pistons connect to it. The way the pistons are arranged, they fire at unequal intervals. No other internal combustion engine sounds like a Harley. On the street, the first motorcycle was joined by what sounded like another hundred. Then the whole flock growled their way to some-where else.

Harley riders, their pockets filled with money, had already begun zipping throughout Bollinger County. The locals loved Harley riders. The couple of hundred riders might spend hundreds of dollars each, keeping the county's economy healthy. Most of the riders camped at Foggy Top State Park. Rosswell hoped the clues were all recorded, because by now they'd been destroyed by the crush of bikes and riders.

The murder investigation wasn't progressing. Rosswell needed to do something. Progress happens when you're out and about, seeking a goal you've set. Progress doesn't happen when you're stoned in a hospital bed. That revelation kicked Rosswell in the butt.

He jerked out the dope line feeding the vein in his arm, tumbled out of bed, dressed himself, and gathered his belongings. Later, when he sobered up, he knew he'd hurt like nine kinds of hell. Future pain didn't matter. He had places to visit and people to comfort.

He wandered all over the hospital. When he discovered Tina's room at the end of a hallway next to a staircase, he barged past Junior Fleming, the city cop he loathed, and saw her.

The cop jumped up from his seat in the hallway and stood in the doorway. "Judge, the nurse said can't nobody go see her."

"Tina." Rosswell leaned over and kissed her cheek. She stirred yet didn't open her eyes or make any other reaction. He ran his fingers through her hair. "Tina, it's Rosswell." Nothing. She lay there inert but still alive. "I'm so sorry, Tina. Can you hear me?" Her voice could heal him. For the moment, he couldn't hear that voice.

"Judge?"

He turned around to face the nurse in charge of everything. "Yes?"

"You can't be in here."

The woman, stick thin and homely as a mud fence, couldn't have been any older than Tina.

"Why isn't she awake?" Rosswell asked the nurse, whose name tag said she was Priscilla Brewster.

"Sometimes anesthesia affects people differently. She's just sleeping."

"Anesthesia? Did she have an operation?"

"No, just a precautionary procedure. No one knew at first if her wounds were serious. The doctor checked her thoroughly. All she needs is rest."

"I put this woman here," Rosswell said to the ugly stick.

Priscilla pursed her lips. "From what I hear, she's not hurt as bad as you were." Rosswell thought she delivered the line as if it were some kind of moral failing that Tina wasn't hurt badly, so why was she taking up space in the hospital?

"If you want me out, then you have Junior there arrest me."

"Do you want to give her an infection?"

No, dreadful tree branch, I don't want to give her an infection. As it so happens, I'm not contagious. Leukemia, acid reflux, allergies, bad eyes, and poor judgment are not contagious.

That's what he thought, although he didn't say it. He wasn't that stoned. Instead, Rosswell said, "Tell whoever runs this place that I've checked out against medical advice to solve a couple of murders."

Although Benita said he wouldn't need a sling, Rosswell rigged a homemade one. It kept his arm from moving which, in turn, eased the pain somewhat. With a buzz from the painkillers running strong, Rosswell's feet weaved the three blocks from the hospital to the sheriff's station. Frizz, of all people, was dispatching. Nobody else was around. Especially no prisoners. Rosswell was sure that Frizz prayed that no one got arrested. Frizz should've been out running the roads, not stuck inside talking on the radio and the telephone. The sheriff shouldn't be doing such things. That's what a dispatcher is for. And Rosswell was responsible for temporarily downing the best dispatcher around.

Rosswell said, "I thought you'd be out making sure the Harley riders spent money on legal substances." He fell into a chair next to the sheriff. "I don't feel so good."

"How's Tina?"

Rosswell squirmed in the chair, trying to get comfortable. "The anesthesia knocked her for a loop. She'll get out later today."

"Neal said he dug a couple of .38 slugs out of your wall."

"Thank God the shooter was a lousy shot. I'll put the slugs in my scrapbook."

"Go home."

"There's nothing at home." A cry of pain escaped Rosswell's lips before he could convince himself that he was too tough for showing pain. "I don't even have a goldfish waiting for me."

"Go sit by Tina."

Rosswell laughed. "The nurse said Tina needed to rest. If I was there, she couldn't rest."

"Junior Fleming will make sure no unauthorized person goes in there."

Rosswell grabbed his stomach. "Junior couldn't keep a dust bunny from getting in Tina's room."

"I promised Junior that if anything happened to Tina, I would personally hurt him bad."

Rosswell belched and clamped his hands over his mouth.

Frizz said, "Are you going to throw up? If you're going to puke, then go in the bathroom."

Frizz's sympathy level hovered close to the bottom of a flimsy barrel.

"My stomach is calmer than it's been for years." Patting his stomach to demonstrate, Rosswell dug a mint from Frizz's candy dish and popped it in his mouth. It was sweet with a whiff of cinnamon. "They give you good stuff at the hospital."

"I've been busier than a whore at a used car salesmen's convention." Frizz covered his face with his hands. "I didn't realize how much I depended on Tina."

"Has anyone reported a missing man or a missing woman?"

"Nope."

"Then we still don't know who the victims are."

"Nope," Frizz said.

"Two bodies and no one has raised an alarm about people missing. Weird."

The radio squawked. One of the deputies needed help on traffic control. Frizz told him there wasn't anyone else available, he'd just have to tough it out. Another deputy asked Frizz where the rescue team should search next. Frizz suggested downstream. That covered a lot of territory since Cloudy River eventually dumped into the Mississippi River, which dumped into the Gulf of Mexico. The phone rang. Rosswell did the gentlemanly thing and answered it.

"Sheriff's department."

"Have y'all found the murderer?"

"Which one?"

The caller hung up. Rosswell could be of real use around here if Frizz would only let him. The sheriff couldn't talk on the phone and the radio at the same time.

Frizz said, "Who was that?"

Rosswell checked the caller ID. "It says payphone. Do we still have payphones in town?"

Frizz slumped in his chair. "I'm exhausted."

That was clear to Rosswell, who waited but said nothing. What was the response to a blatant statement of fact? Hell if he knew.

Frizz continued, "Not only do I have all this shit going on, but I'm dealing with my wife."

His wife? Before Rosswell could ask him to elaborate, the conver-

84

sation jerked to a halt. Rosswell heard the noise of a large Harley right outside. The motorcycle revved a couple of times then went silent.

A huge man, wearing a British bobby cap and sunglasses, rumbled through the front door of the sheriff's station. Rosswell couldn't describe his face, since he could see little of it through the mass of his red hair and beard. After the man removed his sunglasses, Rosswell guessed that his eyes were green. Tattoos of naked women covered his arms. His Harley t-shirt, covered by a leather vest, appeared to be wriggling. What was happening with his shirt? Was the dope making Rosswell hallucinate? The big guy stuck four sticks of Big Red chewing gum in his mouth and leaned on the counter.

"Sheriff?" he said, staring at Rosswell. He pronounced it *Shurff*.

"No," Rosswell said. "Try the man with the gun and the badge." He pointed to Frizz.

An impossibly tiny dog with beady eyes and bad hair sprouting all over its body peeked out of the guy's shirt at his neck. The reason the shirt wriggled. Rosswell wasn't hallucinating.

The faceless mountain said, "Some of the boys and me, we done found something." His accent was pure hillbilly.

Rosswell pointed at the thing in the guy's shirt. "Is that a dog?"

"Yup."

"Is it a Yorkie?" The dog lapped the air in front of it, its tongue flicking in and out of its mouth. A mess of brown hair hung over its eyes.

The motorcyclist gaped at Rosswell, his mouth hanging open, the wad of gum nearly falling out. The guy was six or eight inches taller than Frizz and outweighed the sheriff by a hundred pounds. How he could fit on a motorcycle was an astounding question without an answer.

"That there's Scooby," the guy said. "She weighs right near three pounds."

Rosswell said, "I can believe that."

Rosswell started to express his opinion that Scooby was a stupid name for a weird dog, but Frizz interrupted and instead asked, "Sir, what's your name?"

"Rabil. Purvis Rabil."

Frizz said, "And what did you find?"

"Might have something to do with them there bodies you'uns all are missing."

A blush crept up Frizz's face. "Yes, we had some problems."

Rosswell repeated, "And what did you find?"

Frizz threw daggers at Rosswell with his eyes. "I'll handle this."
Frizz turned to Purvis. "What did you find?"

"There's a bunch of them buzzards a-flying around a deadfall in
the creek." He said *crick*.

"Actually," Rosswell said, "what's flying around that mess of logs
and crap in the river are vultures. Buzzard is an old English word for
hawks or other raptors, not carrion eaters, although the term——"

"Just a minute," Frizz said to the man. "Please wait right there
while Judge Carew and I consult in headquarters."

Frizz forced Rosswell up and dragged him away. When they
lurched into the sheriff's office, Frizz said in a low, menacing voice,
"The hospital called and said you checked yourself out."

"I did."

"You're still stoned."

"I am."

"Then keep your mouth shut while I'm talking to one of our tourists."

"I will."

When they got back to the counter, Frizz said, "Sorry. You saw a
bunch of buzzards flying around a deadfall in a creek?"

Scooby's silky hair invited Rosswell to scratch her ears. Rosswell
gave in to the temptation. Scooby closed her eyes in pleasure. When
he slowed down the scratching, she nipped him until he upped the
rhythm. She farted, sending a tiny cloud of stinking gas down Purvis's
shirt.

The big man said, "Yup."

Frizz said, "Can you tell me where?"

"Up to the state park."

Rosswell sobered up instantly.

Chapter Eleven
Tuesday noon

Frizz radioed the deputy guiding the search team to check out the deadfall in Cloudy River close to Foggy Top State Park.

The bearded giant and his tiny dog waited while Frizz wrote down the man's contact info before running him through the computer. Purvis Rabil of Little Rock, Arkansas, had a cellphone, a driver's license, valid tags for his motorcycle, a Yorkie, and an overdue parking ticket from Paducah, Kentucky.

Rosswell said, "I could take a written statement from him."

Frizz said, "No, you could not."

Rosswell kept his thoughts and responses to himself. Frizz intentionally kept him out of the investigation when he was obviously needed quite badly.

"You ever been to Bollinger County before?" Rosswell asked Purvis.

"No, ain't never been here afore. This here's the first time."

Rosswell said to the good citizen, "I'm glad I got to meet you and Scooby."

Purvis said, "Uh-huh."

Scooby said nothing.

"Thanks for the information, Mr. Rabil. You've been very helpful." After he'd left, Frizz turned to Rosswell. "I need you to do something else."

"Come to your senses, have you?"

"I need you to go home and recuperate. You're not a cop and you will not be a part of this investigation."

"You need me." Plain and simple things are often the hardest to understand. "Rabil's news sobered me up."

"You're not law enforcement."

Rosswell slapped his palm on the desk. "That's exactly what I am. I am law enforcement. Your arrest powers come from the court, which is me." He pointed to his chest.

"My arrest powers," Frizz said in a low, growling tone, "come from the voters who put me in office."

"Bull crap." Slamming his palm on the desk again didn't seem advisable since the first time he'd done it had sent a shriek of pain through his wounded arm. He'd managed not to scream. "Do you want to see the Supreme Court cases that back up my position?"

"Let's have the bitch session later." Frizz swept off his big cowboy hat, peered inside as if divining a secret message from the cosmos. After slapping the hat a couple of times to loosen dust, he screwed it back on his head. "We can argue on down the road."

Inhaling at the wrong time, Rosswell sucked in some of the dust, leaving a scratchy taste that made him sneeze twice.

Rosswell said, "Now would be a good time to air our laundry to see if it's dirty."

"Damn it, let's do that." Frizz picked up a pencil, licked its end, and wrote something on a paper. Rosswell wanted to remind the sheriff he didn't know where the pencil had been but decided instead to listen to Frizz. "Don't you find it odd that no one has reported two people missing?" He made a check mark. For a long minute, he scribbled, the pencil moving on the paper making a scritching sound. "That's odd thing number one."

"Yes, I find that odd. That's why I asked you about it when I first came in. Hermie may've made a connection."

"A connection for what?"

"Hermie saw a white Cadillac leave the park. A big driver. I know several people with white Cadillacs, but none of them are big people. But someone besides the owner could've been driving the car."

"You know them?" Frizz licked the end of the pencil. "Who are these people who own white Cadillacs?"

"Ambrosia Forcade, Turtles Rasmussen, Susan Bitti, and Trisha Reynaud. You know all of them."

"I never see Ambrosia. She must practice some kind of law that doesn't involve going to court."

"Estate planning. On occasion she'll show up in probate court, but she doesn't represent criminals." Rosswell coughed. "Sorry. Alleged criminals."

Frizz snapped his fingers. "Turtles is a guy I've wondered about." He pulled a file from a cabinet. "The guy likes to spend money, but I don't know where he gets it." The sheriff ran his finger down a paper. "He's got to be a con artist, but I've not been able to pin anything on him."

"Maybe he owns a whorehouse in Nevada."

Frizz sputtered. "Where did you get such a ludicrous idea?"

Rosswell evaded the question. "And Susan?" The time didn't seem right to tell Frizz that he'd recently seen a special on the History Channel about sex workers in Nevada who helped the mob launder money.

"Susan is dull as day-old dishwater," Frizz said. "If she's our killer, then I'm returning the couch I bought from her."

"Trisha?"

"Bankers are always taking trips. They never want anyone to know where they're going." Frizz replaced the file folder in the cabinet. "None of them have been reported missing."

"That doesn't mean they're not gone."

"If someone were missing around here, why haven't they been reported?" He wrote again. "Question number two."

"Sheriff, are we playing twenty questions?"

"Indulge me."

Rosswell said, "You told me I'd been fired."

"Shut up and listen." Frizz scribbled something. "You won't leave, so I'm going to pick your brain."

"That's a sordid cliché."

The phone rang and Frizz chatted for a few minutes. When he hung up, he said to Rosswell, "Are you going to talk to me or not?"

"First thing I can think of is that the victims were not from around here. We have a fair amount of folks from other places come through here. Maybe they were driving along with the murderer, got in a big fight, and whoever it is killed them."

"And they took a detour to the park first?" Frizz laughed. "That doesn't make sense. You don't drive through the park going somewhere. You have to find the park. It's way out in the boonies and someone who's never been there could easily get confused trying to find it."

Rosswell stood and paced. "Let's reverse that scenario and assume that the victims and the murderer—"

"Or murderers."

"—were locals. All three or however many of them there were." Pacing helped Rosswell think. It made him feel like he was back in his early days as a lawyer, giving a closing argument to a jury.

"Then why isn't someone around here reporting someone else as missing?"

"There could be several reasons." Rosswell lifted an index finger. "Maybe the dead people were supposed to be on vacation and no one's thought to check on their whereabouts." He raised a second finger. "Maybe no one likes the victims and there are a bunch of people around here who are glad they're gone." He raised a third finger. "Maybe someone knows these folks are missing and they're not telling."

"That's what I really need to know."

"What?"

"I need to find out which one of your three maybes is correct. Or perhaps a fourth or fifth maybe I haven't thought of." Frizz, still sitting, slid further down in his chair. "I don't know where else to start."

Rosswell knew exactly where to start.

Frizz said, "Go home. Your brain is empty. And, remember, you're not a cop."

Rosswell walked home, showered, shaved, and put on fresh clothes. Since he was now sober, he drove Vicky to Merc's. That was the *where* to start. But *how* to start? He didn't have the foggiest notion how he was supposed to find out who the corpses were when they didn't have any corpses. All he knew was that one was male and one was female. That narrowed it down to several thousand people within a hundred miles. Time to go fishing.

When Rosswell sat next to Ollie, the snitch sniffed and pinched his nose. "You still look like shit."

"I'm really tired of your telling me that."

"Then, if I were you, I'd start trying to improve myself."

"I don't stink. I took a shower."

"How's Tina?"

"Stoned and sleeping. She's barely got a scratch on her, but the anesthesia put her under."

"Somebody's a lousy shot."

"Yep." Trying to ignore a sheen of grease on the table, Rosswell filled Ollie in on the detective discussion between Frizz and him. "And, more good news, you're now my official sidekick." With a napkin he'd plucked from the dispenser, Rosswell wiped the table.

"Unadulterated bullshit. I'm not going to irritate Frizz so you can play Sherlock Holmes. And, if we did play that game, I sure as hell wouldn't be Watson. I'd be Sherlock's brother Mortimer."

"Mycroft," Rosswell said, proud as a peacock in heat that he knew some trivia Ollie didn't.

Mabel appeared. "Usual?" She held up the order pad, pencil at the ready.

"Mabel," Rosswell said, "I need to know something."

"I don't know anything."

Ollie said, "Now, honey, you know lots of stuff. Judge here just wants to pick your brain."

Mabel blessed Ollie with a dirty glare. "You know how revolting that cliché is? Would you want someone picking your brain? What do you pick brains with anyway? Toothpicks? I mean, brainpicks? And you can't pick someone's brain unless their skull is gone. What do you do with brain pickings? Eat them? What do they taste like?"

Mabel was a woman Rosswell admired as much as a dog loves a steak.

Ollie laughed. Rosswell half-expected his daughter—Rosswell still assumed she was Ollie's daughter—to grace them with a squeak, but instead she kept the glare on her daddy. She'd inherited from Ollie the ability to cast dirty looks accompanied by biting sarcasm.

"Mabel," Rosswell said, "you've got a regular crowd here, don't you?"

"I could name you a whole list."

"Is there anyone missing?"

"Missing?"

"Yeah," Ollie said, snagging the drift of Rosswell's questions. "Is there anyone who should've come in during the last couple of days but didn't?"

Mabel angled toward Ollie and Rosswell and whispered, "This is about those murders, ain't it?"

"Yes," Rosswell whispered back. "You're quick."

Ollie said, "Two people are dead. A man and a woman, yet no one's been reported missing."

She tapped her pencil against her teeth. *A disgusting habit.* "You know, Mr. Dumey never came in today. He always comes in every day."

"Elmer Dumey?" Rosswell asked.

"No," Mabel said. "Johnny Dan Dumey, Elmer's boy. Elmer's up in the nursing home. Seven Pines, up on the hill."

Ollie said, "We know where it is."

She snapped, "Never hurts to be clear when you're talking to someone."

Rosswell tried to place Johnny Dan. Since he'd never been arrested or had never sued anyone, Rosswell didn't recognize the name right off. He took an educated guess. "Isn't he the guy with a mechanic shop down from the courthouse?" Rosswell had seen the man lots of times, yet had never spoken to him. Then Rosswell made the connection. Johnny Dan was the guy who collected muscle cars. How often Rosswell had lusted after those cars at his shop. "The muscle-car guy?"

"The same," Mabel said.

Ollie said, "Healthy dude. Big shoulders. Blue eyes. Short brown hair. Doesn't say much. Knows everything about cars."

Rosswell said, "How do you know him so well?"

Ollie said, "You saw him talking to Mabel yesterday before Merc ran him off."

"Mabel," Rosswell said, "was he the guy who grabbed your arm?"

"Oh, he didn't mean nothing by that. He gets overly excited sometimes." Mabel blushed. "I been talking to him. He's one smart man. Has an English degree with a minor in theater." She batted her eyes and blushed. Rosswell didn't realize women did that any more. "Ollie, you had lots of conversations with him," she added.

Ollie said, "Guy's sharp as a crackerjack. Says he's working on a book. I've seen him write down stuff he thinks about when he's working on cars."

Rosswell said, "An English major who works on cars. He is indeed one smart guy. He knows where the money is." Rosswell suspected that Mabel's *been talking to him* meant *screwing his brains out* but decided not to get that detailed. And he certainly wasn't going to delve into what *having conversations* with Ollie might entail. "Where's Johnny Dan been going when he doesn't come in here?"

"I don't know," she said. "He doesn't have to check in with me."

Ollie said, "Not yet."

Merc opened the kitchen door, allowing beef stew-scented steam to roll out and hollered, "Mabel, you working or jawing today?"

The good smells set Rosswell's mouth to watering. "Bring my coffee." Later on he would eat something, but coffee came first.

"I'll try some of that coffee, too," Ollie said.

Mabel said, "How can y'all drink coffee in this heat?" She headed for the coffee pot. Back in a second she came, with two boiling white mugs of the black stuff. Nectar of the hyperactive gods.

After she left, Rosswell said to Ollie, "Has Johnny Dan ever hurt Mabel?"

"He's still alive, isn't he?"

Rosswell restrained himself from giving Ollie or Mabel his domestic violence speech. To Rosswell, it appeared that both of them were ignoring clear signs of Johnny Dan's aggressive behavior. Any man who would grab a woman's arm in full view of witnesses should be considered dangerous.

After they finished the fully sugared, slightly salty sludge, Ollie said, "Let's saddle up."

"You don't saddle up a Volkswagen, especially an orange one."

"You're beginning to look like Sherlock Holmes."

Ollie's come around to my way of thinking. I'm evolving into a real detective.

Johnny Dan's place sat a block down from the courthouse. It had an asphalt parking lot completely free of any gravel, stray weeds, or other detritus. There wasn't a spot of dirt or mold on the outside of the white steel building.

The cars Johnny Dan was about to work on sat in neat rows. A yellow 1969 Camaro Z28 with 400 horses, complete with black stripes. A 1969 Shelby Cobra 454, white with blue stripes. A 1978 Trans Am with a 405 and hood scoop, painted black with gold striping. Rosswell's muscle-car lust shifted into overdrive.

Rosswell suspected Johnny Dan was rich. Rosswell didn't use him for the VW, but Johnny Dan reigned as the mechanic of first choice in the entire county. People who buy muscle cars have money to burn, and Rosswell was thinking Johnny Dan tapped into a lot of that money before it got set afire.

"Johnny Dan!" Rosswell yelled when they went into his shop, trying to be heard over the sound of a loud machine. There was no air conditioning. Flies buzzed in the heat. He expected a couple of the bugs to drop dead from the hot air, stale and pungent with motor oil.

"Yo!" Johnny Dan yelled, and the machine went silent. "What you need?" He removed his ear plugs and safety glasses, then wiped his big hands on a red bandana. "Come on back."

Ollie and Rosswell snaked their way around three cars until they reached Johnny Dan at the back of the shop. Rosswell, having decided to pretend that he'd never seen the man before, introduced himself and Ollie to Johnny Dan, who said he already knew Ollie. Obviously. Ollie was Johnny Dan's main squeeze's daddy.

"You the one with that orange VW," he said to Rosswell. "Cute." Cute, to muscle car folks, meant *piece of crap*.

Rosswell said, "Thanks."

"You need it worked on? What is it? '73?"

"1972," Rosswell said.

"If I don't have the parts, I can get them overnight."

"The car's doing fine. If something happens, I'll let you know."

"Yes, sir. Cute."

Ollie said, "Mabel said she's been missing you today."

"What time is it?"

Rosswell showed Johnny Dan his watch.

"Got tied up." He motioned to all the cars he had on the floor of his shop. "Couldn't stop for lunch."

Rosswell said, "You don't wear a watch?" As far as Rosswell could see, there wasn't a clock anywhere in the building.

Johnny Dan said, "You and Ollie need something?"

Ollie said, "Judge Carew wanted to know if you wore a watch."

"Nope. No watch. No ring. No doodads. They get caught in the machinery, you lose a finger." Rosswell wondered why there was a white circle around the middle finger of Johnny Dan's right hand.

Ollie said, "Do you have any help?"

"Ollie, you and the judge are costing me money. I got lots of work to do."

Rosswell said, "I apologize for that, but we're trying to find out about somebody who might be missing."

Johnny Dan pointed to the garage area of his shop. "Nobody's in here. Have a look."

Rosswell said, "We need to know if you have any helpers."

"Nope." He pointed with his chin to the office portion of his shop, also maintained as neat as a new crankshaft pin. "I do my own book-keeping, too. The only thing I can't do is my taxes. I can't understand the forms."

"If you hired another mechanic, then you could get these cars done faster," Ollie said. "What if you need to take off during the day?"

Johnny Dan smirked. "People come to me 'cause they want *me* to work on their cars. Most folks don't have an emergency car repair. I do it at my own pace."

Ollie said, "Point well taken."

"Johnny Dan," Rosswell said, "have you been gone for the last couple of days?"

Johnny Dan picked up a wrench off the floor and hung it in its place on the pegboard fastened to the wall. Rubber bands of various sizes hung each on their own hook. Clear plastic bags holding tiny parts were labeled and alphabetized. Tools and accessories of every variety were displayed on the pegboard.

"Yup. Went to St. Louis to get parts."

Johnny Dan waved toward open shelves groaning under the weight of boxes containing thousands of car parts, all cataloged and labeled. Cocking his eye at two other wrenches on a bench, he clanged them together, then scrutinized them. Apparently satisfied that they were clean, he hung them on the pegboard too. After pumping some kind of hand cleaner from an orange bottle and wiping vigorously, he grabbed a broom and started sweeping.

"Anybody go with you?" Ollie said.

Johnny Dan swept perilously close to Rosswell's feet.

"Nope."

Rosswell said, "Did you meet up with anyone up there?" Ollie and Rosswell made a good pair of interviewers.

Johnny Dan stopped sweeping. "Judge, you need some work done?"

"No," Rosswell said. "We just needed to know a couple of things."

"Then do you mind if we talk later? I'm busier than——"

Rosswell ventured, "A whore at a used car salesmen's convention?"

Johnny Dan belched a great laugh. "That's a good 'un. I'm going to use that."

Ollie said, "See you around. Maybe at Merc's."

"Yeah. And tell Mabel I said hey. Be by later."

The sound of a Harley greeted Rosswell and Ollie when they walked out the front door onto the sidewalk. Purvis Rabil of Little Rock and his little dog Scooby had arrived. Scooby yapped and Purvis tipped his hat.

"Johnny Dan in?" Purvis asked. "Done been looking all over for him."

Ollie pointed inside the garage at Johnny Dan and yelled to him, "Someone's here for you."

"Yo," said Johnny Dan.

"Yo," said Purvis.

Purvis and Johnny Dan walked to the back wall where they stood by a door leading to another part of the shop. With their backs to Rosswell and Ollie, they began an animated conversation.

Parked on the street were two vehicles of interest.

"Look at Purvis's ride," Rosswell said. "That's a 1690 CC twin cam engine. Pivoting foot boards. Breakaway windshield." Inspecting the motorcycle more closely, it was apparent what the thing was. "This is a police edition of some kind."

"Must've stolen it."

"Nope," Rosswell said. "You can buy them used. But this sucker sells for an ungodly amount, even used."

Ollie pointed to a car. A new, silver Malibu with 16-inch tires. "That's Johnny Dan's car," he said. "Johnny Dan's a big boy. Right kind of car. I wonder if that's what Hermie saw?" Rosswell and Ollie both checked every tire. A couple of the tires had suspicious slashes on them. They peeked inside. The car was showroom clean.

"Makes it handy if you wanted to clean up a car after a murder." Ollie pointed to a sign on the garage. DETAILING OUR SPECIALTY! "Let's keep an eye on Johnny Dan."

"Yes, sir." Rosswell gave him a little salute. "And another thing. I've met that Harley rider."

"Great tats." Admiration welled up in Ollie's voice. "Where did you meet him?"

"Purvis Rabil is his name. He came in the sheriff's office earlier and reported buzzards flying around a pile of dead trees in the river at the park. Now here he's come to talk to Johnny Dan, who's been out of pocket for a couple of days earlier this week. Purvis says he's from Little Rock and never been to Bollinger County before. How could he know Johnny Dan?"

"They're not buzzards. They're actually—" Ollie stopped himself. "That's a mighty strange coincidence."

"Mighty strange," Rosswell allowed. "I don't believe in coincidences."

Chapter Twelve

Tuesday afternoon

"Where to now, Sherlock?" Ollie's mannerisms also included references to Rosswell's detecting ability, which Rosswell thought was way better than Ollie's. And, since Ollie called Rosswell "Sherlock," then the snitch was on the judge's side, and Rosswell told him so.

"This means you're helping me."

"No, it doesn't," Ollie said. "I'll tag along for a while. Keep my name out of it when Frizz starts smacking you around."

"I'm not in on this case. I'm just asking questions to satisfy my own curiosity."

"And I'm the Queen of Sheba come to pay my respects to King Solomon."

"Back to Merc's." Rosswell patted his stomach. "I'm hungry."

He ordered tuna on whole wheat with lettuce and sweet pickles, just like his momma made, although he didn't recall her sticking parsley sprigs on the plate. Ollie ordered the same.

"What's this for?" Rosswell said, chomping the sprig. "Parsley has no smell, weak taste, and looks like a weed."

"Some say that French chefs placed it on the customer's plate, signifying that the chef guaranteed satisfaction. Others say that parsley is good for your breath and digestion. Another school of thought—"

"I'm sorry I asked." A slight belch escaped before Rosswell could tamp it down. "Hermie said he saw a white Cadillac around the time of the murder."

"Was he sober?"

"He was sober enough to spot a white Caddy with a big driver. Do you know anyone who drives a car like that?"

Ollie chewed on his parsley while he rubbed his head. "Yeah. That Rasmussen guy. The con artist. Turtles. Let's see who else. Ambrosia Forcade, the shyster. Susan Bitti, furniture lady. Do I win the prize?"

"How about Trisha Reynaud, the banker?"

"Right. Okay, so what?"

"Find out if any of them are missing. And anyone else who owns a white Cadillac in this county."

"Easy. Shouldn't take me more than a couple of hours."

Rosswell didn't ask, because he didn't want to know whose computers Ollie would hack into.

Drinking the sludge after finishing the meal, Rosswell inventoried the other patrons. No one popped up with a MURDERER sign on his, her, or its forehead. He was supposed to interview more people but wasn't clear about whom he was supposed to collar and hit with a bunch of questions. This detective business made his stomach hurt. Or perhaps it was the overdose of caffeine mixed with Merc's tuna sandwich.

A few people stopped by their table and chatted.

One of them, Nadine Blessing, a redheaded real estate agent that Rosswell guessed to be about thirty or thirty-five, pointed to Rosswell and Ollie. "How're you gentlemen this afternoon?" She was the one Rosswell had seen in Merc's yesterday with the young couple. Her late husband, he now remembered, used to run a truck stop out on the main highway.

The purse she carried was a brighter orange than Rosswell's car and larger than his briefcase. And calling them gentlemen? Her inventory of real estate must've been higher than a kite circling in the hot air of a political convention. She was flattering them, trying to butter them up so she could sell some land or maybe a nice house or two.

Rosswell returned her point. "Real good, Nadine. How's it going with you?"

Although she was a big woman, Rosswell found her attractive in a Dale Evans kind of way. Several years ago, he had bought a couple of pieces of vacant land from her for investment purposes. She'd seemed competent and honest enough without the slightest trace of murderous rage. Will Rogers advised buying real estate. He bought it, he said, "for the sole reason that there was only so much of it and no more, and that they wasn't making any more." Made sense to Rosswell.

"Up and down." Nadine peered over her shoulder, then turned back to them. "The real estate market is always going sky high or dirt low." Her hands flew up, then fell down. "You try to even it out." She demonstrated a leveling gesture with her left hand—palm down, moving back and forth—before she searched Merc's with her eyes darting every which way. Maybe she was trying to spot more potential customers. Rosswell noted she wore several rings. He wondered if she'd lost any lately.

Ollie said, "Is your car for sale?" Ollie didn't ask idle questions. He was fishing, too.

Nadine chuckled and pointed to herself. "Honey, everything I got's for sale." Rosswell hoped she wouldn't try to sell herself to Ollie. His genes were already spread out enough in the pool.

Rosswell's sling was binding up on his arm. He rearranged it several different ways.

She said, "I heard you ran into a couple of nasty guys."

"Yes, ma'am," Rosswell said. "It was a close one."

The rumors were getting better. Now it was two bad guys after Rosswell.

Ollie rubbed his head. "I'm in the market for a car. May I look at yours?"

"Yes, oh, yes."

They all paid their bills and headed to the parking lot to inspect Nadine's silver Buick Regal with 16-inch wheels.

"Nice car," Rosswell said, regretting such a lame statement as soon as it passed his teeth. A peace symbol decorated a bumper sticker that proclaimed SAVE THE EARTH. The sentiment was noble, although he'd like to see the plan.

Ollie first checked out the interior, then lowered himself to the ground, slid under the car, and scoped out its belly. "How much do you want?" he said, his voice muffled.

"Fourteen K," Nadine said. "I keep a diary, and part of what I document is every single thing I do to this car. Oil changes, tire rotations, even gas fill ups."

Fourteen K? That sounds like the name of a supermarket. It also sounds like a mighty high price for a used Buick Regal.

"It's clean as a baby's whistle," Nadine added, "and has four brand-new tires."

Ollie scooted out from under the car and perused the interior again. After the scrutiny, he said, "Can you pop the trunk?"

She did. The trunk was spotless except for a small cardboard box full of odds and ends. Rosswell noted that Nadine had a bottle of the same kind of hand cleaner that Johnny Dan had. Fast Orange.

Ollie said, "Thanks. I'll get back with you."

Nadine said, "Yes, oh, yes!" After a little wave, she drove off.

When the pair was seated inside Merc's again, Ollie said, "That car's been detailed lately. Even the tires smell of ArmorAll. If she used it in a murder, it's been wiped clean since. And the tires are new. Our tire impressions might be worthless."

"*Our* tire impressions?"

Ollie squeaked a high frequency squeak. "I meant Frizz's tire impressions."

Ribs Freshwater sidled up to the table. "Y'all alone?" Rosswell didn't know if Ribs had a real name. He got his nickname from his skinniness. Where he got Levi's and blue work shirts skinny enough to fit him Rosswell didn't know. He'd never seen Ribs dressed any other way. Ribs claimed he was a full blooded Cherokee. He wore his long black hair in a ponytail and, adding in his ruddy complexion, he fit the image of a Native American.

"Sit down," Rosswell said.

Ribs stood tall. Would that fit Hermie's description of "big"? He'd have to ask the ranger. Up to that point, the worst thing in Rosswell's mind that Ribs had done was buy a silver Lexus, let it get dirty, and then let it get dirtier. Where he got the dough for such a fancy ride, Rosswell didn't know. Ribs wasn't old enough to retire and live off prudent investments. He had to be working somewhere in order to support a Lexus. Ribs, about the same age as Nadine and Johnny Dan, was wiry and strong. Rosswell figured he had some kind of manual work as an occupation.

"Ribs," Rosswell said, "how's your job going?"

"What job?"

Ollie grabbed the uptake. "You don't work anywhere?"

"Hell, I got lots of work." Ribs—despite his age—cackled like an old man. "I just don't have a job."

Rosswell said, "What is it you work at?"

"That's a good question," Ribs admitted. "I got so many disguises I don't know myself."

Mabel appeared, gracing Ollie and Rosswell with the dirty stares again. "I thought y'all left."

Ollie said, "Honey, we're back."

Ribs blinked rapidly. "Honey?"

Ollie said, "It's a long story." He scratched his head instead of rubbing it. Maybe he was going through the change of life. "Coffee."

Rosswell said, "The usual."

Mabel said, "Y'all are going to die of caffeine poisoning."

Ribs cackled again. "Then let me have what they're having. I want to be high when I die." Ribs' face turned serious. "Judge, I meant a caffeine high. Not, you know, drugs."

"I'm not sitting here looking for business." Rosswell lied. Of course he was snooping around for business. He didn't want anyone to know that searching for criminals was high on his possible to-do list for the day. And the fact that caffeine was a drug was something Rosswell decided not to present to Ribs.

Mabel scurried off.

Ollie said, "Ribs, I heard you were in Memphis a couple of days ago."

Rosswell doubted that Ollie had heard any such thing, yet it was a good place to start. Tripping up a witness with a non-sequitur often made them spill the truth.

"Memphis, Tennessee? I never been outside the state of Missouri, except for the time I went to Piggott, Arkansas, back in '95."

Ollie said, "Why'd you go to Piggott?"

"I wanted to find out why they named their town Piggott."

"Why did they?" Rosswell said.

"Never did find out. I got into a poker game with the sheriff, the moonshiner, the chief of police, the judge, the Baptist preacher, and the undertaker, who was also the biggest pimp in town. Did a lot of business in the back of his hearse. Anyway, lost my car and all my money. They drove me to the state line and kicked me from the Natural State into the Show-Me State. I was drunk. Hitched a ride to Poplar Bluff and rode the Greyhound back home. I figured I done good. Went down there in a two thousand dollar car and come back in a two hundred thousand dollar bus."

It was fortunate that Mabel hadn't brought the coffee yet, or Rosswell might've been spitting it across the table.

I pray that Ribs is the murderer. If he's the killer, then all the cops have to do is wait for him to commit an exquisitely stupid act proving his guilt beyond a reasonable doubt. We'd have our case made. We? I mean Frizz.

The fourth person to join the table was Candy Lavaliere, whom

Rosswell had known for a decade. Now there was a big woman. *Voluptuous, I'd call her. Nice view.* Blonde, with a gentle, stunning face, soft and clear almost to the point of translucence. The woman, tanned and buff, smelled like Ivory soap. Big charm bracelets on her arms rattled and clanked. Rings on every finger. Rumor had it that this expert shooter also lifted weights and had read every book in the public library . . . twice. Ollie's intellectual equal was Candy, the cosmetologist who loved to dance. She didn't have a silver car with 16-inch wheels. Candy owned a golf cart she drove everywhere, including golf cart races in various towns around the area. The tires on the electric cart were only 8 or 10 inches.

"Candy," Ollie said, "pull up a chair and sit your pretty butt down here."

For a moment, Rosswell assumed that Candy, she being of the feminist stripe, would clobber Ollie with her backpack. Instead, she sat between Ribs and Ollie, and tee-hee'd like a teenager, although she had to be around the same age as Ribs, Nadine, and Johnny Dan.

"Here you go, boys." She handed each of the three men a dark fudge brownie wrapped in wax paper. Rosswell's disappeared in a millisecond. Candy's sweet baked goods were famous.

"Thanks," Rosswell said. "That tasted angelic."

Ribs asked her, "You holding up under this heat driving that green buggy all over town?"

"It's not green," she said. "It's chartreuse. And there's no problem since it's not snowing or cold. That's a good thing. You have to search for silver liners in black clouds."

"Linings." Ollie enjoyed correcting people. "You have to search for silver linings."

She tilted her head to one side, her face full of puzzlement. "Why did I say that? I need to check my journal. Must've heard it somewhere." Candy laid a hand on Ollie's arm. "It's hotter than blue bonfires out there."

Candy made goo-goo eyes at Ollie. Rosswell hoped she couldn't see him pulling a forefinger across his throat, signaling Ollie to cut off any more nasty remarks. She apparently had difficulty remembering clichés. No one, especially Ollie, should make fun of her for that. Rosswell found it refreshing that she couldn't remember threadbare phrases.

With a tiny wave of his forefinger, Ollie signaled that he'd seen Rosswell's command. "I haven't seen you in a while," Ollie said to Candy. "Where have you been?"

Ribs said, "You ever been to Piggott, Arkansas?"

Candy said, "Can't say that I have."

Ollie forced the conversation back his way. "Candy, weren't you out of town for a couple of days this last week?"

Ribs said, "Ernest Hemingway lived in Piggott, Arkansas, for a spell. I seen the house."

Ollie quoted Hemingway. "'A serious writer is not to be confounded with a solemn writer. A serious writer may be a hawk or a buzzard or even a popinjay, but a solemn writer is always a bloody owl'."

Rosswell said, "What the hell does that mean?"

Ribs said, "I don't know nothing about birds."

Ollie said, "You're an Indian. You're supposed to know all that nature stuff."

"I," Ribs said, "been busy with other stuff."

Candy scooted her chair closer to Ribs. "I've just been hanging at my own house. Reading in the air conditioning. No one wants me to fix their hair. Think I'll retire." She rubbed her forehead. "Leastways, I think that's what I've been doing. Things are so jumbled up sometimes. I misplace things. Too much on my mind."

Is Candy starting to have memory problems?

Candy asked Ribs, "Are there more flies this summer than there were last year?"

Ribs steadied the coffee cup he held halfway between the table and his mouth. "Can't say as I've counted them."

Candy said, "'The blood-dimmed tide is loosed'."

Rosswell recognized the line from William Butler Yeats' poem about the end of the world. What he didn't recognize was its relevance.

Ollie took Candy's hand. "Are you feeling all right?"

Ribs said, "Maybe she's been counting flies in the heat."

Rosswell noticed that Candy, her hand under the table, was rubbing Ribs's leg. Did Ollie notice? Was Candy doing Ribs and Ollie? If she was, then Rosswell prayed that it wasn't both at the same time. He didn't want to fantasize about that scenario.

Two things happened then. First, Johnny Dan walked in the restaurant. Next, when Ribs saw the mechanic, he threw two dollars on the table, and left through the back entrance without a word of farewell. Rosswell pondered whether these two events were connected when his phone buzzed. Before he could say hello, Frizz said, "You better come to the hospital."

Chapter Thirteen
Tuesday afternoon, continued

"Tina?" Again, Rosswell leaned over her bed. The sheriff's call said that Tina had awakened from the anesthesia. No nurse and certainly no city cop was going to throw Rosswell out. "Can you hear me? I'm here." Her hair had been freshly washed. He pressed his cheek against the side of her head, letting her hair tickle him.

"Rosswell," she said. "Water." She opened her eyes. The afternoon sun shone through the windows on the most glorious vision he'd seen in years. "You okay?"

He helped her sip through a straw. "Yes, I'm fine." He set the glass down and kissed her cheek. "I'm fine and you're fine. You're too cute for words."

She blushed. "Don't feel fine. Won't feel fine 'til we go to our special place."

"You've got one hell of a hangover from the anesthesia."

"We're okay," she said, barely above a whisper.

Rosswell stroked her face. "I love you."

"Someone shoot me?" A scowl crossed her face. "Your house?"

"Yes. A bullet grazed you." Rosswell took her hand. "Are you in pain?"

"Frizz . . . arrest?" Her law enforcement training forced her to think about justice before self. "Who?"

"We don't know who did it." Some liquid in a bag hooked to a tube dripped into her veins. Although it was probably the same painkiller they'd dripped into Rosswell's veins, he worried that she wasn't getting enough. Again, he asked, "Are you in pain, Tina?"

There was no answer. She'd fallen asleep, a natural, healing sleep. The nurse tapped him on the shoulder. Time to go. This time, he left without being an asshole.

Frizz met him in the hallway. "I talked to the doctor earlier."

"And?"

Frizz searched his pockets for his car keys. "Why do they make all these keys look the same?" He flipped through a wad of keys on a circular metal holder. "Everything's going to shit."

Frizz and Ollie fell into the same classification when it came to having a direct and simple conversation. That classification was IRRITATING AS HELL. Rosswell didn't prompt the sheriff, hoping he'd get to the point quickly. Frizz's observation that everything was going to hell wasn't encouraging.

After riffling through about a hundred keys, the sheriff said, "The doctor wants to keep her overnight."

"That means she's going to die."

"Damn it, Rosswell, that's not what that means." He jiggled his keys, the metallic clicks resounding in the sterile hallway of the hospital. "It means he thinks she had a reaction to the anesthesia, and he wants to be careful. He's just not sure. Probably doesn't want a malpractice suit."

"Then he better be finding out. I'm going to move her to St. Louis or Memphis or some other place where they know more."

"It's a minor gunshot wound and a drug reaction, not. . . ." He didn't finish his sentence but Rosswell knew he was going to say *It's not cancer.* "They can handle gunshot wounds here. This is hunting territory, remember? She just needs to rest. I took a deputy off the search who's coming in to spell Junior in a little bit."

They walked to Frizz's car. In front of the hospital, a herd of Harleys roared up and down the street.

Frizz said, "You need to quit."

"Quit what?"

"You don't know what you're doing. I don't want anyone else hurt."

"Whatever you say, Sheriff." An explanation shouldn't be necessary, yet if he wanted Frizz to be straight with him, then he needed to be straight, if not to say redundant, with Frizz. "I nearly got Tina killed, but all I've done so far is talk to a bunch of people who didn't help me one smidgen. I literally do not have one single clue about these murders."

"You didn't almost get Tina killed. The person who shot her could've killed her. Fortunately, your house was dark, and the shooter didn't have a night scope or was a lousy shot or both. I assume."

"You're right about one thing. I can't take any more chances. I love Tina more than anything in this world."

"I know that. It's written on your forehead. You act as goofy as a teenager around her."

Rosswell borrowed Mabel's words. "Never hurts to be clear when you're talking to someone."

"Then you have to do what's right." Frizz slid behind the wheel of his patrol car. "It's your hide. And Tina's."

Rosswell didn't watch him go. Instead, he drifted back to Tina's room. He told the nurse he needed to sit by Tina's side. The nurse relented.

"Tina?" There was no reaction.

He pulled up a chair, sat next to her bed, and scooted close to her face. "I love you." She sighed, but didn't open her eyes. He brushed a stray bit of her hair away from her face. "I'm sorry. I'll never put you in a bad situation again." One kiss. Her lips were dry, yet sweeter than a honeycomb. *I should write love songs.*

"Tina, I promise I'll never do anything that might hurt you."

He sat silently for a while, thinking again, working things out in his brain. Playing detective was just that. A game. He'd had no training in police work. The only thing he knew about law enforcement techniques were what he'd heard in the courtroom. Even then, those descriptions were sanitized, cleaned up by the prosecutor to make the cops look good. The seminars he'd attended about investigating crimes were merely a series of stories by different cops who'd done the right thing or sometimes the lessons they'd learned from doing the wrong thing. Rosswell now didn't know what the right thing was.

To think that Ollie and he could search a death scene that had been flooded and then interview people without even knowing who the victims were was a joke, bottom line, and a bad joke at that.

He needed a soda. A Coke with caffeine struck him as a good idea. He fished in his pocket for change.

The ring.

The ring added to the truth of what a lousy detective Rosswell was. Had there been any fingerprints or DNA evidence, he'd destroyed it when he first found the ring and stuck it in his pocket. Instead, he'd been carrying it around without a thought to its significance.

"Judge Carew?" Father Mike had found him. "May I come in?"

"Please do." He put the ring in his pocket. "I need company."

"How's Tina?"

"She's stoned out of her mind."

The priest grinned. "I've dealt with people in that condition before. I'll keep praying for her." Father Mike traced the sign of the cross on Tina's forehead. "Judge Carew, there's something you and I need to discuss."

"Here?"

"Why not?" The priest pointed to Tina. "It concerns her." He fetched a quarter from his pocket, commencing his coin trick routine. "Do I have your permission to speak?" The quarter disappeared.

"Go right ahead." He stood and offered his chair, which the priest refused. Rosswell remained standing. "Let's hear what you have to say."

"I ran into Frizz out there. He's desperately in need of help right now, but he says you can't help him with the murders. You're a judge, not a police officer. He said you wouldn't be the judge. Some kind of legal technicality that I confess I don't understand."

That made Rosswell feel better. There were parts of his secret knowledge that Father Mike couldn't understand. Lawyers enjoy making the law incomprehensible, just as theologians enjoy making religion incomprehensible.

Rosswell said, "Frizz is right. If it hadn't been for me, Tina wouldn't be in that hospital bed."

"Do you think you have control over that?"

"I don't know if I have control over it, but it's a fact. Frizz doesn't think I have the slightest idea what I'm doing."

Father Mike said, "We discussed all that. You, Tina, everything. He disagrees with you."

"Disagrees about what part?"

"He thinks you know what you're doing. What I meant, however, was you wrongly thinking that Tina is in that bed because she was helping you."

"Father Mike, someone tried to kill her while she was in my house at my request after I asked her to help me investigate this case."

"If you had not asked her to help you, would she still have come over to your house?"

Rosswell slumped into the chair by the bed to ponder his answer. Turning to view Tina, he watched the most beautiful woman in the world snoring. The heart monitor read-outs pumped along in regular, strong patterns. Her chest rose and fell rhythmically. Twitching every few seconds was her only movement. She'd spoken to him earlier. She'd asked him if he was okay. She'd recognized him.

The priest's words stunned him.

Of course, she would've come over. This situation wasn't the same as Feliciana. I hadn't voluntarily disabled myself with alcohol and called on Tina to rescue me. Tina had come to my house of her own free will. And, when she got there, I wasn't drunk. I was being shot at.

There was a wheeze in Tina's breathing. God, Rosswell prayed, don't let her get pneumonia. He pulled the sheets up to her neck. Fear, or perhaps sick realization, rolled around his mouth.

"Yes," Rosswell said. "She would've come to me."

"Then what must you do for her?"

Once again, Rosswell was the student parked at his desk, regarding his instructor with awe, fear, and, yes, dislike. He didn't want this burden thrust on himself.

There was no stopping it. The epiphany bloomed inside his head. There was only one course of action. He formed a plan to catch the murderer so the legal system could exact its punishment. First, he'd find the bodies, and then he'd narrow the list of suspects so Frizz could go after only two or three possible bad guys. Maybe four or five.

That would repay his putting Tina in danger.

No, Father Mike hadn't talked him out of that notion. He'd never believe that his actions hadn't nearly caused Tina's death. She could still die regardless of what the doctors were saying about her condition. He needed to prepare for her death. If it was a minor problem, she wouldn't be in the hospital.

Father Mike said, "She's not going to die."

Holy crap. He's reading my mind.

"How do you know?"

"I've seen this before. It looks worse than it really is. Think of it as her giving in to exhaustion."

Rosswell withdrew the ring from his pocket. "I need to go see Frizz and give him some evidence. We'll need it to solve the murders."

"No, no, no." Father Mike smiled and did a thumbs up. "You miss my meaning completely. Haven't you heard?"

"Heard what?"

"You don't have to be a cop. One of my parishioners called me a few minutes ago. After Frizz left here, he went back to the station. That's when it happened. Frizz made an arrest. The murders have been solved!"

Chapter Fourteen
Tuesday afternoon, continued

At the sheriff's station, pandemonium reigned, with the press and jubilant citizens besieging the place, celebrating the capture of a dangerous murderer. Actually, it was one reporter for *The Marble Hill Tattler*, the local weekly newspaper (one page of news, seven pages of advertisements), and Ollie, who always enjoyed an arrest if it wasn't his. Both were standing outside, chit chatting. That sufficed, in Bollinger County, for pandemonium, especially in the current heat wave and humidity boom.

Several Harley riders, including Purvis, circled the courthouse square in the late afternoon sun. Whether they were pleasure driving or snooping around on the goings-on at the local cop shop was something Rosswell couldn't figure out. Although it didn't matter when he thought of the money they were spending which, in turn, the government taxed. After all, his salary was paid out of tax dollars.

Rosswell pulled Ollie aside. "Who did Frizz arrest?"

"You left Tina's side to come over here to gossip?"

"Ollie." Rosswell stopped for a couple of seconds. "Listen, she's basically sleeping off a big drunk. Junior Fleming is there and a deputy is supposed to come in later."

"Junior Fleming? The city cop? He's incompetent. He couldn't lose his virginity in a whorehouse."

"There are also two security guards at the hospital. There's nothing

I can do for Tina. Besides, she's not in danger. I'll bet whoever shot us has split for Mexico or Canada."

They stood between the American flagpole and the Missouri flagpole. The flags hung limply in the still air. Still air on hot and humid days often presaged savage storms.

The reporter, a girl who didn't appear to be over nineteen, stood at the ready, her sharpened pencil circling above her skinny journalist's notebook, in case someone said something quotable. Around one wrist hung a tiny Canon camera, in case someone did something worth remembering. Tapping her pencil against the notebook, she sounded like a woodpecker urging Ollie and Rosswell to hurry up and say or do something interesting.

Rosswell repeated, "Who did Frizz arrest?"

"Candy Lavaliere. She confessed." Although the petroleum smell lingered, the daily Vaseline coating of his bald head had by then evaporated from the heat. He rubbed his head. Ollie appeared on the verge of tears. He wasn't celebrating this arrest. "She's important to me."

The wind picked up, clinking the grommets of the flags against the flagpoles and blowing grit in Rosswell's eyes, making *him* appear on the verge of tears. There were no clouds in the sky. He assured himself no storms were brewing.

Astonishment hit Rosswell. He recalled Candy making eyes at Ollie while at the same time she was rubbing Ribs's leg. *Candy's libido must soar to the moon. Is she lusting after everybody in town?*

"Ollie, is she your girlfriend?"

"What kind of stupid question is that?"

"Why was she arrested? Does Frizz really think that she killed two people in cold blood?" Candy Lavaliere, a sexual addict and a double murderer? That didn't even begin to compute.

"Candy's not my girlfriend." Ollie spoke with little conviction. If she was his girlfriend, Rosswell was hopeful that she wouldn't become pregnant. "I'm still talking to Benita. She's the mother of my child. She even likes you." Rosswell prayed that Benita wouldn't get pregnant by Ollie. Again.

"Benita's a great nurse."

"The best. She graduated at the top of her class."

"But Candy's got the hots for you. I could tell that from the way she acted around you at Merc's. You would've thought she was fifteen instead of thirty."

"Thirty-five."

"There you go." Something smelled like a fish market here. "Wait a minute. Ollie, why did she confess?"

"She said she'd killed someone. Two someones." He studied the American flag. "I don't believe she killed anyone."

"Did she tell you she was a double murderer?"

"Yes, she did."

"What made her think she'd killed two people?" What was going on in Candy's mind, making her think she'd murdered the pair? To date, Rosswell hadn't heard any gossip that she was suffering from Alzheimer's or any other dread disease that would affect her thinking. Besides, wasn't she way too young for such a thing? "Is she mentally sound?"

"That's the thing, Rosswell." Ollie started up the street, away from the sheriff's station. Rosswell fell in step. The reporter tried to join them but Ollie shooed her away. "Candy's smarter and more rational than ninety-nine percent of the population of Bollinger County." Rosswell believed Ollie, which made Candy's actions even more incomprehensible.

"Then how did this happen?" They'd reached the end of the block. They turned sharply and marched back towards the sheriff's station. The reporter wrote on her pad. Ollie shooed her away again.

Ollie said, "Candy called me about fifteen minutes ago and said she needed to confess to a crime."

"Where was she when she called?"

"That's something else that's strange. From the background noise, it sounded like she was at Merc's. If you're going to call someone about confessing to a crime, wouldn't you go somewhere more private?"

"Was she calling from her cell or Merc's phone?"

"Her cell."

From the way people discussed intimate details on cellphones while standing next to complete strangers, that part of the story made sense. For some reason, the need for privacy evaporated when you used a cellphone.

Other parts of the story, unspoken parts, worried Rosswell. "Do you know if anyone was with her? Do you think someone forced her to call?"

"I couldn't tell."

"Tell me the rest. It can't get any worse."

"I met her in front of the courthouse. I asked her what kind of crime she needed to confess. She said she'd killed those two people at the park. She turned herself in and gave Frizz a full confession."

This could mean the end of dark fudge brownies for a while.

Rosswell said, "You didn't try to stop her?"

Sweat trickled down Rosswell's face. A drop or two of the salty stuff rolled into his mouth before he wiped his face.

"Do you think you or anyone else could keep Candy from doing something?" Ollie was right. If nothing else, Candy was headstrong. "Besides that, I want Frizz to forget I exist. I've seen the inside of that jail enough to do me the rest of my life."

"That's crap." Ollie jerked to a stop. Rosswell said, "I mean the confession. The whole confession thing is crap. How did she say she did it?"

"She told me she stabbed them both after they'd tried to attack her. I don't know what she told Frizz."

"The murder happened either Sunday night or early Monday morning. Do you know where she was then?"

"Not the slightest idea."

"She wasn't with you?"

"This isn't about me."

"You're the research assistant. Find out where she was."

"You heard what she said at Merc's. She said she's been at home, keeping cool, writing in her journal."

"Another thing, where's the knife?"

"She said she threw it in the river."

"Oh, Ollie, that was convenient. There aren't any witnesses. There's no murder weapon. How could Frizz believe someone without any corroboration?"

"Hermie Hillsman identified her as the driver of the silver car. He told me that himself."

"Was Hermie here?"

"He just left."

"Was he sober?"

"Yes, Judge, he was sober."

"Are you sure?"

Ollie said in a low voice. "You and I are drunks. Hermie's a drunk. Drunks can tell when drunks are drunk and when drunks are sober." Rosswell couldn't argue with that.

"She doesn't have a car, much less a silver car."

"But she had the keys to a silver car when she turned herself in."

"Whose car?"

"Johnny Dan Dumey's Malibu."

"What?" Rosswell scratched his mustache, trying to process this information. "She stole a car? Candy stole a car and killed two people? I don't believe any of that crap."

"She didn't tell me how she got the car."

"Does Frizz know she was driving Johnny Dan's car?'

"Got me."

"Where's Johnny Dan?"

"He and Mabel took off somewhere. They're in Mabel's car."
The Harley riders passed them again. Purvis wasn't in the group now. Where had he gotten to?

Rosswell said, "You and I checked the tires of Johnny Dan's Malibu. They don't match the impression."

"I heard that Frizz said they were close enough."

Rosswell blustered into the station, leaving Ollie at the flagpoles. The reporter snapped photos of both men. Rosswell hoped she got his good side. She followed him into the station.

Frizz told her, "I don't have a statement. I'll issue a statement in the morning."

She assumed a journalistic air of hatred and skepticism. Then left without a word.

"Frizz," Rosswell said. "Why did you arrest Candy?"

The light inside the station appeared dim compared to the glaring sun outside, and the air was several degrees cooler. Not cool, but cooler.

"Calm down," Frizz said. The sheriff was the only one in the place except for the single prisoner he now held. "Stop scratching your mustache. There's not much left of it."

"It's grown back as much as it's ever going to grow since I took my last dose of chemo." In other words, it was as scrawny as ever.

"That's a good reason not to scratch it."

"I doubt that Candy could kill a small fly, much less two grown people."

"Sit." Frizz indicated a chair. "Let's talk."

Rosswell sat. "Talk." He reached up to his face to scratch his mustache again but thought better of it. It had taken him too long to grow the emaciated thing.

The telephone rang. Frizz grabbed it as if he feared Rosswell would answer it. More media types apparently, since he told whoever it was on the other end the same thing he'd told the reporter. When he hung up, he closed his eyes for so long that Rosswell thought he was taking a nap. To pass the time, Rosswell ate a couple of Tootsie Rolls from the sheriff's candy dish. Chocolate helped him think. Then Frizz opened his eyes and gave Rosswell his full attention.

Frizz said, "With all the sugar you eat, one of these days you're going to blossom."

"Thanks for your concern, but tell me about Candy."

"She came in here a few minutes ago and said she was a murderer." Frizz removed his hat and finger combed his hair. "I stuffed her in one of the female cells. She's got paper and pen, writing her confession."

"Did you book her?"

"Not yet, but I did call the public defender. She talked to Candy and told her to keep her mouth shut and stop writing."

"But she's still writing."

"The public defender can't sit back there and babysit her. And I can't take pen and paper away from a prisoner."

"Has the search team found the bodies yet?"

"I sent them out to the park, but the water's still too high. It's dangerous to explore that deadfall. They'll have to wait until the river goes down."

The sheriff was stuck in town at the jail, guarding a woman who claimed to be a double murderer. She hadn't been booked yet, so she wasn't officially in jail, and the prosecutor wouldn't charge her until she was booked. Frizz was smart enough to notify the public defender. If she came over to talk to Candy again, perhaps the lawyer could persuade her to withdraw her ludicrous confession, whatever that confession might say.

Frizz couldn't take the chance that Candy might be guilty. If she were guilty and he didn't keep her behind bars, the wolves would gather around the sheriff's station and howl for his body to be thrown to the pack.

On top of all that, Frizz had no help. The three deputies were exhausted, having been on overtime duty, searching for the bodies. The only dispatcher was in the hospital.

Junior Fleming was a standing joke. Every Saturday night, the cop issued one traffic ticket, always to a driver between the ages of 16 and 21. The tickets usually ran around $50. The kids in town (and some adults also) had started a ticket fund. Whoever got the ticket that weekend was given $50 to cover the cost.

"Frizz, did Hermie tell you that he saw Candy driving a silver car out of the park?"

"You aren't a detective. You aren't on this case. You aren't going to stick your nose into my business."

114

"If you're right about the killer going after Tina, then it is my business."

"No, it's cop business." Frizz's face grew red. He drummed his fingers on the desk. However this turned out, the two would still be working together after it was over. Rosswell didn't want to burn any bridges he might need to cross in the future, and he hoped the sheriff felt the same. Eventually, Frizz said, "Do anything you want as long as you don't do it under the porch and scare the dogs."

"I guess you're going to have to arrest me next." Rosswell drew out the ring and stuck it in Frizz's face. "For withholding evidence."

Chapter Fifteen

Tuesday afternoon, continued

"What's this?" Frizz said. He turned the ring in all directions, inspecting it closely.

"It's a ring I found at the crime scene." Rosswell told him the whole story.

Frizz shoved it under a lamp, appraising its every detail. For a long time, the only sound Rosswell heard in the sheriff's station came from the static on the radio. An old clock, probably evidence in a long forgotten crime, chimed every quarter hour. A ticking from the computerized tape recorder for the telephone system rose to Rosswell's consciousness. He grew tense, waiting for the wrath of Frizz.

"Judge, why in the hell do you have Ollie Groton helping you?"

"He's my research assistant."

"That's shit and you know it. You don't need a research assistant. Ollie's a criminal, plain and simple."

"Don't you believe in rehabilitation?" That line hadn't worked on Tina, and Rosswell doubted that it would work on Frizz.

"People don't like to see judges hanging around with criminals in social settings."

"Social settings?"

"Merc's."

"Ollie knows a hell of a lot of stuff about people and computers. And he doesn't ask for legal advice. Sure, he's got a spotty past, but we all have secrets that we don't want everybody else knowing."

Frizz didn't reply. Instead, he returned to examining the ring. Eventually he said, "No use trying to lift prints off it now." He studied the ring one more time. "You and Ollie are probably the only ones who have left prints here. I've almost dismissed you as a suspect, even though you were the first one on the scene by sheer happenstance."

Rosswell hung his head. "I picked it up without thinking and stuck it in my pocket. It's not often I discover two corpses." Rosswell's body language must've showed remorse to the point that Frizz didn't blast him with any more sarcasm.

Father Mike marched through the door, letting a blast of hot air into the air-conditioned semi-comfort of the station. "Sheriff, may I speak to you, please?" Always the gentleman.

"Rosswell was just leaving," Frizz said.

Father Mike waved his hands in a dismissive gesture. "Oh, no. This isn't private." He focused on Rosswell. "The judge can stay."

Not wanting to miss anything, Rosswell propped his bad arm on the desk behind the counter, relaxed, and listened.

"What is it?" Frizz verged on sounding brusque. Rosswell fought back the urge to tell him that maybe the priest had important information. About what he didn't know, although you should never brush aside people who may have information.

"Do you have Candy Lavaliere locked up?"

"Yes, I do." Frizz closed his eyes and shook his head. Rosswell could tell that the sheriff longed for a catnap. Frizz said, "I should say that I have her locked up in a manner of speaking. Why do you need to know that?"

"I'd like to post her bail."

"Father Mike," Frizz said, "she's not been charged with anything yet. That means there's no bail. She claimed she committed the murders. Right now, she's writing a confession. I think she's loony."

Candy wasn't loony. Arguing with Frizz about that in front of the priest wasn't going to happen. In fact, arguing with Frizz about anything in front of anybody wasn't going to happen. Rosswell kept his mouth shut.

Father Mike said, "If she's not been charged, then can she leave?" Apparently, he wasn't going to argue the loony charge either.

"No, she cannot." Frizz stood. "I wish she could leave."

"Then I want her."

"You can't have her."

The priest's eyes widened. "I want to talk to her."

Frizz strolled to Candy's cell.

Although Rosswell couldn't make out the words, Frizz and Candy engaged in a lengthy conversation. After a moment or two of silence, the sheriff returned with Candy in handcuffs. Frizz was playing this by all the rules.

She took a gander at the priest. "What do you want?"

Rosswell decided that covering his mouth with his hand to hide any smiles seemed advisable in case there were a fight between Candy and Father Mike.

Father Mike said, "People are worried about you. I want to take you home."

"What people?"

Father Mike said, "Sheriff, could I talk to her in private?"

"Yes. Lawyers and clergy get that privilege." Frizz showed them the room adjacent to the dispatch area that was divided by a heavy glass partition with a grille for speaking. Each side had a passage door. Candy sat on one side and Father Mike sat on the other. Rosswell didn't think either one of them looked pleased with the situation. Each side had a call button. "One of you press your button when you're through."

Candy said, "I can't do that with my handcuffs on!"

"Sure you can." Frizz shut the doors.

Rosswell said, "You'll have to charge her and get another judge to set her bail."

"Already in the works," Frizz said. "The prosecutor's taking care of it. Now, what about this ring?"

"Maybe the killer left it. Maybe it belonged to one of the victims. Maybe someone lost it there years ago and it has nothing to do with anything."

"Do you have any idea whatsoever who could own this?"

"I don't know who owns that ring."

Frizz paused a moment before he continued. "EJD. Do you know anyone with those initials?"

Frizz caught my equivocal answer.

Rosswell said, "I searched the phone book. Nothing there."

"Maybe EJD doesn't have a phone. Or maybe he has a cellphone."

"Why do you say he?"

"This is a man's ring. And you said Ollie told you it was a Mason's ring."

"*Maybe* it's a Mason's ring."

118

"What else could it be?" Frizz said. "If it's not a Mason's ring, then what could it be?"

"Maybe it's a gang symbol, although I don't know of too many gangs who have Latin mottos."

Frizz grunted. "Nothing surprises me these days."

"One of my language professors at Mizzou told us that if you learned Latin, you wouldn't become a criminal."

"Do you believe that?"

"No. He's serving time for embezzlement."

"Studying Latin must actually lower your morals."

"I'm not sure this ring is evidence."

"You're not on the case, remember?"

"What case?"

"Damn it, ANY case!" Frizz removed his hat, mopped his brow, ran the handkerchief around the inside of the hat, and then punched it back on his head. "I need some rest."

"Yeah, and a happy pill."

That made Frizz chuckle. "Yeah. If only a pill could solve my problems."

A loud clunk signaled that the air conditioning system had failed. Again. Frizz had fought with the cooler for the last two years. The system was held together with bailing wire and pink bubble gum. Humidity and heat began rising inside the sheriff's station.

Rosswell watched Frizz go outside and stomp to the air conditioner where he kicked it. When he came back, the uncooperative machine, subjected to the sheriff's magic foot, returned to service. Frizz said, "Works every time."

Rosswell said, "Did you know that Candy had the keys to Johnny Dan's car?"

"She had keys when I arrested her. How do you know they were Johnny Dan's?"

"Ollie told me. Candy told him on her way in to jail."

"Shit." Frizz consulted the phone book and then punched in a number on the phone. Rosswell could hear an answering machine click on and a voice deliver a message. Frizz hung up. "At least he left his cellphone number." Frizz punched in the number. "Johnny Dan? Sheriff Dodson here." Frizz picked up a pen and scribbled on a legal pad. "Yeah. Did you loan Candy Lavaliere your car?" Frizz wrote something. "Okay. I'll wait." He covered the mouthpiece and said to Rosswell, "He said, hell, no, he doesn't loan his car to anyone. He's going to check it out." Johnny Dan came back on the phone. "Thanks. I'll call the Highway Patrol and report it stolen."

Rosswell thought about that exchange. Hadn't Ollie said that Johnny Dan and Mabel had gone somewhere in Mabel's car? Of course, it was possible that Mabel was close and drove Johnny Dan past his shop to check on the car.

Rosswell said, "All this excitement has worn me out."

"Do me a favor."

"What's that?"

"Go home. Rest up. Heal."

"I appreciate your concern, Sheriff." He grew weary at Frizz always telling him to go home. An inferiority complex would sprout next if Frizz didn't treat him better. "You don't want me to wait around until Father Mike gets through talking to Candy?"

"No. Take care of yourself before you keel over dead." The sheriff patted Rosswell on his shoulder. "I wouldn't know what to do with all the peace and quiet if you weren't around."

"That's what I'll do. Go straight home and go to bed."

I hate lying to the sheriff.

Chapter Sixteen
Wednesday morning

The first thing Rosswell thought when he woke up in the chair next to Tina's bed was (again) that Frizz had no one else to help. *Except for me and my duty is clear.*

Junior Fleming showed to up to start guard duty. "Judge," he said in a whisper. "Come here."

Rosswell followed the cop into the hallway.

"Is that ugly nurse here?"

Rosswell said, "I haven't seen her."

"She's so ugly, anybody who'd try to get in her pants is too damned lazy to jack off."

"Junior, just keep your mouth shut, your eyes open, and your zipper zipped."

Rosswell returned to Tina, who was groggy but awake.

"Go away," she told Rosswell. "I just need rest."

Rosswell left the hospital and called Frizz from the parking lot.

"Did Candy finish her confession?" Rosswell unlocked Vicky the Volkswagen and got in.

"No, she did not."

"Crap."

"Candy's gone."

Rosswell grabbed the steering wheel with the hand that wasn't holding the phone, sending pain up the arm he'd accidentally cut. "What happened?" The other hand, the one holding the phone, felt like it could crush the device.

Frizz told him that the prosecutor had filed charges and another judge from two counties away had set bail. "Then," the sheriff continued, "she posted bail. Or, I should say, Ribs Freshwater hired a bail bondsman who posted her bail."

"Did you find Johnny Dan's car?"

"Nope."

Rosswell calmed himself. He didn't want to give this part away. "Okay. Thanks." He hung up.

Rosswell knew that if Candy was the murderer, she'd be heading only one place in Johnny Dan's car. Tina was no threat. She lay on a hospital bed, out cold or, now, groggy. If Rosswell was in trouble with Candy, then he'd take his chances, but she wasn't heading for him or she'd already have gotten him. There was only one immediate concern. If Rosswell was wrong, Frizz would never know. If Rosswell was right, he'd be a hero, and Frizz would pin a medal on his chest while at the same time excoriating Rosswell for playing detective.

Hermie Hillsman was in danger.

Hermie was the guy who'd fingered Candy. Rosswell still couldn't believe that Candy was the murderer, but she had confessed and Hermie had witnessed her in the area driving the now famous silver car. Rosswell had been wrong before. But not this time.

Damn it! Rosswell knew he couldn't withhold the information. He called Frizz again.

"Hermie Hillsman is in danger."

And Rosswell told Frizz's voicemail why he thought that.

He hung up, started the convertible, and gunned it for Foggy Top State Park. Unfortunately, he had no blue light to clear the traffic. Motorcycles clogged the streets of Marble Hill. He nearly clipped several, trying to pass them. Once he got out of the town and zoomed onto the Confederate Trail heading for the park, the traffic thinned, but not much. Storm clouds gathered in the sky. The Weather Channel warned of supercells forming yet again over the area. Ozone from lightning strikes to the west tinged the air with a biting odor.

The motorcyclists clumped into a group on the blind curves of the main highway, a road carved into the side of the hills. Once, in a flat stretch in a small valley, Rosswell passed seventeen bikes at one time, floorboarding his sweet Vicky. Seventeen motorcyclists and each carrying a female passenger. That meant thirty-four birds flipped his way when he and Vicky overtook them. Rosswell waved back. He tooted Vicky's horn as he boogied through the cloud of stinking Harley exhaust.

Still in the proverbial one piece, Rosswell eventually arrived at the park, although more frazzled than when he started. No cars were visible and no one occupied the guard's rock-covered gazebo. That was a good thing. Maybe it was Hermie's day off. Maybe no one was looking for him.

Tooling Vicky slowly down the road, Rosswell yelled "Hermie!" several times. No answer from Hermie or anyone else. On the bright side, no one screamed for help. Honking the horn didn't raise anyone. As they say, no news is good news.

Rosswell hammered to a stop, jumped out, and vaulted up to where Hermie usually stood guard.

He rushed to the front of the guard shack and peered inside.

Too late.

Hermie lay flat on his back. Dead. The cause of death was unmistakable.

Rosswell's sword pierced the ranger's heart.

Frizz and Neal hovered over the body. Rosswell stayed back, waiting for the storm that he knew was coming.

Neal asked, "Ross, why do dead bodies seem to follow you around?"

There were several things wrong with that question. Main among the reasons was that his name wasn't Ross. Next, "dead bodies" is redundant. Finally, nothing "seemed" to follow Rosswell anywhere. Yet he kept his peace.

Frizz said, "Nothing's following the judge. I'd say he's following the bodies."

Hermie's wife and son wouldn't be celebrating the kid's birthday next week after all. Instead, they'd be attending a funeral. Poor kid. Poor wife.

Neal said to Rosswell, "What're the chances of you finding three corpses in the state park?" The medical examiner's face burned red and his breath came in gasps. "And one of them's killed with your sword?"

Rosswell said, "I'd say the chances are one hundred percent."

"You son of a bitch."

Frizz tugged Rosswell aside. "Neal's sister is Hermie's wife."

"Now that," Rosswell said, "is awful. Neal, I'm sorry. My God, who did this?"

Neal said, "I'm going to find out." Neal transformed instantly from a grieving relative into a scientific crimefighter. "This crime scene will be documented in more detail than any other scene in history." Rosswell believed Neal's words. Neal held up his camera. "I want someone else to back me up on the photos. This one is too close to home. Do you have your camera?"

"Yes. And it's at your disposal."

After each of them had snapped several hundred shots, Neal motioned Rosswell to stop.

Neal then started his examination by withdrawing the sword from Hermie and placing it in a long cardboard box. After that, he barked commands to the EMTs who'd arrived after he had. There would be nothing overlooked by Bollinger County's version of a big city's crime scene investigation unit.

Frizz and Rosswell walked to his patrol car. The sheriff said, "You know what's next?"

"You're going to arrest me for murder?"

"If the evidence is there, that's exactly what I'll do." He wasn't joking. "But something else needs to be done first. A search."

Rosswell said, "Your main priority is finding Candy. I can't believe that all of us failed to see how violent she can be."

"Anyone can hide his plans. Her plans. Anybody can do that when they're devious enough. It's not hard to fool people. That's what makes my job difficult."

Frizz and Rosswell faced off in the grilling sun, Rosswell certain that the sheriff's brain boiled as fiercely as his own did. The sky to the west had grown a deep gray. Rosswell heard rumbles of thunder and smelled the lightning.

Rosswell said, "We'd better make sure that this body doesn't wash away."

Frizz contemplated Neal working the scene. "He'll make sure that he doesn't miss a thing."

"Yes, you'll need to search my house and car." The salty taste of sweat dripping from Rosswell's mustache into his mouth nauseated him. "Probably want to give my office the twice over."

Frizz regarded Rosswell without making a motion or saying a word. Guessing the next thing that needed doing was easy.

Rosswell said, "I'll have the consent to search ready by the time you get to town."

"Vicky?"

"Search her now."

Frizz scoured the car and, finding nothing, finished only seconds before the storm pounced on them.

After reaching Marble Hill, Frizz and Rosswell dashed through the rain from their cars into Rosswell's house. Once inside, Rosswell wrote and handed Frizz the consent to search.

Frizz said, "I need a deputy here."

"Call one. We're in no hurry."

"They're all still looking for the bodies and controlling traffic."

They stood together at the front door and listened to the thunder and the rain pounding on the tin roof. Then, after flicking on every light in the house, Rosswell rejoined Frizz.

Rosswell said, "Call the Highway Patrol."

"They're swamped. They're trying to work loose an investigator to come down here and help us."

"Listen, Frizz, you search however much you need to. I'll check into a motel. You can seal the house until you get more help if you don't think you've done a thorough enough job."

"Let me do it and I'll tell you what I decide when I finish."

"Sounds good to me."

Frizz searched the kitchen. Nothing unusual there except that Rosswell's fingertip test revealed that the countertop by the sink wasn't as clean as normal. There were knives, but nothing that any other kitchen in the whole nation wouldn't have. As expected, no guns. The only gun Rosswell owned resided in the desk of his bench in the courtroom at the courthouse.

Next, Frizz prospected the living room. He found nothing until he knelt and peered under the couch. Without turning around or standing up, he said, "You need to make reservations at a motel."

As if Frizz's words had called down an Old Testament sign from the Lord, a lightning bolt struck nearby, filling the air with ozone and damn near deafening Rosswell. Coldness prickled his skin. He felt nausea rising and his vision blurring. Something itchy ran up and down his spine.

Rosswell said, "What is it?"

With the barrel of his gun, Frizz teased out the object under the couch.

A knife that had to be a foot long, covered with blood and gore.

"This knife," Frizz said, "is a polycarbonate quasi-resin."

"What the hell does that mean?"

"It's a super tough plastic that's extremely sharp and a metal detector can't find it. Terrorists love them."

"Terrorists? Are you telling me that terrorists attacked me in my own house?"

"I don't know who attacked you."

"Of course you do. Candy. When she tried shooting Tina and me, she couldn't pull off a kill shot because it was dark. After we got carried off to the hospital and everyone cleared the scene, she came back and planted that knife. It's a message that she cut the throat of that poor guy out at the park. Then she probably shot the woman. After that, she killed Hermie, which makes three. I'm going to the hospital to make sure it's not four."

"I've put a twenty-four hour guard on Tina," Frizz reminded Rosswell.

"Candy is after Tina. And me."

"Candy never mentioned one word about trying to shoot you two. Her confession is so full of holes it looks like a hunk of Swiss cheese after Ollie the rat got through with it. Why would she confess to two murders but forget about two attempted murders? It doesn't make sense."

"It doesn't have to make sense to Candy. She's nuts."

"If there had been trouble at the hospital, we'd already know about it. Rosswell, you act like I don't have a stake in Tina being safe. She's going to be fine."

"I'll call you if you're wrong."

The ugly stick, sitting on duty behind the desk of the nurses' station, didn't greet Rosswell's appearance with streamers and confetti. Instead, she glanced up from her *People* magazine, giving him a glare that would've killed Samson before he got his haircut. Her portable television was tuned to *The Price Is Right*. On the small screen, people cheered and clapped.

"Judge, do you want me to call security?"

Rosswell, on the drive over, decided the non-cautious approach would be the best. Where else would Candy go?

"Yes, immediately." Rosswell galloped past Priscilla. "Tell them to get here on the double. And call Frizz, too."

126

"What?" She sprang from her chair, knocking a plastic bottle of Diet Coke to the floor where it thunked and spewed. "Wait. Don't go in there."

Junior threw down an *X-Men* comic book he'd been looking at and said, "Judge, what the hell's going on?"

When Rosswell reached Tina's door, he turned and faced the cop and the nurse. "Call security. Tell them it's an emergency. Tell them to get here right now."

Junior said, "There's no emergency. I've been here the whole time."

The stick gasped an unprofessionally loud gasp when she followed Rosswell into Tina's room where they discovered Candy roosting on a high stool by his sweetie's bedside. Candy, draped over a sleeping Tina, was tangled in the tube going from a hanging bag into Tina's arm. If Candy moved the wrong way, the needle in Tina's arm could be torn loose. Above Tina, all the machines purred, giving no sign that there was distress in the room. For that small favor, Rosswell was thankful.

"How did you get in here?" the nurse asked Candy. "Who are you?"

Rosswell said, "Candy, you have to leave right now."

Junior said, "Lady, you're under arrest."

Rosswell said, "How the hell did she get in here?" Neither the nurse nor the cop seemed to know. Rosswell suspected Candy had slipped up the stairwell and sneaked in when she saw Junior take a break. Candy was crazy, not stupid.

Candy didn't budge.

The nurse said, "Candy?" Then, to Candy, she said, "He's right. Get out of here."

Candy, dressed in baggy blue jeans, gray sweatshirt, sunglasses, big bracelets, and a John Deere cap, hummed and rocked back and forth. Her clothes stunk of old sweat. She didn't speak. Instead, she sat stroking Tina's hair and whispering to her in sounds that didn't quite form words. Tina lay in a deep sleep. Rosswell hoped Tina wouldn't remember anything Candy did or said to her.

Rosswell said, "Nurse, did you call security and Frizz?"

Junior found his handcuffs and said, "Judge, I can cuff her right now."

Rosswell said, "Let's try the easy approach first. Candy, you need to move away from Tina. Right now."

Candy removed the large sunglasses she had pushed up on her head but otherwise didn't change position. Her big bracelets clanked when she moved her arms. The ugly stick hustled over, unwound the tubing off Candy, then inserted herself between Candy and Tina. Rosswell regretted his nasty thoughts about Priscilla Brewster after he witnessed her brave devotion to a patient under her care.

Priscilla punched two buttons on her pager that, he guessed, called security. Rosswell's eyes never left Candy. As far as he could tell, she had nothing in her hands. If Candy had a weapon on her, it wouldn't be noticeable in the baggy outfit she wore.

The nurse said, "I've called Father Mike."

Rosswell said, "We don't need a priest. We need security."

Priscilla said, "I paged security."

Rosswell said, "Junior, radio Frizz."

Junior clicked his radio several times. "Battery's dead."

Rosswell said, "Junior, do you know how to use a telephone?"

Father Mike strolled into the room, not at all hurrying as Rosswell thought he would've done had he known the situation he was entering.

Rosswell said, "Father Mike, call security and Frizz. Tell them we need them right now."

"Candy," Priscilla said, "shouldn't be here. And I already called security. We're not going to let anything happen to our patient."

"That's right," Junior said. "Not on my watch."

Father Mike said, "A guard is on her way."

Rosswell, at that point, still couldn't tell if Candy was armed. There was no way of determining if Candy even realized that the priest, nurse, cop, and Rosswell were in the room.

"Judge," Father Mike said, "I was a St. Louis City cop until I went into the priesthood at age thirty. I've faced down people a lot scarier than a young woman in a running suit." The priest turned to the cop. "Back me up, Officer Fleming."

"Yes, sir," Junior said.

The priest wasn't armed, but his police background would help. He headed for Candy.

Rosswell said, "After Candy posted bail, she found Hermie Hillsman and killed him."

"Candy," Father Mike said, without the slightest surprise in his voice about Rosswell's accusation, "did you kill Hermie?"

Candy said, "Hermie is a bad man." She hadn't answered the question.

Candy reached around Priscilla, trying to touch Tina. Priscilla slapped Candy's hands.

"Candy," Rosswell said, "you need to come out in the hallway with me." She didn't move. Father Mike, Junior, and Priscilla all three stood over Candy. Rosswell hoped the priest would check Candy for weapons. Soon.

The security guard appeared. She marched into the room, surveyed the situation, then asked Junior, "We can carry her to the sheriff's station."

Father Mike said, "Wait a minute, please." He asked Candy, "What are you doing here?"

"Am I my sister's keeper?" Candy said. "Yes, I am. True religion is helping our brothers and sisters in their time of need."

Father Mike and Rosswell exchanged glances. Rosswell said, "You're the expert in that field." Rosswell nodded, hoping the priest understood him. Hoping to make it plainer, Rosswell said, "You need to take over here." Rosswell was part of law enforcement. If he dragged a confession out of Candy without giving her the Miranda warnings or got other evidence from her, everything could be thrown out during her trial. As a former cop, Father Mike should know that.

Father Mike said to her, "Candy, listen to me."

"I'm listening."

"We need to leave here right now."

Candy said, "Tina needs me to soothe her brain. She's had a lot of trouble."

Father Mike said, "Yes, she has indeed. And what she needs now is sleep and rest."

Candy slipped her hand somewhere deep into her outfit and pulled out a slender object. Father Mike bent to see what it was. Rosswell leaned over Candy and screamed, "Knife!" Rosswell pushed Priscilla aside and jumped between Candy and Tina, ready to take the cut himself rather than letting his sweetie suffer any more trauma. The cop and the guard rushed Candy.

"Stop!" Father Mike said, "That's an MP3 player."

Rosswell swallowed hard and breathed deeply. "A what?" His voice screeched like a dry hinge on a heavy door.

Candy said, "It plays music downloaded off the Internet. I selected a lot of comforting New Age melodies for Tina." She turned the thing on and stuck ear buds in Tina's ears. Father Mike lifted Candy away from Tina. Candy left in the custody of Junior and the security guard. Father Mike and Priscilla followed them out of the room.

"Officer Fleming," Rosswell hollered after him, "take her directly to Frizz."

He said, "Not to worry, Judge."

After everyone else left the room, Rosswell unplugged one of Tina's ear buds and listened. Soft, tinkling noises, occasionally interrupted by a chord, joined random notes running up and down the scale. In the background, wind sighed. It didn't sound like music, but it was better than rap. After he removed the second ear bud, he stuffed the thing in his pocket.

He'd give it to Ollie, who needed to hack the thing to make sure there were no terrorist secrets stuffed in it. Such as how to sneak a polycarbonate knife onto an airplane. Or stuff one under a judge's couch.

Rosswell wanted Tina to perk up. Damn it, the anesthesia shouldn't have knocked her down this long. It had been nearly 48 hours. There were, to Rosswell's way of thinking, only three things that could be happening: First, Tina was sicker than anyone realized; or she was suffering a normal reaction to whatever anesthesia she'd gotten; or, number three, something else. The third possibility, he thought, made him feel paranoid.

Someone's pumping her full of dope.

Tomorrow, he'd arm himself.

Chapter Seventeen
Thursday morning

After Rosswell and Ollie went through the breakfast buffet at Merc's a couple of times, they tramped to the courthouse, where Rosswell unlocked the front door of the three-story brick building. The perpetual stink of the place greeted them. Although smoking had been banned several years ago, the wood of the building remained permanently stained a dirty brown from generations of tobacco clouds, and continued to release the soaked-in odors.

Rosswell was glad the courthouse was closed for the Hogfest, so he and Ollie could have a little privacy to discuss the case. They climbed the steps to the second floor courtroom where Rosswell clicked on the brass chandeliers. He shuffled—the activity lately generating muscle pain—to his chair on the high, old-fashioned bench. The bench and the paneling in the courtroom were dark, polished oak.

Rosswell nearly tripped over a wrinkle in the carpeting. *I feel like death walked me home from the dance.* Placing his hand on the paneling to brace himself, he winced at the state seal hanging on the wall behind the chair. The defective thing never failed to irritate him. Some illiterate craftsman cast it in plaster before World War II. The date of Missouri's admission to the Union, written in Roman numerals as MDCCXX (1720), was wrong. The correct date was MDCCCXX (1820). A word in the motto was misspelled, reading, "United We Stand, Divied We Fall." Early in his career, he'd offered to buy a new, correct seal for the county and pay for it himself. There was a fancy copper style he'd found in a catalog. The descendants of the original craftsman pitched a hissy fit at the thought of replacing the old seal. Fearing the loss of votes, Rosswell dropped the matter. He understood that you don't irritate voters, especially if they were taxpayers.

Now, something else bothered Rosswell. "I've viewed every inch of this courtroom for years, yet I wonder how much of it I've really seen." He pointed to the tin ceiling. "For example, what ran through the mind of the guy who designed those weird curlicues in that tin? No one can tell what that stuff's supposed to be. They're random patterns dreamed up by a fellow who made tin ceilings. They're meaningless."

Ollie peered at the ceiling for a moment. "It's the beveled clover and thorns design. A similar design was popular during medieval times on the plaster works in the great houses and castles around Oxford, England."

By now, Rosswell was beyond amazement at Ollie's vast knowledge of obscure facts. That Ollie knew arcane trivia was why Rosswell had hired the mouse as his snitch. Sometimes an obscure fact is a key to a riddle.

Rosswell said, "My thoughts exactly."

I can't see any damned clover and thorns on the ceiling, much less any that were beveled, whatever the hell that means.

"Interesting, Judge. Have I caused you to think?"

"Yes, as a matter of fact, you have."

"We didn't come up here to talk about tin ceilings."

"That's not my point."

"Is it that crappy seal with the mistakes on it?"

"Ollie, listen." Rosswell paced behind the bench. The space there afforded little room for a major pacing. He did his best in the cramped area with a minor pacing. "I came on the death scene first. I saw it before anyone else did."

Something sticky glommed onto the bottom of Rosswell's shoe. The janitorial service in the courthouse had gone to hell.

Ollie said, "Besides the killer."

"Or killers."

Whatever it was on the bottom of Rosswell's shoe smelled of wintergreen.

Ollie said, "Or killers. Plural. I know we haven't established how many bad guys or girls there were."

"That's what bothers me."

A muted thumping began. The courthouse air-conditioning unit ranked down there with Frizz's system. Mildew scented air oozed from the registers.

Ollie said, "You lost me."

"I saw something or smelled something or heard something or felt something out there that I can't recall."

Scratching his mustache, Rosswell found that the scrawny thing had trapped a crumb of something that he flicked onto the floor, which didn't smell all that good since the carpet hadn't been vacuumed in two or three weeks. Budget cuts.

Ollie said, "How do you know you can't remember something, if you don't recall knowing it in the first place?"

"When I was studying the bodies before anyone else got there, I noticed something that was strange."

"What?"

"If I knew, I'd tell you. But I keep thinking that it's important."

"Two corpses in a picnic area is strange. And important."

"Yes." Rosswell scratched his mustache, took his glasses off, and then put them back on. Picking up a pencil, he beat a quick rhythm on the bench. "That's strange, but something tickling my brain tells me that something about the bodies themselves was strange."

Rosswell unlocked and slid open the drawer under the bench to reveal a box. He unlocked and lifted its lid, then laid his hand atop his sidearm, a Smith & Wesson 442 Airweight .38 Special. He withdrew its holster, stuck the gun in it, and shoved the holstered pistol in his pocket.

Ollie showed no surprise. "Do you know how to use that?" Maybe he thought every judge had a weapon handy when holding court.

"I didn't want a gun," Rosswell said. "I had enough of firearms in the military. In fact, I earned the expert badge."

"You're a sharpshooter?"

"You're not listening, Ollie. I said I was an expert. Pistol and rifle. Sharpshooter is the middle, marksman at the bottom. I was at the top."

"I hate it when you know something I don't."

"Frizz insisted I buy the weapon. I stored it on the bench in case there was ever some kind of desperate problem in the courtroom."

"A problem in the courtroom requiring a gun to solve it?" Ollie bowed his head, as if in prayer. However, it wasn't prayer. A bad thought must've struck him. "You mean that you had access to that gun every time I came before you?"

"Yes."

His head was still bowed. "I'm proud I behaved myself."

"I came close to shooting you between the eyes a couple of times."

Ollie jerked his head up. "That's not funny."

"It's hilarious."

Ollie rubbed his head and pouted. Rosswell loved it when he made Ollie pout.

Ollie said, "What the hell did you see? Or smell? Or taste? Or hear?"

"You mean out at the park?"

"You're as dense as Nordic bread."

"I certainly didn't taste anything out there." Rosswell again pawed at his mustache and adjusted his glasses. Neither action helped him think. "I give up."

"No."

"No, what?"

"You can't give up. Think! What was there that you can't remember?"

"Can you hypnotize me?"

Ollie squeaked. The mouse noise verged on pushing Rosswell to commit physical harm on his snitch. Ollie said, "Hypnotism's a bunch of unadulterated bullshit."

"I've been meaning to ask you about that phrase."

"Which one?"

"Unadulterated bullshit. Is there such a thing as adulterated bullshit?"

"Unadulterated bullshit is pure bullshit, just like the bullshit you tasted out there at the park."

"I didn't taste anything," Rosswell said. "I smelled the worst smell a human can smell. I didn't feel anything. It was quiet so I didn't hear anything. It must've been something I saw, but I don't know what it was."

After double checking the gun to assure himself it was fully loaded, Rosswell scooped up a handful of cartridges, each feeling a little greasy, smelling of gun oil, and stuffed them into his pocket.

"Let's go," Rosswell said. "The next time anyone comes after me, I'll be ready."

"You could take that sword you're so proud of."

"That sword is in the evidence locker." Rosswell explained about his weapon being found stuck through Hermie, Frizz's search of Vicky, and the knife Frizz found under his couch.

"Holy shit," Ollie said. "Why aren't you in jail?"

"Because I didn't kill anyone. Frizz is smart enough to see that."

"Let's hope so."

Rosswell shoved the gun back in the holster and then pocketed his weapon. The oily cartridges in his pocket gave off a metallic clicking sound when he walked. "The smell of a clean gun in a new leather holster raises the spirit of courage in me." Rosswell smiled.

"That's scary."

"Ollie, we need to see a man about a dog."

"You need to pee?"

"No. The dog in that Sherlock Holmes story."

"The one that didn't bark in the night?"

"The same. The one that isn't there." Rosswell corrected himself. "I mean, the *ones* that aren't *here*."

They set off to track the killer.

###

The streets of Marble Hill were crowded. A good place to hunt for the murderer.

The Harley riders, as expected, made up the bulk of the traffic. When bunches of people show up in a little town year after year, other people also show up to sell things to them. It's called capitalism.

The lemonade and sweet tea vendors were dipping up drinks as fast as they could pour. Ollie and Rosswell stopped at one stand and each got a large sweet tea. Rosswell's caffeine and sugar levels had fallen to a precarious low since breakfast. Watching some of the local artists sketching portraits of a couple of motorcyclists took up more of their time, as did buying two cheeseburgers from a sandwich vendor. The smell of frying onions had prodded Rosswell's taste buds into a slobbering fit that could only be quelled by cheeseburgers. Boy Scouts demonstrated their signaling skills with mirrors and semaphore flags. A woman who specialized in making copper jewelry had sold out of nearly everything she'd brought to town. Crafters who had made all kinds of wooden do-dads hawked them to the crowd. Scented candles perfumed the air. The cotton candy guy had a line twelve deep.

In general, there was a street fair going on.

"Ollie," Rosswell said, "how do we find two people who aren't here?"

"My grandpa said when he was a kid that if someone left Bollinger County for a visit to somewhere else, everyone knew it. It's not like that anymore. Now people go to Europe and no one ever knows it until they get back and spread the word."

"Why is that? The population hasn't gone up in this county for a hundred and fifty years."

"Simple," Ollie said. "Cheap cars and cheap gas. The population is mobile. You don't even realize how much people travel anymore. It's too common."

"Gas isn't cheap."

"Comparatively speaking, it is."

Since Rosswell knew he was going to lose the argument, he shut up.

They stopped on a street corner and soaked in the view. There might have been five hundred tourists in the little town, running up and down the streets. Money on the hoof.

Who, if anyone in that crowd, was suspicious? No one. At least on first inspection.

Rosswell reassessed everything. Harley riders. Portrait artists. Jewelers. Boy Scouts. Crafters. Cold drink vendors. Sandwich sellers. Cotton candy guy. A mass of confusion. In his mind, he separated each person or each group, scrutinizing them anew.

When Rosswell watched several people standing still, moving their arms in slow motion, a glacial coldness slugged him in the gut.

Rosswell pointed. "Ollie, they have our dog."

Chapter Eighteen
Thursday morning, continued

Three Boy Scouts, standing a half block down from the courthouse, brandished semaphore flags. An Eagle Scout in charge of the demonstration faced the other two scouts. Rosswell approached the black-haired leader and told him, "I want to show you two positions. You tell me if they're semaphore signals."

"Sure," he said. "Let's see them."

Rosswell stood erect with both arms pointing downwards at a 45 degree angle, the same as the male corpse. "What's that?" Sweat ran from his armpits down his torso, tickling him.

"The letter Y."

"Great," Rosswell said. "What's this?" He pointed his left arm upwards at a 180 degree angle, his right downwards at a 180 degree angle, the same as the female corpse.

"That's an E."

"Thank you very much," Rosswell said to the boy before he motioned Ollie to head out. "Ollie, that tells me something."

"The letters E and Y. What does that tell you?"

They skedaddled back to Rosswell's office where they reviewed the pictures of the bodies on Rosswell's camera. "Check that out," Rosswell said, indicating a photo with both corpses visible. "I'll be right back."

The fountain in the hallway gave him a cold pint or so of thirst quenching water before he returned to his office. Heat exhaustion wasn't on his agenda. Cold water would dampen the possibility.

Ollie said, "The bodies are giving semaphore signals."

"Exactly. Y and E. Or, if we look at it the other way, E and Y. All we have to do is figure it out."

"If it means anything."

Rosswell considered giving Ollie one of his own squeaks. Instead, he said, "Of course it means something. There's nothing accidental about the way the corpses were arranged. Bodies don't just fall into the positions that I found those two."

"I'll assume that. Tell me what it means."

Rosswell chewed on the inside of his lip for a few seconds until he bit himself and tasted blood. "Oh, crap!"

"What? What does it mean?"

"I bit myself."

"You're not helping here."

Rosswell massaged his cheek. "Now, listen, E and Y don't make any words. E and Y, Y and E. Nothing."

"YE is Old English for *the* and also for *you*."

"That's pretty esoteric."

"I'll tell you something else. YE is the Internet notation for Yemen and YE is also a common Chinese surname."

"Yemen?" Visions of terrorists danced in Rosswell's head. "China?" Maybe a band of Commies was behind the dual murders. "What about EY?"

Maybe Commie terrorists planted that knife under my couch.

"EY," Ollie said. "Election year?"

The sounds of the street fair conjured up memories of political rallies, complete with hot air and noisy speeches signifying nothing.

Rosswell admitted, "Election year is scary, but the word or abbreviation has to be something common, very common. Let's assume the murder or murderers arranged the bodies that way."

"Assuming here."

"Yeah, you know you don't really have to say it that way when you're agreeing with me. Nod your head or say *okay* or something."

"Agreeing here."

Rosswell's head hurt. Sometimes, instead of talking to Ollie, he'd rather rub his head against a cheese grater. He closed his eyes for a beat before he started again. "Since those letters don't spell anything, then they must be an abbreviation."

"Initials." Ollie had segued into one of his pissy moods, obviously hoping to distract Rosswell from doing anything completely stupid.

It was an old trick the snitch used. When, in the past, Rosswell had started thinking goofy, Ollie pissed him off and then Rosswell came up with good ideas.

"A name," Rosswell said. "My thought exactly."

"Who do we know who has the initials E. Y. or Y. E.?"

They consulted the telephone directory. Yes, it could be someone who didn't have a telephone or had a cellphone. They could check the voter registration and tax rolls during regular office hours. Now, Rosswell suggested Elizabeth Young, Yancey Eberhardt, and Yardley Edgeworth, names he'd spotted in the phone book.

Rosswell said, "Do you know any of those people?"

"All of them. Elizabeth Young is a teacher who regularly screws up her computer at home and at school. Yancey Eberhardt works at a sawmill. He doesn't own a computer. Yardley Edgeworth is from London, England. Quite computer literate. How he found Marble Hill, I don't know."

"Are they all present and accounted for?"

"Only one way to find out." Ollie handed Rosswell the desk phone. "Start calling."

Rosswell dialed each of them. Elizabeth Young's answering machine picked up, but he left no message. Yancey Eberhardt didn't answer and didn't have an answering machine. Yardley Edgeworth picked up on the first ring. Rosswell put the call on speakerphone.

"Are you there?" Eberhardt said, in a proper British accent.

Well, yeah, I'm here. What did that mean?

"Umm . . . yes," Rosswell said. "I'm here. Is this Mister Yardley Edgeworth?"

"It is."

"This is—"

"I know who it is, Judge Carew. I have caller ID."

Damn. Rosswell hadn't thought of that. *Good thing I didn't call from my cellphone.* He didn't want that number made public.

Rosswell said, "Mr. Edgeworth, have you heard of the unfortunate deaths we've had here in the county?"

"Beastly."

"Yes. They were pretty bad." A mint that he'd previously missed on his desktop begged him to eat it. Rosswell obliged. The sharp cinnamon flavor cleared his sinuses. Breathing made him happy.

"When I moved here, I didn't realize we'd be competing with St. Louis and Kansas City on murder rates." There was a distinct sniff from Edgeworth.

"I'm working on a press release and, for additional human interest, I'd like to know how you, a Britisher, feel about such things happening in your adopted land."

If Ollie had rolled his eyes any harder, he'd have fallen over. As it was, suppressing his laughter made him wobbly. Rosswell put his finger to his mouth, hoping to shush Ollie.

"Judge Carew," Edgeworth said, "it's bloody beastly, pardon the foul language."

"I appreciate your time. Thank you."

Edgeworth hung up without saying good bye.

"Press release?" Ollie said. "*Britisher?*"

"You're not supposed to say Chinaman anymore. I didn't think Englishman was still politically correct. I had to think fast."

"The British don't use the term *Britisher*."

"Tough. We're in America and we won that war."

At this point, Rosswell had come up with exactly one clue. The only thing he knew now that he didn't know when he spotted the corpses was that the bodies had been arranged in a way that mimicked semaphore signals. And he had no idea why the killer had the bodies signaling an E and a Y. Or a Y and an E.

"Judge, maybe they're not letters."

"What do you mean they're not letters? Y and E are letters."

"Maybe the clue isn't using those letters as letters, but as part of a symbol or picture."

"Yes." Ollie's mind worked differently than Rosswell's. Speaking of clues, Rosswell didn't have one when it came to understanding what Ollie was talking about. "I was thinking along those lines. You go ahead and elaborate."

"Let me draw my guesses." For two or three pages' worth, Ollie scratched stick men, strange symbols, and gibberish. Eventually he threw down the pencil. "This is crap. Let's put that idea aside for now."

"How many people do we have on the really good suspect list?"

"Counting the names we put on there today?"

"Yeah."

"None."

"I'm a crappy detective."

I'm a damn good detective. Ollie knows that. He'll back me up. He'll make me feel better.

"Yes, you are one lousy private eye."

Well, at least he didn't say, Agreeing here.

Rosswell said, "I'm giving up. I'm going to find Frizz."

"Frizz already told you to give up."

"I want to tell him the semaphore clue. Then I'm giving up."

"I'm going back to Merc's. I could be missing a lot of juicy gossip."

Rosswell was locking the outside courthouse door when he heard a small voice say, "Sir, may I talk to you about signaling?"

Rosswell turned around to find Ollie staring down at a young Boy Scout. The round-faced scout had no rank on his uniform, which meant he was a Tenderfoot. Rosswell recognized him as being one of the boys under the tutelage of the Eagle Scout at the mirror and semaphore demonstration.

"Sure," Rosswell said. "Talk away."

"Bobby doesn't know what he's talking about." The kid's uniform was immaculate and his short brown hair was perfectly combed.

Ollie said, "Who's Bobby?"

The kid stared up at Ollie, probably amazed that human rats could talk. "The Eagle Scout."

Rosswell said, "What's your name?"

"Franklin Pierce Hillsman."

Another glacial coldness slugged Rosswell in the gut. "Are you Hermie's son?"

"Yes, sir."

Rosswell was stunned into silence. Ollie proved to be the better man than Rosswell because he said, "We're sorry about your daddy."

"Thank you, sir." Franklin drew himself to attention, clicked his heels together, and saluted. "I miss my daddy. He helped me a lot." Tears rolled down his cheeks.

What is the child doing here? Hermie's funeral isn't until Monday. There's no nice way to ask.

A woman dressed in black from neck to shoes strode up to the boy. "I'm Emma Borland Hillsman." She stuck out her hand to shake hands with Ollie first, and then with Rosswell. "I'm this young Scout's mother and proud of him." Her pale red hair and square head gave testimony that she was indeed Neal's sister.

Rosswell was astounded. This woman's husband had been murdered yesterday, yet here she was at a street fair with her son. He said, "I'm sorry about Hermie. He and I had some long talks."

"One talk you didn't have with him, Judge Carew."

"What was that, Mrs. Hillsman?"

"Our ancestry. We come from good Scots stock, Hermie and I do.

We landed in Virginia in the seventeenth century and made our way in a wild land."

Rosswell, although naturally proud of Scots folks making good in the world, was baffled. "That's wonderful, Mrs. Hillsman."

She continued. "We fought disease and the British. We nearly froze to death in the winter. We came close to starving several times. We crossed half this country to settle in these hills a hundred and twenty-five years ago, our families did. I'm going to bury my husband on Monday, but if he were standing right here, he'd tell Franklin that he should be doing his flags because Franklin comes from good stock."

Ollie said, "Wow." Rosswell made a mental note that he needed to keep Emma Borland Hillsman in mind the next time Ollie needed a good lecturing. Hearing her warmed the cockles of Rosswell's heart.

Wait. What's a cockle?

Franklin said, "My momma said that my daddy would want me to participate today, especially since he and I had been practicing our flags." He wiped his eyes and straightened his neckerchief.

"Your momma is right." Rosswell pulled a handkerchief from his pocket and, not bothering to remove his trifocals, wiped his face. "And, thank you, Mrs. Hillsman, for raising such a fine son. I know Hermie was proud of him." Rosswell prayed for forgiveness because he knew no such thing for sure, and besides, he added to the prayer, he hoped young Franklin never touched booze.

Two girls walked by, toting huge sticks of cotton candy that carried a cooked sugar smell. The hamburger guy poured freshly cut onions on the grill, their sizzle sending out sharp scents. Four or five Harleys started at the same time. The noise level made hearing the boy difficult.

Emma said, "Franklin needs to tell you all something about Bobby."

Ollie said, "Franklin, what was it you wanted to tell us?"

"A lady gave money to Bobby when she saw you all coming."

Rosswell said, "A lady? What lady?"

He directed their attention to the crowd. "That lady right over there."

Chapter Nineteen
Thursday morning, continued

Rosswell's eyes followed where Franklin Pierce Hillsman's finger pointed.

Rosswell would never fire a gun in a crowd, but the woman could be dangerous. A murderer. Patting his .38 to make sure it was still in his pocket, he prayed he'd never have to use it. Especially in public.

Rosswell said, "Which woman?"

Ollie craned his neck to search the crowd. Being taller than Rosswell, he might've been able to spot the woman in question before Rosswell did, who couldn't see who the boy had pointed out. Ollie gave no sign that he saw her either.

Franklin shook his head. "She's gone."

Rosswell asked him, "What does she look like?"

"Big. Old."

The boy would be 12 next week. Anyone over 21 years of age would look old to him.

Ollie said, "What color hair does she have?"

"I'm colorblind," he said.

Rosswell said, "Was it dark or light hair?"

"Medium. Maybe gray."

Candy doesn't have gray hair. The kid's colorblind. Candy's dirty blonde hair could've looked gray to him.

Ollie lined up next to Rosswell. "Was she as tall as I am or as tall as the judge?"

Franklin studied the two men. "In between."

Rosswell said, "Franklin, this is really important."

"Yes, sir."

Rosswell said, "What was she wearing?"

The boy thought for a moment. "Blue jeans. But not the tight kind. The kind that's loose and floppy. And a sweatshirt and a ball cap and sunglasses." Franklin closed his eyes, perhaps envisioning the woman. His eyes popped open. "One more thing. She had a big bracelet. Maybe two or three bracelets on each wrist."

Ollie said, "That's a good description. Your daddy would be proud of you."

"Thank you, sir."

Rosswell said, "Anything else?"

"She smelled funny."

"What," Ollie said, "did she smell like?"

"Vegetable oil."

Rosswell said, "Franklin, you're quite observant."

"Thank you, sir."

The young scout shook Rosswell's hand. Franklin's small hand, warm and sweaty, still managed a firm grasp on Rosswell's hand. The boy gave the handshake of a man.

Rosswell said, "Do you know why the lady gave money to Bobby?"

"She wanted him to lie to you."

"We need to know something." Ollie cleared his throat. "What did she want Bobby to lie about?" Ollie began rubbing his head, a sure sign of nervousness. He was a hound dog on a hot scent.

"What the semaphore signals meant."

The lady murderer had bribed Bobby, an Eagle Scout. Or at least an Eagle Scout got bribed by someone who knew about the murders. An Eagle Scout accepting a bribe! The world was spinning out of control. The bribery of an Eagle Scout will never make my report. I don't want anyone knowing that an Eagle Scout could stoop so low. Wait. Report? What report? I'm not making a report because I'm quitting this nonsense.

But.

Rosswell couldn't help but wonder how the murderer knew where he and Ollie would be. The answer was simple. Without a doubt, he was being tailed. And so was Ollie. Why hadn't the murderer, using a gun with a silencer, simply sneaked up on them and popped them in the middle of that noisy crowd? The bad girl could be gone before anyone realized that they were dead.

Does Candy want us alive for some reason?

"Franklin," Rosswell said, "do you know if Bobby told me a lie?"

"Yes, sir, I do." He glanced over his shoulder, apparently to make sure Bobby couldn't hear him before he answered. The fallen Eagle Scout chatted with two girls who appeared to be inspecting merit badges on the sash he wore. "He told you two lies."

Franklin was perceptive way beyond his years. Rosswell hoped that Hermie had recognized that quality in his son.

"You know a lot for being as young as you are," Ollie said.

"My daddy always said that."

Yes! Good for you, Hermie.

Rosswell asked, "What two lies?"

"This—" Franklin demonstrated with his arms "—isn't the letter Y. It's an N."

Rosswell said, "I'm guessing the second lie was about the letter E."

"Yes, sir." Again, Franklin demonstrated. "That's a D, not an E."

Rosswell said to Emma Hillsman, "We're proud of your son."

Emma said, "It's a requirement for a merit badge, what he's doing here today. Hermie would've wanted him here. Franklin promised Hermie last year that if he got to join Boy Scouts, he'd make his daddy proud and become an Eagle."

Franklin said, "Yes, sir. Thank you, Judge Carew."

Rosswell said, "Mrs. Hillsman, would you and your son walk around with us awhile to see if you can spot the woman?"

Emma said to Franklin, "Answer the man."

"Yes, sir."

After 15 minutes, they aborted the mission. None of the females in the crowd came close to Franklin's description. Surely, Rosswell thought, the woman hadn't been stupid enough to hang around after the bribery. Rosswell thanked the boy and his mother. After the two melted into the crowd, Ollie and Rosswell ran for Rosswell's office. Rosswell leafed through the D's in the telephone book, the pages rustling.

Rosswell said, "We need to find someone who smells like vegetable oil."

"Franklin was describing someone we know."

"Candy."

"She does a lot of cooking but she's not old."

"Ollie, crap. The kid is eleven, twelve next week. He thinks if you're twenty-one, you're at death's door."

"Then . . . yeah, okay." Ollie thought for a moment. "Yes, the kid was describing Candy. But she's in jail."

"Scratch Candy. By the way, what's a cockle?"

"A clam. Why do you ask?"

"Just curious." Rosswell refused to form the picture of Emma Hillsman warming the clams of his heart.

Then, starting toward the back at the N's, Rosswell found the only ND in the telephone book. "Ninepins Dixie? Isn't that supposed to be Dixie Ninepins, the bowling alley? I didn't think businesses were listed that way."

"This is the phone company."

"Yes, of course."

That time of day, the sunlight shone on his desk. The telephone book, lying square in the light, couldn't help them. Words, even when brilliantly lit on the page, mean nothing if the reader can't interpret them. The phone book was useless.

Ollie said, "I can't believe that's the only ND in the whole book."

"Believe it. That won't help us unless someone's been bludgeoned with a bowling pin."

"Especially, since the bowling alley uses ten pins, not nine. Ten pins are big and common. Nine pins are smaller and not too common around these parts."

"Why do they call it Ninepins?"

"Must be some kind of marketing ploy."

"A ploy that's lost on me." Rosswell riffled through the D's. "Dahlbert Nathaniel. That's the name of the detective in those P. D. James novels."

"No, that's Adam Dalgliesh. Not even close."

"And you didn't know who Mycroft Holmes was?"

"I don't know everything." Ollie straightened to his full height to give Rosswell his best pronouncement. "Most everything I know. But not everything."

"Is this guy another Britisher?"

"Weird guy. He moved here from Miami last year. I set up his computer system. Nathaniel sells used books online."

Rosswell dialed Dahlbert's number, thinking that Ollie would definitely know weird when he saw it. No answer and no answering machine. "Why don't these people have answering machines?" After fifteen rings, he hung up.

"I used to get irritated when I connected to an answering machine. Now I get irritated if I don't."

After noting his address, they drove to Nathaniel's house, a trim cottage about four blocks from the courthouse. Parked next to the blue house under the carport, was a silver Infiniti with 15-inch tires. Several potted ferns sat in the shade of the front porch. A hummingbird feeder, full of red hummingbird nectar hung above one of the ferns.

Rosswell said, "Think we should call Frizz?"

"And tell him what? We found one of the two hundred vehicles that might match the description that Hermie gave you?"

Rosswell wrote down the car's tag number. They walked to the door and Rosswell knocked. The curtain on the front window drew back about an inch. Someone was checking them out. After a moment, a tall man with close-cropped bright red hair answered. He didn't appear to be an albino. Nonetheless, he was one of the whitest men Rosswell had ever seen.

"Yes?"

"Mr. Dahlbert?" Rosswell asked.

"The same. And whom might you two be?"

Rosswell introduced himself and Ollie. Nathaniel invited them in. After all, the two visitors didn't appear to be common burglars. Rosswell thought that he himself looked like a vacuum cleaner salesman, maybe, but not like a burglar. Ollie looked like a hoodlum. The star-shaped purple tattoo on his bald head must not have bothered Nathaniel.

Rosswell said, "I'm trying to track down the driver of a silver car that was out at Foggy Top the other day."

Nathaniel tilted his head, a sign of curiosity. "Sit down." If he thought the question was odd, he gave no indication.

Ollie and Rosswell sat on the long, green couch in his living room. Nathaniel commandeered the tartan La-Z-Boy recliner.

Nathaniel picked up a cup of steaming black tea, squeezed a lemon slice in it, and asked, "Join me in a cup of tea?"

There were several white cups, thin enough to read a newspaper through, snuggled next to a silver tea set.

"Sure," said Ollie. "Plain."

"Make mine six lumps," Rosswell said. "No milk. It dilutes the sugar taste."

The end table next to Nathaniel's chair held the telephone and the answering machine. Every inch of the room was crammed with books, categorized by their Library of Congress number. His house was neater and cleaner than Rosswell's, who was anal about house-keeping. The thought that maybe there was a Mrs. Dahlbert flitted across Rosswell's weary brain, and then he dismissed it with the real-ization that no woman would allow a man to keep all his books in the living room.

Ollie drank half his cup of tea in one gulp. "Mr. Dahlbert, have you been in the vicinity of Foggy Top lately?"

"I don't believe that I've ever been in that vicinity." His puzzled appearance seemed genuine. "Or if I've been close, it was by accident. I'm not sure where it is. I'm not even sure what Foggy Top is."

What was Ollie expecting? That the guy would break down crying and confess to being the murderer? The man had never even heard of the park.

"It's a state park," Rosswell said, and explained how to get there. Then he said, "Have you loaned your car to anyone recently?"

When Nathaniel folded his hands together, Rosswell spotted an exact duplicate of the ring that he'd found at the crime scene. Nathaniel wore it on his right hand. There wasn't a wedding band on his left hand.

"No," he said. His voice sounded strained.

"That's a nice ring," said Rosswell.

"*Virtus junxit mors non separabit,*" Ollie said.

Nathaniel sipped from his cup. "That's the motto on the inside of the ring."

"Are you a Mason?" Rosswell asked Nathaniel.

"Yes, I am."

Ollie said, "Do you know a Mason around here with the initials EJD?"

Nathaniel chuckled. "Those letters aren't the initials of a person. A breakaway group from the Masons kept a lot of the rites and symbols, but they added EJD to the motto you just spoke."

Rosswell stirred his tea before drinking it. "What's the translation of the original motto?"

"'Virtue unites us, death won't separate us'. That's a loose translation. A lot of Latin scholars cringe when they hear the motto translated that way."

Ollie said, "What's with the EJD then?"

"Those are the first letters of an English motto: Even Just Die. The *just* in that motto is a noun, meaning 'just ones'. Sloppy English, but you get the drift."

Nathaniel stood and retrieved a thick volume from a shelf. "You gentleman are investigating the murders." He leafed through the book. Its cover was brown.

Neither Ollie nor Rosswell answered. They didn't have to. They were that obvious.

"Maybe," Nathaniel said, "you need to buy this informative book on forensics." Always the salesman, he handed the book to Rosswell.

Rosswell declined the book. "Thanks, but right now I don't need that."

"I've got books on every aspect of criminal investigation, from how the mind works to talking to suspects to how to do autopsies." He swept his arm around, pointing to all the shelves. "And if there's a title you need that I don't stock, I'll get it for you at the lowest cost anywhere."

"I'm his research assistant," Ollie said. "Maybe I'll come back and we can go over a few things I need. I'm sure you'll give the judge good credit terms."

Rosswell stood. "We need to go before Ollie mortgages my house."

Rosswell slipped the key into Vicky's ignition. "Do you think it's a coincidence that the only guy in the county—at least the only guy in the telephone book—whose initials are ND has a ring like the one I found at the scene?"

"To quote a snarky friend of mine, 'I don't believe in coincidences'."

Nathaniel peered through his curtains. Good detectives shouldn't sit in front of a suspect's house and discuss the interview they just had with the possible bad guy. Not only is this bad form, it makes the suspect nervous. Nervous suspects do stupid things.

Ollie said, "That guy looks like a clown. White as a ghost with screaming red hair."

"You've got a bald head with a—"

"Stop right there. Please. Judge."

"Change of subject. Why were we pointed in Nathaniel Dahlbert's direction?"

"The murderer pointed us in his direction? Or maybe it is coincidence that the arms of the corpses were signaling the letters D and N?"

"My guess is that there are more people involved in these murders than we suspect." Rosswell's mouth savored the memory of the drink they'd been served. "Damn good tea." He started Vicky but didn't put her in gear.

One of Nathaniel's neighbors, an elderly woman dressed in a black pantsuit, walked out of her house and began sweeping her sidewalk. She was probably part of the Neighborhood Watch, memorizing the description of two men in a bright orange Volkswagen parked in front of the nice book salesman's house.

Ollie said, "Nathaniel poured from a Reed & Barton pointed antique tea set. Sterling silver."

"They sell those at Wal-Mart, right?"

"The cheap ones on eBay sell for two thousand dollars."

"Selling used books must be quite lucrative."

"If they're full of dope."

"You noticed the answering machine."

"My eyes notice everything. I'm the research assistant."

"The missed-call light was blinking. That can mean only one of two things."

"Judge, you're giving me all the easy ones. He either genuinely missed the call or saw who it was and didn't want to answer."

"But—"

"Let me finish. I vote for genuinely missed the call. If he'd seen who it was on the machine, then when he peeked out the curtain and saw us, he would've erased the call before he let us in."

"That's right."

"And he's the only one in the county with the initials ND. Or at least the only one we know about."

"There's someone else with the initials ND."

Ollie said, "Who?"

"The murderer."

"That's crap. Candy is the murderer and she's in jail. It's time for us to close up shop."

"Let's just talk about this as an intellectual exercise."

Ollie made a sound low in his throat, suggesting he'd just stifled a squeak. "The murderer is the woman who bribed Bobby."

"They're one and the same person."

"Agreeing here."

"Ollie, check out Nathaniel, top to bottom."

Rosswell's phone rang.

Frizz said, "I got good news and I got bad news."

Rosswell said, "I'll bite. What's the good news?"

"Purvis Rabil says he wants to meet us at the station. He says he's got mighty important info for us about the murders."

"I'll bet. And the bad news?"

"Ribs hired a fancy attorney out of Saint Louis who filed papers to keep Candy out on bail. The lawyer says Candy didn't commit a crime by going to Tina's room. She was just visiting a sick friend."

"No judge is going to buy that bull crap."

"One already did. Candy never went back to her cell."

Chapter Twenty
Thursday noon

At the station, Rosswell eyeballed Purvis while Frizz greeted the big motorcyclist when he came through the door.

Before Purvis had arrived, Rosswell had said to Frizz, "If Candy's running loose, then I'm headed for the hospital."

Frizz said, "I've got Junior guarding her door and a female reserve deputy inside her room. Candy's nowhere in town. I checked myself. Ribs told me she's in Saint Louis talking to her lawyer."

"I'm going to the hospital."

"Rosswell, damn it, you'll just be in the way. You've got to talk to Purvis. He insisted you be here."

Now, Purvis nodded in Rosswell's direction. "We need to have a talk about a ring that the honorable judge found." Rosswell wondered where the hell Purvis learned about the ring. Like Ollie had said, there were no secrets in Bollinger County. That, however, didn't satisfy Rosswell as a good answer.

Purvis's shirt was drenched with sweat and his face was redder than when Rosswell had seen it before. Scooby's hair was wilted and she panted incessantly.

Frizz motioned Rosswell over. "Take my gun and lose Ollie."

Rosswell looked first at his own gun and then at the sheriff's. Rosswell said, "You want me to shoot him?"

"He doesn't belong here. He's not law enforcement."

Rosswell ordered Ollie outside.

Ollie never peeped, scared as he was of Frizz. Good thinking, Ollie.

Frizz said to Purvis. "I'm patting you down."

Rosswell aimed Frizz's gun and his own gun at the motorcyclist's head. If Purvis tried hurting anyone, Rosswell could get two shots at the hog rider. Purvis grasped his hands behind his head in a prisoner of war stance and stood with his legs far apart. He knew the drill. Frizz patted him down so thoroughly that it made an airport screener's groping look like a limp handshake. Satisfied that the man wasn't armed, the sheriff took back his gun from Rosswell but didn't holster it. Rosswell held his gun down at his side, finger outside the trigger guard.

Frizz ordered Purvis, "Spill it."

"Sheriff, if you don't mind. Before we go any further, I need you to verify who I am. I've got info in an envelope on the inside pocket of my vest." Purvis Rabil pointed as he spoke. His hillbilly accent had mysteriously disappeared, replaced by the speech of a cultured Southern gentleman. "Let me retrieve it and then you call the numbers I've written on the paper. All my identification is there also."

Frizz nodded, and Purvis handed the envelope to the sheriff. He dumped the contents, read the information, and scoped out the identification cards. "Holy shit." Riffling through the info once again, he let out a low whistle. "I'll do the calling in private." Frizz disappeared into headquarters and shut the door. Apparently, the sheriff wasn't scared that Purvis would murder Rosswell while he skedaddled to make a phone call.

Rosswell asked Purvis, "What's your story?"

"I'll tell you when the sheriff returns."

"There's a killer loose. Three victims—three that we know of—are dead. Earlier, a woman we think is the killer visited Tina in her hospital room. Fortunately, we stopped her before she could hurt Tina. I suggest you be very forthcoming with the sheriff."

"I'm sorry, but I will not speak until Sheriff Dodson returns."

"How did you know about that ring?"

Purvis hooked his thumbs in the belt of his jeans and said nothing. His silence scared Rosswell. Scooby lapped the air with her tongue and yapped. The dog's bark wasn't as loud as a baby's fart.

"Judge," Frizz said when he came back to the dispatcher's area, "meet Special Agent Purvis Rabil of the ABI."

Purvis made a slight bow from the waist. "Glad to meet you."

Rosswell said, "What's the ABI?"

"Alabama Bureau of Investigation," Purvis said.

"Alabama?"

"That's right, Judge."

"You're using your real name?" Rosswell said. "I take it that your apparel is not a standard uniform for the ABI. That means you don't want anyone to recognize you. Why are you using your real name?"

Purvis said, "I use my real name because no one could ever connect me with any law enforcement agency."

"An attempt at deep cover," Rosswell said. "Anyone can hide with the right hacking of a couple of different databases." Ollie had taught him that. "Sounds like a spy novel."

Purvis said, "Judge, it is a spy story. But a true one, not a novel."

Frizz said, "Purvis, tell the judge everything but, Rosswell, remember that it's confidential."

Scooby farted. The rotten smell of dog gas dissipated quickly.

Rosswell said, "I'll never tell anybody anything about what you tell me. I'd be kicked off the bench and disbarred for violating a confidentiality."

Not true, but the lie should work.

"Let's start with Johnny Dan Dumey," Purvis said. "I'll give you the short version. Johnny Dan buys and sells cars—mostly old muscle cars—all over Missouri, Illinois, Tennessee, Arkansas, Alabama, Kentucky, and Mississippi."

Purvis fished around in one of his pockets, came up with a new package of Big Red, and stuffed five sticks of the gum in his mouth.

He continued around a big wad, "On one of his trips to Alabama, Johnny Dan went after a car in Birmingham. The fellow selling it had the vehicle stored in a meth lab. Johnny Dan came to the ABI headquarters in Birmingham, and I talked to him. Thanks to his info, we busted a huge meth operation. One of the biggest in the Southeast."

"That's great," Rosswell said. "But Alabama is a long way from Missouri. What does it have to do with the murders here in Bollinger County? And what's that got to do with someone trying to kill Tina and me?"

Frizz said, "Give the agent a chance to tell the whole story."

Purvis said, "The meth lab in Birmingham was backed by interests in St. Louis and Kansas City. We recruited Johnny Dan. He signed on as undercover. His car business gave him the perfect camouflage. Add to that Johnny Dan's acting ability and he was a natural. He's been in several little theater productions. And the guy keeps the best notes of any snitch I've ever had. Most of my informants can barely read or write."

"Purvis," Rosswell said, "this is interesting and all, but someone tried to murder Tina and me. Can you help us on that?"

Frizz said, "You interrupted the man's explanation. He's fixing to shed light on the crimes we've been suffering during the last few days."

Rosswell said, "I think he's an overgrown hippy riding a motorcycle."

"Thank you, sir," Purvis said. "That was what I intended to look like. Glad it worked."

"So far," Rosswell said, "you've not said anything interesting."

Purvis said, "Johnny Dan Dumey witnessed the murders at the state park."

Frizz curled his hands into fists. "Just why in the hell did you and Johnny Dan forget to tell us that bit of information? I should arrest you both for withholding evidence. In fact, I should arrest you for impeding an investigation since you didn't report to me the second you got in this county."

A gaggle of motorcyclists sallied down the street in front of the sheriff's station. Purvis' motorcycle was parked out front. The hog riders no doubt wondered what one of their own was doing talking to the sheriff. They revved their engines, flooding the area with the strange Harley engine sound.

"The reason for not telling?" Purvis said. "The ring."

"You," Frizz said through clenched teeth, "couldn't tell me about an eyewitness to two murders because of some fricking ring?"

"Let's talk about the term 'eyewitness'," Purvis said.

"No, let's talk about the fricking ring," Frizz said.

"As far as an eyewitness, there's nothing to talk about," Rosswell said. "The term 'eyewitness' is well defined. It means the person was at an event, saw what happened, and can testify to it."

"The first part about being there is correct," Purvis said. "But the next part about seeing what happened is not correct."

Frizz said, "You're playing word games. Tell us who the murderer is so we can go after her."

Scooby furiously licked Purvis's neck. Without breaking stride, Purvis pulled a small cup and a bottle of water from a pocket, poured Scooby a drink and set her down to enjoy the break. Until she finished, every three seconds she'd growl and bark at Purvis. When she belched, obviously a signal that she was through, Purvis stuffed her under his shirt.

Purvis said, "I can't guarantee that your killer is a woman."

Rosswell said, "That's a load of crap."

Frizz said, "Rosswell caught Candy in Tina's room."

"And," Rosswell said, "a woman tried to plant a false clue at the street fair."

Frizz looked at Rosswell for a moment with an unspoken question.

"I'll tell you later," Rosswell said.

Purvis clasped his hands behind his back and stared at the ceiling, reminding Rosswell of professors he'd known long ago. A lecture was aborning.

"What," Purvis said, "did this woman at the street fair look like?"

"She looked like Candy," Rosswell answered. "At least that's the description we got from an eyewitness." Rosswell didn't mention that the eyewitness was an eleven-year old Tenderfoot Boy Scout. "Baggy blue jeans. Gray sweatshirt." Something else. What was it? "Oh, yeah. Her hair tucked under a John Deere cap. Dirty blonde hair. And sunglasses. Big sunglasses. She wore big bracelets on each wrist."

"Baggy." Purvis still stared upwards. "Baggy clothing hides a lot."

"That's what my wife says," Frizz said. "Women wear baggy clothing to hide something."

"And the cap part?" Purvis said. "Judge, are you sure it was a John Deere cap?"

Rosswell said, "I didn't see the woman at the street fair. Purvis, you sound like a defense lawyer, not a cop."

"I sound like a defense lawyer because I want to get rid of the defense lawyer's arguments before the prosecutor takes the case to court."

"Then," Frizz said, "get on with it. I'm still considering arresting you and Johnny Dan."

"It's impossible at a distance to say that was a woman," Purvis said. "The Judge couldn't have identified this person's sex from her hair, which was covered by a cap, nor by the shape of her body, which was clothed by baggy items, nor by her eyes covered by sunglasses."

Rosswell said, "In other words, if I'd seen her from a distance, I'd have identified the person by face alone."

"You're quick." Purvis smiled at Rosswell, then said, "And you are correct about the face. At least the part of the face that was visible."

"And," Rosswell said, caught up in the spirit of the question-and-answer session, "the killer could've made herself look like a man or vice-versa."

Purvis said, "Unless you're a man who has a beard or mustache, if you cover yourself, all but your face, most people can't identify your sex during a period of stress."

Frizz said, "I learned all that crap, too. But Rosswell knows the woman. If he saw her from a distance, then he could still identify her as Candy."

"Johnny Dan is who I'm talking about." Purvis began pacing. All he needed was a chalkboard behind him and he'd fit the professorial image one hundred percent. "He was definitely present at the murders."

From the look on Frizz's face, Rosswell thought the sheriff would shoot Purvis.

"That does it," Frizz said. "Purvis, you son of a bitch, you're under arrest."

Purvis stuck both hands out and Frizz slapped on the cuffs.

Rosswell said to Purvis, "Why in the hell didn't you say something the first time you came to the sheriff's station? You should've identified yourself."

Frizz said to Rosswell, "Let me handle this. I've got him under arrest for withholding evidence. Purvis, let's go to your cell."

Purvis spoke in a low voice to Frizz. "I can deliver the murderer to you."

Frizz moaned. "But Johnny Dan didn't see if the killer was a man or a woman? That's a crock of shit. I'm going to arrest Johnny Dan, too. He's impeding this investigation."

Purvis said, "Hidden in the woods, keeping out of sight, Johnny Dan was too far away to hear or see anything distinct. He thinks the murderer was a woman."

Frizz said, "You and Johnny Dan are going to be in separate cells far apart. You won't be able to cook your story."

Rosswell said, "Couldn't Johnny Dan tell if the killer was wearing a woman's clothes?"

"A woman's clothes?" Purvis scowled at Rosswell. "Go out in the streets and take a look around. When was the last time you saw a woman wearing a dress or a skirt?"

"Crap," Rosswell said. "Of course. Not a lot of dresses or skirts around these days. I guess I need to pay more attention to women."

Frizz said, "That still doesn't explain why Johnny Dan didn't tell us about the murder."

Purvis said, "I can help you with the investigation or I can sit in jail." He shot a glance at the handcuffs. "Sheriff, your call."

Rosswell said, "I need to get back to Tina."

Frizz said, "Not yet."

Purvis said, "Johnny Dan knew one of the victims. The male victim. It was Eddie Joe Deckard."

"EJD," Rosswell said. "That explains the initials on the ring." In other words, Nathaniel lied to Ollie and Rosswell about what the initials meant. Why the lie?

Purvis said, "Eddie Joe Deckard was one of the biggest dope dealers in your county."

"I know Eddie Joe Deckard." Frizz removed his hat, wiped his forehead with his sleeve, then stuck the hat back on. "I've never had one whiff of a suspicion on that boy. How could he be the biggest dope dealer around here?"

"Simple," Purvis said. "He didn't do business in this county. As far as we could tell, Eddie Joe wasn't a user. All he did was deal. And he was making a healthy profit. He was the linchpin between Birmingham, Memphis, St. Louis, and Kansas City."

"And yet no one bothered to tell me?" Frizz said. "That's a crock of day-old shit."

"The ring?" Rosswell prompted Purvis.

Purvis said, "Johnny Dan made a buy from Eddie Joe. Johnny Dan claimed he didn't have the full amount of money for the dope. Eddie Joe gave him credit but wanted some kind of collateral. Johnny Dan gave Eddie Joe his ring."

"The initials?" Rosswell again prompted Purvis. "How did Eddie Joe's initials show up on Johnny Dan's ring?"

"Johnny Dan told me that Eddie Joe refused to return the ring. Somewhere along the line, Eddie Joe had his initials engraved inside the band since he decided to keep the ring."

Again, Rosswell thought, that story didn't fit with Nathaniel Dahlbert's story, which was that a schismatic group of Masons added the first letters of Even Just Die to the Latin motto. And those letters happened to be the same as the initials of Eddie Joe Deckard? This possible coincidence seemed especially ludicrous.

The gaggle of Harley riders who'd circled the station a couple of times did a complete tour again. Maybe they were growing suspicious. Purvis talking to the sheriff. And for a long time. Rosswell was happy that the hog riders couldn't see the handcuffs on the big guy.

"Let me get this right," Rosswell said, staring straight at Purvis. "One of the biggest dope pushers in the country lived in Bollinger County, but nobody in Missouri knew. Only y'all in Alabama knew."

Purvis hid an ace or two up his sleeve. The problem, however, was that Rosswell had no idea what the game was. And he doubted that Frizz knew either. "And the tale gets better. Johnny Dan gave Eddie Joe his Masonic ring as collateral on a dope deal? And Eddie Joe decided to have his initials engraved inside the ring and keep it?" Rosswell toyed with the idea of trying to imitate Ollie's squeak, but gave up on the idea.

Purvis said, "Judge, do you think that only when a criminal's rational plans get screwed up that charges are brought? These dopers do a lot more stupid things than you ever dreamed of."

Rosswell said, "And Johnny Dan followed Eddie Joe out to the park?"

"Yes," said Purvis. "We asked him to keep an eye on Eddie Joe."

"And," Rosswell said, "Johnny Dan *almost saw* who murdered Eddie Joe and the woman?"

"Correct." Purvis stroked Scooby's head. The dog licked Purvis's hand. "Johnny Dan can't swear to it in court, but he's almost certain that the killer was a woman. That's why we didn't want Johnny Dan to talk to you, Frizz. We didn't have a sure footing yet."

The whole story sounded like a load of crap. Rosswell had heard loads of crap before. Yes, there's plenty of jurisdictional squabbling when it comes to law enforcement agencies, but Purvis's story reeked of something made up during a late night of drinking. From his squinted eyes and downturned mouth, Frizz didn't seem to be buying the whole load either.

Frizz said, "Now would be a good time to bring Johnny Dan in for questioning."

Purvis nodded to Frizz. "You can have Johnny Dan. That's why I'm here. You should have full access to him all you want. As far as we're concerned, he can tell you anything."

Rosswell said, "And blow his cover?"

Purvis said, "Undercover operatives don't last forever. Eddie Joe is gone, and we consider that a major accomplishment. Time for us to move on to different targets."

Frizz said, "You're not worried that the other bad guys in the dope ring won't try to kill Johnny Dan?"

Purvis stood silent.

"Answer me."

Purvis said, "I can't guarantee anyone's safety. Johnny Dan knew that when we signed him up."

"Frizz," Rosswell said, "I need to head back to Tina's room. I've got to make sure she's being guarded correctly."

"Yeah," Frizz said to Rosswell while staring at Purvis who hadn't satisfactorily answered Frizz's really good question. Frizz seemed distracted. "Purvis is headed for jail."

###

A half hour later, Frizz knocked on Tina's door.

Rosswell said, "Come in."

Tina was sleeping. Housekeeping had visited earlier after Junior patted down the man on duty and checked his cart for hidden weapons. Priscilla came in after housekeeping left. She made Rosswell turn his back while she bathed Tina and fitted her with fresh pajamas, if those rags you get in hospitals could be called any kind of sleepwear.

Frizz said, "Are you by yourself?"

"Yeah. I relieved the female deputy. Hope that's okay."

"Sure. Listen, I've been asking around about Eddie Joe. I can't find out who he'd been hanging around with lately. We're still searching for the bodies, but the volunteers have dwindled down to two or three."

Rosswell said, "Have you been to the deadfall yet?"

"Nope. Going there tomorrow. The river's still too high but it's going down."

"Sounds dangerous."

"There's something funny about Eddie Joe."

"Funny?"

"I couldn't find out where he lived. The closest I came was an address that's six months old. Somebody else stays there now, but it's like Eddie Joe disappeared after he moved."

"And now he's dead?"

"Seems so, if Purvis knows what he's talking about." Frizz rubbed his nose and sneezed. "Something's floating around in the air. Anyway, Purvis talked me into helping. I didn't throw him in jail. He's out trying to track down info on Eddie Joe."

"Maybe Eddie Joe had moved off somewhere and came back for a visit."

"Anything's possible," Frizz said. "He owned a house in Marble Hill. He sold it and left no forwarding address. That's not unusual. I've talked to a couple of people who've seen him around in the last few months, but no one knows where he stays."

"Where did he live in town?"

Frizz told Rosswell the address.

Rosswell gasped. Loudly. Detectives shouldn't do that since it removes the element of surprise.

"That," Rosswell said, "is where Nathaniel Dahlbert lives."

Chapter Twenty-one
Thursday afternoon

"Who the hell is Nathaniel Dahlbert?""

Rosswell gave Frizz what he knew about the book salesman.

Frizz said, "Do you think he's mixed up in this in any way? Sounds like Nathaniel knows his way around a computer. It wouldn't be hard for him to set up dope deals on the Internet."

"I don't know who is doing what."

Tina moaned. Frizz moved over to her bed, watching her sleep. "She'll be fine."

Rosswell reached under the covers and touched Tina's hand. She moved. The bedding crinkled, signaling it was clean. He tucked the crisp-smelling blanket around her neck. This being a hospital, the temperature in the room hovered around 5 degrees below comfortable.

"Frizz, there are lot of reasons that I hope she's fine. More than fine." Secretly, he'd been praying that Tina lived long enough to attend his funeral, not the other way around. A world without Tina was unimaginable. "Her reaction to the anesthesia is beginning to worry me. She should've been out of the hospital by now."

"Tell you what." Frizz practically fell into the chair next to Tina's bed. "Go talk to this Nathaniel guy again, knowing what you know now."

"I thought you wanted me off the case."

"I'm so tired I don't know if I've found a rope or lost a horse.

You've talked to Nathaniel. He'll be more likely to talk to you than me. He'll tell you more than he would me."

"I'm not leaving Tina."

"You go and I'll stay." When Rosswell didn't consent immediately, Frizz continued, "I'll stay behind a locked door and not move from this chair until you get back. I'll threaten Junior with a slow, painful death if he bothers us."

Rosswell could see that Frizz was indeed exhausted. If the sheriff wasn't useless now, he soon would be. Maybe a nap was in order. If the worst happened and the crazed murderer made another run at Tina, Junior would probably shoot the bad guy—or was it a bad girl? If Junior failed, Frizz could stop the killer, even if he had been napping. A nap? Close your eyes in any hospital and listen to the noise. How could a nap be possible with all the clanking and talking going on? Rosswell's mother had always said that a hospital was no place for a sick person. He wondered if an orderly would wake Tina for a sleeping pill.

"All right." Rosswell gave a half-hearted salute. "I'll talk to Nathaniel."

Frizz listed the specifics of what he wanted to know and then Rosswell walked out the door of Tina's room. After he heard the click of the lock, he left the hospital.

When Nathaniel opened his door, he said, "Judge, good to see you again."

Yes, you're about as happy to see me again as I was when I found out I had leukemia.

"Come in."

If Nathaniel was trying to hide anything, he was putting on a happy face. A secretive person doesn't ask an investigator—thanks to Frizz's request, Rosswell considered himself a detective now—to come into his house with such warmth if there's something to hide. Right? Maybe Nathaniel hadn't heard that Rosswell was a detective now.

After the formalities, Rosswell asked, "When did you buy this house?"

"Tea?" The silver tea service, shiny and clean, sat ready for service. "It's time for my afternoon tea."

"Could you answer the question?"

Any warmth Nathaniel had shown disappeared in an instant. "Is it true that in law school they teach you never to ask a question in court unless you already know the answer?"

The rich fragrance of Golden Steed Eyebrow flooded the room when Nathaniel poured his cup. China's Fujian Province is the only place in the world where that tea grows. With the dollar in the toilet, the beverage had to be the most expensive imported drink in America.

Rosswell said, "I don't recall anyone in law school saying specifically that you should know the answer before you ask the question, but it's certainly a good idea."

He'd never heard that taught in law school. Maybe some professor said it when he was trying to catch a nap after a big lunch.

"Then you already know that I bought it six months ago?"

And what secrets, Nathaniel, do you have? That's the question Rosswell wanted to ask but didn't.

"Yes, I already knew that." As with his discussion with Father Mike about confession, Rosswell again felt as if he were in the fifth grade being interrogated by an irritated teacher slapping a chalkboard eraser on her palm. The memory of chalk dust made him sneeze. "Who did you buy it from?"

"You already know the answer to that, also." Nathaniel leaned back in his recliner. "Eddie Joe Deckard."

Rosswell had heard the cliché about blood boiling all his life. Now with the fire of anger sizzling his insides, he realized how the phrase started.

Keep it steady. Don't lose this guy. You need info from him.

"Nathaniel, why didn't you mention him when we were here the first time?"

"You didn't ask me about him."

"Sure, I did."

"No, you did not. Ollie asked me if I knew a Mason around here with the initials EJD."

"And you told us that the letters EJD weren't the initials of a person. You gave us an unadulterated bullshit story about those letters standing for a motto."

Again, Rosswell sneezed. It wasn't the memory of chalk. It was dust on the books. Why hadn't it bothered him the first time he was there?

"I certainly did, but it wasn't, as you say, unadulterated bullshit." Nathaniel scratched his ear. "What is 'unadulterated bullshit'?"

"It's something Ollie says."

162

Nathaniel scanned the books in his living room. Perhaps he searched for a dictionary or thesaurus. "How can something as nasty as bullshit be considered unadulterated?" He'd been cleaning house, stirring up dust. A spray can of Endust and a rag gave mute testimony to Rosswell's conclusion.

"If you knew Ollie better, you wouldn't ask that question." Rosswell found it hard to talk with clenched teeth. "You especially wouldn't want to ask Ollie that question. The answer might last an hour."

Nathaniel pushed the recliner down and stood. "Would it make you less curious if I gave you permission to talk to my real estate agent?" He opened a desk drawer and rifled through it. "I've got nothing to hide."

"What would I learn from your real estate agent that you couldn't tell me?"

"What is it that you want to know?"

"First of all, I want to know where Eddie Joe Deckard went after he sold you his house."

"I wouldn't have the slightest idea." Nathaniel stopped leafing through the papers in the drawer. "Here it is."

"Who is your real estate agent?"

Nathaniel read from a business card: "Nadine Dumbarton."

"I know a Nadine but her last name isn't Dumbarton. Never heard of Nadine Dumbarton. Is she from around here?"

"A native if I'm not mistaken. She's the head of one of the largest real estate agencies in the county. Blessing Land Company."

Nathaniel handed Rosswell the card. Rosswell said, "Blessing Land Company is owned by Nadine Blessing, not Nadine Dumbarton."

"I'm sorry." Nathaniel chuckled. "I knew her when we went to college. Her maiden name was Dumbarton."

Rosswell choked. The card crinkled when he crushed it in his hand. He felt as if he'd broken the neck of a baby bird. Nathaniel backed away a couple of steps. A crazy judge in his house. First, he wads up a business card for no reason. What will he do next? That's what Nathaniel was thinking, Rosswell was sure of it.

And what had propelled Rosswell into the weird action?

N. D. Nadine Dumbarton? Nathaniel Dahlbert?

The murderer arranged the bodies with the initials ND. Bragging about her work. Or his work. One of the two is the killer. Or maybe they worked together, thinking it was cute to make a subtle ND clue.

From somewhere back in the recesses of Nathaniel's house, Rosswell heard a telephone ring. Nathaniel made no move to answer it. The telephone by his recliner was not ringing. He had two telephones with two different numbers. After three rings, the telephone stopped. If it was hooked to an answering machine, Rosswell couldn't hear the message.

Nathaniel returned to his recliner, sipped from his cup, remained silent. His eyes never left Rosswell. Now, Rosswell assured himself, if Nathaniel felt he was a threat, he'd splash lukewarm tea in his face. A lot of good that would do. Rosswell's skin would merely soak up the caffeine which would give him a burst of energy.

Rosswell pulled himself away from the distraction back to the main point. Nadine Dumbarton Blessing was the murderer. Or at least she was the first name on Rosswell's really good suspect list. Dampening his thrill and agitation was a Herculean task. Rosswell didn't want Nathaniel to see his excitement. Nathaniel could be involved with the murders. Nathaniel had known Nadine since college. Perhaps he and Nadine had cooked up some scheme to murder two people, for what reason Rosswell didn't yet know. Warning Nadine that Rosswell would call on her, to snoop in her business would be the first thing Nathaniel would do if the real estate agent and the bookseller were cohorts in crime, but there wasn't much he could do to prevent that.

Another thing bubbled to the surface of Rosswell's brain.

He concluded that Nathaniel Dahlbert had shot at both Tina and him.

Or Nadine Dumbarton had shot at them.

One or both of them wanted Tina and me dead. We were snooping and getting close to the truth. ND would risk killing us before we could discover her guilt. Or his guilt. Or their guilt.

Either way, Nadine and Nathaniel were in cahoots. Rosswell couldn't turn his back to the man. And he couldn't leave Tina alone for another second. He'd talk to Frizz and tell him what he'd learned, but talking to Nadine could wait until morning, His wounded arm hurt and he felt close to collapsing.

Rosswell graciously excused himself from Nathaniel's presence, with a recollection of an urgent appointment, and headed back to the hospital.

Chapter Twenty-two
Saturday, early morning

Saturday morning, Rosswell left the sleeping Tina in the care of the city cop, who'd groused about not getting enough sleep the night before. Rosswell went to gather Ollie at Merc's. Crowded as usual, Merc's smelled of bacon and eggs, the breakfast special.

"Mabel, I need six chicken biscuits to go."

Rosswell sat and spilled the news about Nadine to Ollie.

Ollie asked, "We're going to talk to her?"

"Right now."

"I've got news on the Cadillac owners," Ollie said. "Rasmussen is home in bed with both the flu and his wife's sister, conning her out of money while he's screwing her and passing on the flu. Bitti is in the Bahamas on vacation, undoubtedly looking for a new line of furniture. Ambrosia's in North Carolina at a legal seminar. Reynaud is supposedly out of town, but no one knows where. Probably at a bank convention."

"Maybe Susan Bitti and Trisha Reynaud are lovers, and they're sunning themselves on the beach at St. George's."

"That's in Bermuda, not the Bahamas. But I have heard some rumblings that they're both lesbians hot to trot."

"And this valuable information came from Merc's?"

"My lips are sealed."

After a few minutes, Mabel brought the chicken biscuits, hot and fresh from the smorgasbord.

Ollie had been talking to Nadine about buying her car, so she'd not think it odd that the pair of them showed up at her office to talk some more about the vehicle.

Standing outside, Rosswell asked Ollie, "Doesn't Mabel ever go home?"

"She's got a lot of bills to pay. She needs to work as much as she can."

"She won't be able to pay many bills if she falls over dead from exhaustion."

"She's young."

Before they boarded Vicky the Volkswagen, Rosswell tapped her peace symbol for luck.

"I've seen you do that several times," Ollie said. "Why do you touch that chicken claw?"

"It's to bring good luck. Get in the car. We don't have time. . . ." Rosswell choked again. "What did you call that?" He indicated the peace symbol.

"A chicken claw. Some people think the peace symbol represents a chicken claw."

Rosswell laid a hand on Vicky's peace symbol. "That's what Hermie called it. He said that the silver car that he saw out at the park had a chicken claw on it."

"You know where I've seen one of these, don't you?"

"On Nadine Dumbarton's car."

Nadine's assistant said she'd taken Saturday off, which Rosswell thought was odd for a real estate agent. There was an abundance of potential customers milling around today. He asked for Nadine's home address, but the girl refused to provide it, handing over Nadine's cell-phone number instead.

Ollie and Rosswell went back to the courthouse, fired up Rosswell's computer, and Ollie found Nadine's address within seconds.

"Ollie, can you find anything and everything on the Internet?"

"Sure. Give me something to find."

"Find my cellphone number. It's unlisted."

About five minutes later, Ollie displayed Rosswell's number.

"Crap," Rosswell said. "Let's go."

The real estate agent lived off the Confederate Trail on a gravel road that wound up a small hill. The log house was isolated, nestled in the deep forest, its nearest neighbor three miles away.

By the time they pulled up to her house, Rosswell had wolfed down all six of the chicken biscuits. Fortunately, none of the chicken had claws. However, his greasy hands messed up Vicky's steering wheel. After her soaking at the park and his assaulting her with greasy paws, tomorrow he'd have to do a complete detailing on her.

Rosswell recalled that Nadine's husband, Guilford Blessing, had died three or four years ago, leaving her the sole owner of the small residence. She'd never remarried and had never latched on to a boyfriend. Or girlfriend. That he knew of.

"Do you have your gun?" Ollie asked when the house came into view.

"Hell, yes, I've got my gun. I'm not getting caught with my pants down around my ankles again."

"I prefer you never use that figure of speech in my presence again. How I'm going to stop that visual from rattling around in my brain, I don't know."

Rosswell checked his cellphone. No service. What else could he expect? That would've been too convenient. When he stuck the thing back in its holster, it beeped. Nothing like a sarcastic cellphone.

A porch ran the full length of the front of the house. The sidewalk leading from the driveway to the porch was lined with lilac bushes in full bloom, pumping a sweet aroma into the air. Their smell reminded Rosswell of Tina's perfume. Every log of the house shined. The lawn, although small, had been freshly cut without the least sign of a dandelion or any other weed. There wasn't a garden gnome in sight. Nadine clearly had good taste.

Nadine's silver Buick Regal was parked in the double garage. The garage door shuddered down. Rosswell mulled it over. *Either she'd seen us coming and closed the door or she'd just arrived and was closing up. She could've been hiding. Or setting up an ambush.*

A red-winged blackbird, clinging to a cattail growing in the ditch in front of Nadine's house, screamed an alarm. The bird probably knew something they didn't. At least the bird wasn't out trying to capture bad people.

What Nadine was doing inside the house was anyone's guess. But they didn't have to wait long before they found out.

Nadine bounced out her front door, waving to them, smiling broadly. "How nice of y'all to come over." Perky as hell, dressed in tight white shorts and a loose blue kind of a blouse thing.

Rosswell said, "Ollie wanted to look at your car again if that's okay."

"Yes, oh, yes. Get out. I'll open the garage."

Nadine disappeared into the house, pulling the front door shut. When the door closed, it boomed, sounding like a thunderclap.

Ollie said, "Little house, damned big door."

"Let's stand over there, where we can't be seen from any windows."

"Or be fired at from any windows."

Ollie and Rosswell jumped out of Vicky and scuttled to the front of the garage door. Rosswell kept a watch on the windows of the garage door while Ollie surveyed the rest of the area. Ambushes were Rosswell's least favorite activity, especially if he was the ambushee.

After a moment, the garage door rumbled up. Rosswell found his gun but kept it hidden. No use telegraphing his intentions.

Nadine had come out her kitchen door into the garage. "Come on in." She waved at the two men.

Ollie mumbled, "Said the spider to the fly."

The garage smelled of fertilizer and bug spray. Fifty-pound sacks of white sand and pea gravel lined both sidewalls. Small barrels of potassium nitrate, calcium nitrate, potassium phosphate, magnesium sulfate, and other chemicals lined the back wall. There were two five-gallon cans of gasoline and a lawnmower. There must've been one hell of a garden out back. Odd. There weren't any shovels, rakes, hoes, things you'd associate with gardening. And no weed killer. On one shelf, sat a row of diaries, the year number stamped on the spines, beginning ten years ago and continuing to the present.

Nadine said, "You want me to back it out?"

"No," Ollie said. "I've already had a pretty good look at it."

Beef stew was cooking in the kitchen. The odor of something else—cherry pie?—had wafted out the kitchen door when Nadine opened it.

She flicked on the garage lights. Like Nathaniel, if Nadine were trying to hide anything, she did a lousy job of it.

Brushing a smudge off the SAVE THE EARTH bumper sticker, Rosswell asked her, "Where did you get this bumper sticker?"

"I bought it from the Greenies."

"Greenies?" Ollie said.

"It's the Ecology Club at Sterling Price," she said, referring to the local high school. "Or maybe it's the Environmental Society. Something like that."

Rosswell said, "They were selling these stickers?"

"That's what the woman said," Ollie said unnecessarily.

Nadine said, "Yes, oh, yes. They sold around a thousand of them."

The stickers were the peel off plastic kind, the ones that would clog up a garbage dump for five or six hundred years.

Ollie said, "What's that slogan mean? *Save the Earth.*"

Nadine said, "I have to be careful with my politics. I don't want anyone knowing how I vote or what I think about controversial subjects. You have to do that when you want everyone of every persuasion using your services. Those kids, though, they're cleaning up creeks, maintaining abandoned cemeteries, stuff like that. I thought *Save the Earth* was so general that no one could be against it."

"Yes," Rosswell said. "No one's in favor of destroying the Earth. It would be hard to keep track of your stuff."

Ollie and Nadine gawked at him. Neither one laughed. *Oh, well. I thought it was funny.*

"Then," she said, "there's the real reason I bought the bumper sticker."

Ollie said, "Which is?"

"My initials."

Playing dumb would be a good idea here, Rosswell thought, so he said, "Nadine, you lost me there."

"This is the letter N and this is the letter D." She semaphored N and D with her arms. "Some people think ND stands for nuclear disarmament. But I think it stands for Nadine Dumbarton, my maiden name."

Superimpose the N and the D and you get a chicken claw. Or peace symbol.

Either way, the murderer had left that clue. The answer shone clear and bright in Rosswell's mind.

"Nadine," Rosswell said, "you're under arrest."

Nadine froze in position. Rosswell had his hand on the gun, resting in his back pocket, just in case. He would never shoot anyone, but if he aimed at someone, that person wouldn't know that he couldn't shoot him, her, or it.

Then she burst out laughing. "You looked so serious, Judge. You do have a reputation for being a joker. Now I know how you got it."

Ollie said, "He's not kidding."

"Get in my car," Rosswell said. "We're going to see the sheriff."

"You want to carry me to jail in a red Hyundai? That's even funnier."

Rosswell said, "Vicky is not a Hyundai and she's not red. Vicky is a 1972 Volkswagen Cabriolet, colored Monarch Orange Pearl."

"Vicky?" Nadine clapped her hands to her face, shrieking. "You're too precious for words! You named your car?"

Each of her fingernails was painted with a different color and a different design. On each ear, she had a couple of earrings, all of varying hues. Five rings with unusual gemstones. She must've been going through a rainbow stage.

Rosswell said, "My mother named that car."

Nadine said, "What's a Cabriolet?"

Ollie said, "It's from a French word that means leap in the air like a goat."

Rosswell thought Nadine would choke to death, she laughed so hard.

Ollie said, "Rosswell, get her in the car."

Nadine stopped laughing long enough to threaten Rosswell and Ollie. "Do y'all have handcuffs? I'm not going anywhere with y'all. Judge, if you want to carry me off anywhere, then you and this rat-faced drunk are going to have to handcuff me and drag me to wherever you want to take me. And after my lawyers get through with you both, y'all won't have a straw to piss through."

Ollie said, "Rat-faced drunk?"

Rosswell said, "I think she's insulting us."

Nadine started again, leaning against her car in a paroxysm of laughter that threatened to cripple her. If it kept up, she'd slither to the driveway. Rosswell signaled to Ollie, and each of them grabbed one of her arms.

"Rape!" she yelled.

She tried to yell it again but fell to guffawing. Nadine's threshold for humor was exceptionally low. It's difficult to arrest someone who's laughing at you.

The surreal scene turned deadly when a gunshot shattered the back window of her Buick.

Chapter Twenty-three
Saturday morning, continued

Nadine shrieked again, but there was no humor in this scream. "My God, they're shooting at us!"

"They?" Rosswell said. *Why had Nadine referred to more than one shooter? Had some of her disgruntled clients paid a visit?*

Ollie and Rosswell hustled her to the passage door leading to the house. Rosswell slapped the garage door switch. Before the door hit the ground, another bullet screamed into the garage. Another round hit the outside of the garage door but didn't penetrate it. Rosswell found it odd that the door was so exceptionally strong. The three of them bolted into the kitchen. Nadine clicked off her oven. Someone was trying to kill them and she worried about her baking. The cherry pie or whatever it was that smelled so good would have to wait.

"Where's your phone?" Rosswell said. She pointed. He lifted the receiver, praying that the bastard (or bastards) shooting at them hadn't destroyed the phone service. The receiver had a slight odor of perfume. His sweaty palms would soon obliterate the pleasant aroma. The receiver grew slick with sweat while he waited. Then, a dial tone. *Thank you, Lord.* He dialed 911. The phone rang. *Thank you again, Lord.* And rang. And rang. No one was at the sheriff's office. He clicked off and then dialed the operator.

"Operator."

Rosswell told the man on the other end the situation, gave him directions, and told him to call the highway patrol.

The operator said, "Dial 911 if you have an emergency."

Rosswell said, "What's your name?"

"Sir, I'm not allowed to give out that information."

"Operator, I don't want a date. I want to beat you senseless unless you call the highway patrol."

Another gunshot slammed into Nadine's front window, yet it only spider webbed the glass without breaking it. Who puts bulletproof window glass in a house? Was Nadine connected with the mob?

The operator said, "Was that a gunshot?"

Rosswell said, "You're damned right that was a gunshot. There have been lots of gunshots out here, and three people are the targets."

"I'll connect you with 911."

Rosswell yelled, "You call the highway patrol or I'm going to personally cut your nuts off."

A gasp, followed by, "You can't talk that way to me."

"Operator, I'm going to castrate you and make you eat your testicles. Then I'm going to—"

"I'm putting you through to my supervisor."

"About time."

After a few clicks, a lot of static, and what seemed like a century, a woman came on the line. "My operator tells me that you've threatened him with bodily harm."

Roswell said, "Then call the cops and report me. Call the highway patrol. Call the FBI and the Secret Service. Someone is shooting at us. Call the CIA. Call NATO and the UN."

"The number you are speaking from is registered to Nadine Blessing. Is Ms. Blessing available?"

"Nadine," Rosswell said, "the operator wants to know if you're available."

Nadine grabbed the receiver from him. "This is Nadine Dumbarton." She held the receiver out so Rosswell could hear the conversation.

The supervisor said, "The telephone is registered to Nadine Blessing. I must speak with her."

"Dumbarton is my maiden name, which I started using when my husband died."

Then why was her real estate agency still called Blessing Land Agency? Rosswell didn't understand that at all.

"Here's what you need to do," the supervisor said. "Send in notarized proof of a legal change of name to us, complete with—"

"Listen here, you bitch, you call the cops right now, or I will personally shove your headset up your ass so far that a team of surgeons won't be able to find it." Nadine held the receiver close to her ear and listened for a few seconds, then said, "Good," and hung up the phone. "Woman to woman. You just have to be meaner than the one you're talking to. She's calling the cops."

Three rounds spanged against the front window. None of them made it through.

Ollie said, "Nadine, do you have a basement? Somewhere we could hide?"

They had positioned themselves away from any windows, but going underground seemed like a good idea. When someone's shooting at you, make yourself hard to find.

"Follow me," she said. "I have a . . . it's what you could call a safe room."

For a moment, Rosswell considered asking her to carry the cherry pie downstairs. There was no reason not to have something to snack on while waiting for assailants to run out of ammunition. Her kitchen smelled the same as a long-ago kitchen did on Saturday afternoons when Grandma Carew baked goodies. Stress sends your mind spinning in odd directions.

Nadine opened the basement door. "Get down there. I'll lock this door. Hurry."

Ollie and Rosswell clumped down the steps, Rosswell's hands brushing the sides of the stairwell. Fear of falling made him careful in strange stairwells. The walls were slick and cool to the touch. Nadine followed Ollie and Rosswell and slammed the door, which gave out a metallic thud. A metal door inside a house? She rifled through a mess of keys on a yellow daisy key fob until she found the right key. She locked the door. A door lock on the *inside* of the basement door? Why would Nadine ever want to keep someone on the ground level of her house from opening the basement door?

At the bottom of the steps, she unlocked another heavy door by punching five letters on the keypad of a combination lock. They zoomed through the door and she locked it behind them. Next, they scorched through one more door and locked it. They found themselves in a hydroponics greenhouse, exceptionally well equipped. Rosswell had paid attention in all the drug seminars the state forced him to attend. Nadine Dumbarton was the proud possessor of about one hundred plants of White Widow, one of the most potent marijuana strains known to man. Or, in this case, woman.

She fondled the leaves of a vigorous plant. "It's strictly for medicinal purposes."

On one wall, a bank of instruments with red LEDs reported the time, temperature (inside and out), humidity, and wind direction outside. Another bank of instruments reported the percentage of each chemical necessary in the water of the setup. A third operated the lights, ventilation, heating, and cooling. This was no amateur's outfit.

Rosswell said, "I don't give a crap if you bake brownies with it, as long as we're safe."

Ollie, obviously stupefied by the amazing setup, bent over the apparatus, examining every inch. "The solution goes directly to the roots. Good. No more misting. And the lights. Lots of red spectrum. Great for strengthening the stems and encouraging leaf growth."

"Ollie," Rosswell said, "how is it that you know so much about growing pot?"

"This is one of the best set-ups I've ever seen."

"What?"

"I mean, you know, pictures of hydroponics gardens. This is the best pot growing set-up I've ever seen. Pictures of, I mean."

"Judge, we're safe," Nadine said. "Those are steel-lined doors. Unless that son of a bitch has an atomic bomb, he's not going to hurt us. All we have to do is wait for the highway patrol."

Ollie said, "Frizz has been trying to get the highway patrol down here to help on the murders. No luck. I don't think we're going to see them today."

Nadine said, "I don't care if it's Junior Fleming who comes out here."

Rosswell said, "Nadine, you could be sent away for a long, long time."

The look of surprise on her face seemed genuine. "I save a judge and his . . . his. . . ."

Ollie said, "I'm his research assistant."

Nadine said, "I save a judge and his research assistant, and I get sent to the pen because I have a few measly marijuana plants for recreation and medicinal use?"

"At first," Rosswell said, "you told us it was strictly for medicinal use, which, by the way, is not legal in Missouri."

The pungent marijuana plants would stone Rosswell if he breathed any deeper. Dizziness would soon set in unless he breathed fresh air. The plants reminded him of fresh-cut alfalfa but with a punch that kicked his taste buds into gear when he gulped in another breath. If he was going to die, perhaps he'd die stoned. Shot while stoned. He could already see that written on his gravestone.

"Recreation," Nadine said, "can be considered medicinal. If you're really stressed out, there's nothing like a joint to mellow you." She was beginning to sound like a hippie character in a movie from the 1960s.

"Nadine and Ollie," Rosswell said, trying to act the sober judge, "let's concentrate on saving our butts. All we have to do is wait until the shooter gets tired or runs out of ammo. Then we can leave."

Ollie said, "He's right, as always. Let's just relax. We don't need the cops. They're too busy elsewhere. All we need is time."

Rosswell patted the seat of an available chair and sat. The wooden chair's comfort ranked down there with a football stadium's bleacher.

"You're right, Judge," Nadine said. "Let's not worry. We're safe now."

This was her safe room. She knew how secure it was. Her voice was soft, calm, reassuring. They would merely bide their time. Everything was copasetic.

Rosswell smelled smoke.

He touched the crucifix Father Mike had given him and uttered a prayer.

Chapter Twenty-four
Saturday morning, continued

The pounding noises, they agreed, came from the other side of the basement door in Nadine's kitchen. The noises stopped when the asshole must've grown tired of trying to beat his way through a steel door. Gunfire erupted. More unintelligible shouting on the other side of the door. Whoever was after them was shooting the door, obviously hoping to knock it down. That didn't work either. The thought of the rage boiling in the shooter clutched Rosswell's gut in a cold grip. Giving up didn't appear on the shooter's agenda.

"Nadine," Rosswell said, "are you positive that the door can stand up to gunfire?"

"Yes, oh, yes," she said. "Unless they have a bazooka. The door's never been tested before, but I'll stake my life on it."

Rosswell said, "I thought you said we were safe from an atom bomb."

Ollie said, "Do we have another choice? We have to stay here."

Whatever was burning put off a caustic odor. Rosswell placed his palm on the door. Its surface began warming. All three of them coughed intermittently.

"You keep saying they," Ollie said to Nadine. "Who's after us?"

Nadine scanned the area around them, as if searching for something. "It's a manner of speaking."

"Unadulterated bullshit," Ollie said. "Tell us what you know. We could be dying here."

Ollie rubbed his head and his eyes grew wide. After he clenched and unclenched his fists several times, his shoulders slumped, as if the fist exercises relieved tension. Rosswell hoped that Ollie wasn't on the verge of a screaming panic fit.

Nadine said, "If I knew who the hell is trying to kill us, I'd tell you."

Nadine's red hair wilted in the heat. Her face ran with sweat. Rosswell could tell her breathing was becoming labored by the wheezing sounds she made. She sounded as if she were on the edge of suffocation.

A few more rounds slammed into the door. Ollie cocked his head. "Doesn't sound like an automatic weapon. Guy's just got a fast trigger finger."

"I'm not sure how that helps us," Rosswell said. "Dead by one bullet or ten. Doesn't make much difference."

The smell of smoke grew even stronger. Something plastic was burning. They would die from inhaling toxic fumes before the fire reached them. That was comforting. Suffocation should always be preferred over immolation. The advantage of suffocation is, of course, that you pass out before you die. Burning to death didn't strike Rosswell as having a single advantage.

Rosswell said, "Is there a back way out? Some way we can get out without going through your kitchen?"

"That's it," Nadine said, pointing to the door. "This isn't supposed to be a tourist stop. You come in here and you're safe from the outside world." She sobbed. "Ha. My plans didn't work out so good."

Ollie said, "How did you ever get a building permit for this if you didn't include at least two ways out?"

Rosswell had noted in the past that sometimes, when Ollie was under stress, his brain took a vacation. This was one of those times. Rosswell wasn't strong enough to slap him upside the head. And he doubted if Nadine had it in her either.

Rosswell said, "We're stuck. A fire and a gun between us and safety. Pick your favorite way to die." He backed up against a wall and slid to a sitting position on the concrete floor.

Ollie said, "What about the ventilation? Does the system bring in fresh air from the outside?"

Nadine gaped at Ollie as if he'd asked her if she kept alligators in her basement. "What difference does it make if the house is on fire?"

More deadened yelling from the kitchen, but Rosswell couldn't understand the words. The voice at first sounded male, then female. There could've been two people. Rosswell couldn't begin to identify the voice. It could've been Frizz or Tina, yet Rosswell wouldn't have recognized the voice.

Rosswell doubted that whoever was shooting wanted to invite them to tea. A sustained rattle of gunfire peppered the upstairs door. The smell of gunpowder mixed with the stink of burning plastic, the combination giving Rosswell thoughts of sneezing or puking. He couldn't decide which to do first.

Rosswell said, "I think he found a machine gun."

Ollie said, "Maybe it's a she."

The temperature inside the safe room escalated, according to the thermometer. Although no smoke was yet visible, the stench of it had increased. The next thing Rosswell would see would be puffs of the nasty stuff rolling in under the doors. Then death.

He pointed to the ceiling and asked Nadine, "You don't have a sprinkler system?"

Ollie squeaked the mouse squeak, possibly the last one Rosswell would ever hear. "The plants are sitting in water. Who would expect a fire?"

Rosswell said, "There are lots of other things down here that could burn."

Nadine said, "Judge, you have bullets?"

"Plenty. Do we want to shoot ourselves in the head, burn up, inhale deadly smoke, or run out in front of the shooter?"

Ollie and Nadine exchanged glances, then looked at Rosswell.

Ollie said, "I vote we run."

Nadine said, "Me too. Anything else is certain death. If we run, we might have half a chance."

Rosswell stood, put one hand on Ollie's shoulder, and grasped Nadine's hand in his other one. "Half a chance is better than no chance."

Rosswell's esophagus, coated with bile that tasted of copper and vinegar, nearly squeezed shut. Perhaps he'd die from choking on his body's own fluids. Only one place where he'd stand in this parade.

Rosswell said, "And I'm supposed to be in front?"

Nadine said, "You've got the gun."

Ollie said, "And if he shoots you, then I'll take over."

"And," Nadine said, "if he shoots Ollie, then I'll take over."

Rosswell said, "That's comforting."

The smoke increased. The temperature rose. Rosswell made his decision.

"Does anyone have any famous last words?"

Ollie said, "I've got an overdue library book."

Nadine chuckled. "I'm laughing on the gallows."

"If you make it out and I don't, tell Tina I love her," Rosswell said. He threw back his shoulders in a gesture of bravery that he didn't feel. "Follow me."

Hoping the air close to the floor was breathable, he crouched low, reached his arm up to the knob, and opened the hydroponics garden door. They duck-walked to the bottom of the steps leading to the kitchen. Another blast of gunfire, but still the door held. When they gained the top of the steps, Rosswell drew his pistol and reached for the door to the kitchen. The doorknob was warm, but not hot. There was a possibility he could open the door and they wouldn't get fried. They'd still get shot, but they wouldn't get fried first.

"Get ready," Rosswell said.

Nadine said, "We don't have much time."

Rosswell turned the knob. Tried to turn the knob. Nothing happened.

"Nadine," he said, "the door knob is stuck."

She patted herself down. "You need the key. The knob won't turn unless it's unlocked." Seconds like hours passed, but still she didn't hand Rosswell the key. "It locks automatically when you shut it."

"We know that," Ollie said. "We need the key."

"The key, Nadine," Rosswell said. "Give me the key."

"I can't find it." She patted herself down more thoroughly. "It's on that big ring of keys. How could I have dropped it?"

"Ollie," Rosswell said, "check the floor downstairs."

Ollie scooted down the steps and along the floor until he reached the garden door. Nadine wheezed, then slumped against Rosswell, barely conscious.

"Ollie, you better hurry."

No answer. At least Rosswell couldn't hear Ollie over the noise of the fire if he had said anything. Had Ollie already gone back into the hydroponics room to search for the missing keys?

Eventually, Ollie yelled, "The door to the garden is shut."

Chapter Twenty-five
Saturday morning, continued

"Open the door, damn it! Nadine's passed out and I don't know how much longer I can stay conscious."

The smoke thickened. It felt like it was over a hundred degrees.

"It's not just shut. It's locked," Ollie said. "It's a combination lock."

"I know that. She already unlocked it when she opened it."

"It's locked now."

"Nadine," Rosswell said. He slapped her across the face. Her half-lidded eyes showed no response. He doubted that she could see him. "Nadine, can you hear me?" He slapped her again, harder. The thought of assaulting anyone, especially a woman, sickened him. The situation, however, seemed to warrant the rough treatment. He'd deal with his bad acts later. "What's the combination?"

Rosswell latched on to her shoulders. After he shook her, she muttered, "Initials children Israel sealed." Her eyes, barely open now, grew dimmer, then shut.

"What? Nadine, the combination!"

Ollie hollered up from the basement, "What's the combination?"

"Nadine's spouting nonsense. I don't know."

"What's the nonsense?"

"She said, 'Initials children Israel sealed'."

"Yes! Yes! Yes! That's it!"

What? Rosswell heard the click of the buttons Ollie punched. Then heard the door open. What the hell kind of clue had Nadine given Rosswell? It sounded Biblical, but she hadn't told him any series of letters. Ollie needed those to punch into the lock. Rosswell promised himself that if they got out of this alive, he'd have to reward Ollie. Maybe give him a couple of days' credit on his next jail sentence. Ollie would appreciate that.

Ollie scrabbled his way back up the steps.

Rosswell said, "Did you find the keys?"

"No." Ollie's breathing sounded labored. Rosswell wheezed. Nadine still breathed, but Rosswell couldn't get any response out of her. Ollie said, "Give me your phone. Need light."

Rosswell patted himself down, praying his luck was better than Nadine's. His cellphone was in his right pocket. "Here. Go get those keys."

When Ollie reached the bottom of the steps, another fusillade rammed the other side of the door Rosswell leaned against. Even if Ollie made it back in time and Rosswell found the right key on the key ring, when he opened the door to the kitchen, they were all dead. On the other hand, if they stayed there without opening the door, they were all dead. No other alternative existed.

Ollie crawled back up the steps with the keys in his hand.

An explosion sounded on the other side of the door.

"Crap, now he's bombing us."

Another explosion sounded.

"Find the key. If I'm going to die, I want to get shot."

There had to be about a hundred keys. Rosswell picked a likely looking one and tried it. No luck. He noticed that it was a Lockset lock. Flipping through the selection of keys, he stopped when he reached a heavy one with a triangular handle.

"This one," he said. "Try this one with the triangular handle."

Rosswell had weakened to the point where he couldn't reach the doorknob. A lot of good he'd do with his pistol.

"It's called a bow, not a handle," Ollie said, taking the shiny key from Rosswell, who toyed with the idea of shooting Ollie himself. They teetered on the verge of death and Ollie was playing trivia games.

But the key worked. The answer was clear. The right key had to be big, barely used. The key slipped into the lock like a perfect honeymoon. Ollie turned the key. "It won't unlock."

"Christ."

"I think, we're fixing to meet him."

"Turn the key."

"The heat." Ollie gasped. "The heat is screwing up the lock."

Nadine's wheezing stopped. Rosswell said, "Nadine's dead."

Ollie never paused. He drew out the key and spit on it, then stuck it back in the lock. It unlocked, the moisture of the spit reducing the friction enough to allow him to turn the key.

Rosswell pushed open the door, stood, and commenced firing. The pistol's recoil, small as it was, knocked him down. Panting, he fell to the floor, waiting for the shooter to drill him through the head.

Nothing.

Through the smoke, he could make out the kitchen. No one was in there.

"Come on, Ollie. Help me drag her out."

They reached the livingroom door. Apparently, the evildoer had set the back of the house on fire near the kitchen and garage. The front of the house had yet to be fully involved. When they struggled through the front door, Rosswell waved the gun around but found no target.

"Come out here, you son of a bitch," he yelled.

Where had the bastard gone?

Ollie said, "Vicky's still with us."

The garage, a whole wall blown out, was the victim of the two cans of gasoline. Vicky sat far enough away to miss any real damage. Or so Rosswell prayed.

The fresh air revived Ollie and Rosswell. Rosswell put his ear next to Nadine's nose and mouth. The noise of the fire made it impossible to hear. There was no way to tell if she was still breathing. Rosswell stretched her out and pumped her full of air with mouth-to-mouth resuscitation. The sirens reached his brain.

"God almighty," Nadine said. Jerking upright, she launched into a coughing spasm that sounded like it would end with her expelling a lung. When the seizure ended, she said, "Let's get the hell out of here."

Disoriented, she shot up and ran the opposite way from Vicky. Ollie tackled her.

Nadine pounded on Ollie's head, screaming at him. Rosswell grabbed her in a full nelson and yelled in her ear, "Follow Ollie."

Ollie and Rosswell had been destined to beat up the same woman today. Rosswell hoped Nadine would forgive them. Rosswell hoped Tina would forgive him for slapping and then deep kissing Nadine.

"Okay, okay, okay," she said. Rosswell released her, and the three of them dashed for Vicky. Nadine yelled, "Stop screaming at me."

Something was wrong. Rosswell wondered why no one was shooting at them. The shooter wouldn't have simply given up and gone home to check what was on cable television.

Vicky started, Rosswell backed out, and they ripped down the road of the long, narrow valley that led to Marble Hill. Coming toward them were sirens. The telephone supervisor must've gotten enough power on the horn to send rescue troops their way. How was that possible? Frizz couldn't get extra help but a telephone operator could call out an army of cops?

The sound and feel of the house burning reminded Rosswell of a hot tornado whipping itself into a fury behind his back, fixing to chase him. Another sound overrode the sound of the fire. The deduction was clear as the sky after a storm moves through. The shooter had heard the sirens and beat feet. The bastard had to be close. But where? Was he in a car or on foot?

"Damn it." Nadine turned her head to watch her house burning to the ground until Rosswell turned a corner and it left her view. "Everything I worked for . . . gone."

Ollie said, "It was a nice house. I'm sorry, Nadine."

She smiled. "The good part is that my little . . . garden . . . it's gone now."

Ollie said, "Meaning?"

"I won't be going to jail for my illegal garden."

"Garden?" Rosswell said. "What garden?"

"All my beautiful White Widow. Up in smoke." Nadine faced forward. "I meant for it to go up in smoke. But not that way."

"White Widow?" Ollie said. "Marijuana?"

Rosswell said, "I didn't see any marijuana. Did you see any marijuana, Ollie?"

"Nope. Never saw a thing. I've never seen any marijuana anywhere, except in the movies. Or television. Or pictures of it. But never in real life."

Rosswell tried imitating Ollie's squeak without success.

Nadine said, "Both y'all look and smell like the shit you're full of."

A fire truck screamed past them, heading for Nadine's.

Chapter Twenty-six
Saturday morning, continued

"Maybe they didn't recognize my car," Rosswell said when none of the firefighters paid them a mouse lick of attention.

Nadine said, "They'd have to be blind to miss an orange rind packed with grubby scoundrels."

Ollie said, "They don't care about us. Just the fire. Someone must've called the fire department."

The three of them were covered with soot and ash the color of dog-vomit gray. Rosswell's face felt like the business side of a piece of rough grit sandpaper. He couldn't smell anything but burning house and contents.

Ollie said, "Judge, you can talk to them back in town. We need to get to the hospital. We could be injured."

"I'm not stopping for anything. Coming close to dying once a day is one time too many."

In front of Rosswell on the road, a woman in blue jeans, a gray sweatshirt, big bracelets, sunglasses, and a ball cap stood in a shooter's stance, pointing an AK-47 at them. The same woman that bribed the Eagle Scout.

Candy Lavaliere.

Frizz had, after all, arrested the right person. He just didn't know it.

Blue and red lights flashed in front of Rosswell and a siren squawked. A firefighter in his personal vehicle who was following the trucks waved at Rosswell, who stomped on the brakes and jumped out.

"Over there," he yelled and pointed.

At nothing. Candy had disappeared, no doubt fleeing into the woods.

The firefighter stopped and scowled at Rosswell. "I'm on my way to a fire."

Rosswell said, "You got a radio?"

"Yeah. Why?"

Rosswell leaped back into the car. "Call Frizz. Tell him that Candy Lavaliere tried to kill us. We need medical attention." The pedal hit the metal, and they flew down the road. Rosswell assured himself that no firefighter in his right mind would turn away from a fire to chase a judge on his way to get medical help. The firefighter must've lost his mind because his lights flashed and his siren screamed behind Vicky. Rosswell stomped on the brakes again.

"What?" Rosswell said when the man approached the car. "We're headed to the hospital. We're suffering from smoke inhalation. We nearly got killed by a madwoman who's on the loose back there." Although Rosswell was tempted to use another finger, he jerked his thumb backward, pointing to the place where Candy had tried to way-lay them. The firefighter gave him the okay sign, returned to his pickup truck, and Rosswell answered his cellphone. He hadn't noticed he'd drifted into one of the few 10-foot-wide ribbons of service the phone company draped across the county in random patterns.

"Frizz, I'm headed for the hospital. Candy Lavaliere is our murderer."

Frizz said, "You've been eating hallucinogenic mushrooms."

A warning that the phone's battery was about to die beeped. Rosswell turned it off. They needed medical help before they developed pneumonia or some other nasty complication from breathing in fumes from a burning house and pot, and died on the back roads of Bollinger County. If an emergency arose before they reached the hospital, Rosswell didn't want to be without the phone. The phone's car charger had been secured in Rosswell's desk in the courthouse. Frizz would have to save his bitching for later. Rosswell figured the stupid telephone might have enough juice for one more call. If he was lucky.

At the city limit sign, Candy Lavaliere puttered along the highway in her chartreuse golf cart. She'd made it into town before the trio and switched vehicles. Misdirection. Candy was smart enough not to use the silver Malibu she'd stolen from Johnny Dan.

Nadine, being a woman, also noticed something else about Candy. "She changed clothes." Nadine pointed out that Candy still wore jangly bracelets, but they were different from the ones she'd had on out on the road. She'd donned a crinkly muumuu, featuring a green background splattered with red, yellow, and blue flower prints. Had she been wearing that outfit when she rushed into the woods at the sight of the firefighter, she would've stood out like a hair in a biscuit. She wasn't wearing sunglasses.

Ollie said, "She's good. Sneaky." His eyes watered, leaving tracks in the dirt on his face. It couldn't have been tears at the realization that a buddy of his was a murderer. Ollie didn't cry. Never ever. Although Rosswell suspected that Ollie and Candy were more than just friends, he decided to reserve that conversation for later.

Rosswell said, "Candy's no dummy. She's trying to confuse us. I admire her for her quick thinking."

He pulled in front of Candy, forcing her to the shoulder. She eased up on the accelerator, causing the golf cart to jerk to a halt. The three tumbled from the car and surrounded her. Rosswell pointed his gun at Candy's chest.

"You're under arrest, Candy." Although this was the second arrest he'd made that day, saying the words didn't thrill him. In fact, since the first arrest had been the false arrest of Nadine, his confidence scraped the bottom of what was left of Nadine's grow tank. Candy, to his way of thinking, floated around town, a harmless young woman who'd never thought an evil thought in her life. Yet the human mind breaks down for unknown reasons. Who knew what dark tunnels her train of thought rushed through? If the firefighter had been one second later in coming up in front of them on the road leading to Nadine's house, Candy would've wiped them out with the AK-47. Rosswell had lost all sympathy for Candy.

Pointing a gun at me makes me angry.

"Arrest?" Candy belched. "For what?"

Had she been drinking? Rosswell wasn't about to get close enough to smell her breath. She leaned down as if she were about to pick up something from the floor of the cart. Her hands needed to stay visible, whether she was drunk or sober. Her gun could be hidden anywhere in the cart or on her person. She picked up a squeeze bottle of Fast Orange and started cleaning her hands.

Rosswell said, "Keep your hands on the steering wheel. We're calling the cops." He sounded like a bad crime show on late night television. He didn't care. All he needed was to deliver the message to her that he was going to be safe from her violence. She grasped the steering wheel as if waiting for a tornado.

Thrusting his phone into Ollie's grasp, Rosswell said, "Turn that thing on and call Frizz. Tell him we've got Candy cornered."

After a few minutes, the cellphone finished booting up. By that time, a crowd had gathered. Someone must've called Merc's because a clump of the regulars now gathered behind Rosswell, perhaps hoping that they'd witness a judge shoot a pretty young woman. Rosswell heard one of the coffee drinkers say, "I told you he'd go off his nut." Another one offered, "One too many whiskey sours, if you ask me." A woman's voice said, "Playing blackface ain't politically correct no more. Them three needs to be ashamed of theirselves, acting racialistic." Rosswell made a mental note to wash his face as soon as possible.

Ollie dialed. "Frizz," he shouted, "Rosswell has Candy cornered at the south city limits. She tried to kill us." Ollie listened for a few seconds, then shoved the phone into Rosswell's hand. "He doesn't want to talk to me."

Rosswell holding his gun steady in his right hand, held the phone in his left hand and talked to Frizz. "She's down here. She tried to kill us. She's the murderer."

Frizz said, "Candy Lavaliere? A murderer? I don't believe it. We've already been through this."

"You already arrested her for murder. Remember?"

"Judge, I had to arrest her but I didn't believe she was a murderer the first time. And I don't believe it now."

"Believe it now. Ollie, Nadine, and I witnessed her standing in the road with an assault rifle, trying to kill us."

"Two drunks and a doper. What a trio of witnesses." Frizz, no doubt understanding that he'd crossed a line that he shouldn't have, waited a few moments before he continued. Rosswell heard him breathing. There was a rustle on the sheriff's end. Frizz was probably wiping his face with his handkerchief, wondering how he was going to remove his big foot out of his big mouth. "Rosswell, sorry, but listen. Are you sure you saw her?"

"Yes. She was wearing blue jeans, a gray sweatshirt, sunglasses, and a ball cap, the same as the woman who tried to bribe that Boy Scout."

"I'll be right there."

"No, I'm bringing her in."

"Don't you dare. Stay where you are."

Purvis Rabil and Scooby arrived, perched on Rabil's police edition

Harley, currently the biggest, baddest hog in the county. "Judge," Purvis said, "what're you doing?"

"Who's that?" Frizz asked.

"Purvis. Since he's a cop, I'll have him help me."

"Damn it," Frizz screamed into his end of the phone. "Are you deaf? Don't do anything until I get there. You let Purvis help you and I'll arrest him again!"

"I'm holding my gun on her as we speak," Rosswell told Frizz. "She damned near killed three people today. You should've kept her in jail when you had her."

The phone died. In a couple of seconds, Rosswell heard a siren and squalling tires in the direction of the courthouse. Frizz had no doubt left a trail of burnt rubber in his haste to reach Rosswell and his motley crew.

Purvis said, "Judge, can you tell me what's going on?"

"Frizz is on his way. I'll deal with him."

That's when Frizz blasted past them, never slowing a bit, lights and siren going full tilt boogie.

Ollie said, "Must be something big going on out that way."

Rosswell watched Frizz disappear. What could've been more important than the arrest of a murderer?

Purvis said, "Now will you tell me what's going on?"

"Candy Lavaliere tried to kill all three of us," Rosswell said, motioning with the phone to Nadine and Ollie. "I arrested her."

Nadine said, "She set my house afire while we were inside. And shot at us."

"We've sucked in a lot of nasty stuff," Ollie said. "We need medical help." He coughed.

Candy said, "I was on my way to the library when Rosswell started waving a gun in my face. I hope it's not loaded."

Scooby growled.

Purvis cut off his bike and faced the crowd of onlookers. "Show's over. Go home."

"Who the hell are you?" said the woman who'd accused Rosswell, Nadine, and Ollie of racial insensitivity. "You gotta badge there, big guy?"

Rosswell saw that no one in the gaggle of people stirred, apparently unwilling to be shooed off from a potentially exciting showdown. Would Purvis whip out his Alabama Bureau of Investigation badge? Would the good citizens of the Show-Me State be convinced that the Hell's Angels version of the Age of Aquarius was a cop? And if they were convinced, would they listen to an out-of-state law enforcement agent?

As if in answer to an unseen signal from Purvis, ten hog riders materialized, encircling the spectators, gunning their engines, yet careful to keep the bikes in neutral. The mirrored sunglasses the riders wore must've convinced the folks. That and the unsmiling faces. The crowd scattered, no doubt heading to Merc's to grow their accounts of the incident to monumental proportions. This bit of gossip would no doubt live for a century or two in the annals of weird local things.

Rosswell wondered if the motorcyclists knew Purvis's secret identity. Rosswell wasn't going to tell them. He suspected that the arrest of Purvis, and then Frizz freeing him shortly thereafter, only raised Purvis's standing among the Harley bunch.

Through the mass of red hair covering the face of Purvis, Rosswell recognized the big man throwing him an evil eye, clearly signaling danger.

Purvis headed straight for Rosswell.

Chapter Twenty-seven
Saturday morning, continued

"We're going to see Frizz," Purvis ordered. "All of us." His tone of voice offered no compromise.

"That's what I've been trying to do for the last fifteen minutes," Rosswell said. A gentle reminder was in order. "She's armed," he said to Purvis. "Or at least she was the last time I saw her."

Candy laughed. "Do I look like I'm armed?" She planted both feet on the shoulder of the highway and shimmied magnificently. "Where am I going to hide a gun?" Shooting both hands into the air, she shook some more, prancing and dancing fancy steps. The Harley riders whooped and clapped. After she sank into the driver's seat of the cart, Candy blew them kisses. The crowd from Merc's, which had formed again, laughed and hooted.

Purvis said, "Weapons come in all flavors. If you don't have a gun, you could have a knife or a Taser or who knows what."

Ollie, his eyes locked on Candy's face, said, "Purvis, I don't feel like giving her a second shot at me today."

Candy said to Ollie, "I'd never shoot you." Ollie turned his head, no doubt feeling like Judas.

Purvis pointed to Nadine. "Search Candy so we can get this show moving on down the road."

Rosswell took up a position on Candy's left, Purvis on her right. Nadine said to Candy, "Exit the vehicle, madam." Nadine had obviously watched too many episodes of *Cops*. Candy stepped to the ground. Nadine felt her up in a manner that would make a TSA agent proud, reminding Rosswell of Frizz's search of Purvis. "Clear," Nadine said and stepped back.

"Clear?" Rosswell said.

Nadine said, "That's what they say on television."

"They say that in CPR scenes, not in TSA training videos," Ollie said. "Let's get her to Frizz."

"I agree," Rosswell said. The sooner Candy was placed in custody, the better. "Purvis, you lead. Candy, you follow this nice man. I'll follow you."

"Don't I get a phone call?" Candy asked Ollie.

Ollie said, "I'm not the cops."

"Then why are you helping them arrest me?"

"Candy, you stood in the middle of that road and pointed a gun at me."

Candy stared into the cloudless sky. "Everybody's gone crazy."

Purvis said, "Let's go, people."

The caravan lurched forward. From Vicky's back seat, Ollie said, "Don't let her escape."

Rosswell said, "If she gets above seven miles per hour, I'll ram her."

Nadine said, "She doesn't seem dangerous."

"Right," Rosswell said. "I also heard Stalin was charming."

The trip took 15 minutes. Thanks to practically everyone in the county owning a cellphone, they had a flash mob—six people would constitute a flash mob in Marble Hill—lining the route from the southern city limits sign to the jailhouse. The town's impromptu parade headed downtown. The caravan had it all: a mountainous furry man, his head topped by a British bobby's cap; a Yorkie sticking out of the big man's tee shirt; a good-looking woman in a garish muumuu, piloting a chartreuse golf cart and waving to the crowd; and three dirty people in an orange VW. A couple of jokers along the route waved Confederate flags for reasons unknown to Rosswell. *This arrest had nothing to do with the war.* Did it? He made a mental note of three or four teenagers waving a green flag with a red marijuana leaf in the middle. Ollie would be assigned to give him the straight dope on the kids. And, in addition, The Friends of Purvis rode as guards, zipping up and down the outside of the cavalcade, making certain the taxpayers didn't stone them. The only thing missing were vendors selling refreshments and souvenirs. This day would never be noted on Rosswell's résumé.

Sweat pouring down Rosswell's face, mixing with the grime of the fire, burned his neck and, after running into his eyes, ruined his vision. He had to stop several times to wipe his face with a McDonald's napkin he found in a side pocket of Vicky's door. It smelled of old cheeseburgers. If the heat wave didn't kill him, he'd never be cool again the rest of his life. And that could be a long life. The research he'd done told him that the kind of leukemia he had was not necessarily fatal. What was he thinking? Life itself is fatal and always ends the same way. His death could still be a long way off. Rosswell thought that Paul Newman said it best in the movie *Hud*: "No one gets out of life alive."

When they arrived at the sheriff's station, Frizz reappeared, zooming up to Purvis.

"Sheriff," Purvis said, "she's all yours." He pointed to Candy.

Frizz jumped from his patrol car and stalked over to Purvis.

"That's right," Candy said. "I'm back. I missed you, Frizz. I want to work on my confession some more."

Frizz's face, red as three beets, poured sweat.

Rosswell said, "Where have you been?"

Frizz said, "False alarm."

Ollie said, "That was convenient."

Frizz stormed over to Ollie, still sitting in Vicky's back seat, and towered over him. "I'm tired of your mouth."

"Frizz," Ollie said, "I was simply pointing out that you got a false alarm about the same time Rosswell arrested this murderer. Don't you find that strange?"

Frizz pivoted and marched into the sheriff's station.

Purvis asked Rosswell, "Who stuck a burr under his saddle?"

Rosswell said, "He's exhausted. He's got too much to do and not enough people to help him."

They all followed Frizz into the sheriff's station.

The sheriff had sailed through many episodes in the past without breaking a sweat. Granted, this was the worst of the lot, yet Rosswell couldn't convince himself that Frizz's actions were totally the result of simple exhaustion. Rosswell had just lied to cover for the sheriff's personal problems.

Frizz booked Candy, then said, "Let's go back to your cell."

"I need to know your full name," she said. "My lawyer will need to know your name for the lawsuit I'm going to file against you, Rosswell, Purvis, Ollie, and Nadine." She withdrew a large red handkerchief from a pocket and blew her nose. After silently crying for a few moments, she said, "And a whole bunch more people. I may sue the whole damn county."

Frizz said, "Don't make me drag you back there."

Candy said, "Just you try."

Purvis, Nadine, and Ollie must've been thirsty because they all wandered back to the kitchen for a drink of water. Rosswell didn't appreciate their desertion. Frizz may need witnesses if he got sued.

"Candy," Frizz said, "let's do this the easy way. You go back there, I lock you in, you work on your confession, and when I get back, I'll let you call your lawyer."

"Promise?"

"I promise."

"Let's do it."

After locking Candy in the cell, Frizz ordered Rosswell to stay in the sheriff's station. The three who'd gone to the kitchen must've slaked their thirst. All of them wandered back into the dispatcher's area.

Frizz said to Rosswell, "I'm going to the deadfall. The river should be down far enough for me to check if there's a body stuck out there."

Ollie put a hand over his heart. "'That only needs a finger touch from God, to spring it like a deadfall and the fault, in nature would wipe out all human fault'."

Rosswell gave Ollie a finger slice across the throat. "Shut up."

Ollie said, "Robert Frost."

Frizz said, "I'm going to give you Jack Frost up your butt if you don't keep your mouth shut."

"I'll assist you, Sheriff," said Purvis. "I mean, search."

"Stay out of my way," Frizz said. "I'll take your help, but remember, you don't have any authority in Missouri."

Purvis said, "Yes, sir."

Frizz said to Rosswell, "You three stay here and write your statements. I'll need them for the prosecutor."

Rosswell saluted and said, "Yes, sir."

Frizz and Purvis left.

Rosswell said to Nadine and Ollie, "What the hell was that combination business?"

Nadine said, "I needed something simple to remember the combination."

"Simple?" Rosswell said. "'Initials children Israel sealed' is simple? Ollie, you punched only five letters. All the letters of the alphabet make for thousands of combinations."

"Not even close," Ollie said. "Eleven million, eight hundred eighty-one thousand, three hundred seventy-six."

"That's why," Nadine said, "I wanted something simple. I remembered something out of the Bible."

Ollie said, "As in, 'And I heard the number of them which were sealed: and there were sealed a hundred and forty and four thousand of all the tribes of the children of Israel.' Revelation 7:4."

Rosswell said, "You didn't type all that onto the combination pad."

Nadine said, "No, of course not. I picked the initials of the number: OHFFT. One hundred forty-four thousand."

Silently thankful that Ollie figured out the bizarre clue from a half-conscious Nadine, Rosswell handed them yellow legal pads and Bic pens. Blue ink. "Start writing and don't leave anything out." Rosswell was a lawyer. Lawyers love yellow pads and blue ink.

"I need medical attention," Nadine said. "I'm filthy. I want to go to the hospital and then check into a motel and scrub down. I'll need new clothes. I'll go to Walmart first, then—"

"You'll live," Rosswell said. "Shut up and write. It won't take long."

Nadine and Ollie smelled as bad as Rosswell did. There was no doubt that they could feel the film of smoke and grit inside their mouths and smell nasty burning things lodged in their noses, stopped up with soot, as Rosswell's was. Too bad. Fresh memories required narratives written as soon as possible after the event. When Candy faced a jury, Rosswell didn't want some slick defense attorney attacking their statements because they weren't made at or near the time of the event. He'd seen that done before. Knowledge is preparation.

Rosswell bent to the work and wrote steadily for 10 minutes. He'd have continued writing, but Ollie tapped him on the shoulder and motioned to come with him. Nadine kept writing. They went to Frizz's office—*Headquarters*. Frizz had nailed a hand-lettered wooden sign over the doorway, proclaiming the same in a thick scrawl. Rosswell flashed on the sign, noting the childish scratching.

Rosswell said, "What the hell were you doing in here?"

"Working on my statement." Ollie pointed to the pile of papers on Frizz's desk. Rosswell recognized Ollie's handwriting, small and crowded, decorating both sides of several pages.

"Get your statement and come out front where I can keep an eye on you. Frizz would throw your ass in jail if he knew you were back here. Let's go. Now."

Instead of leaving, Ollie shut the door. "You know, as well as I do that something's eating Frizz."

"And?" Rosswell put his hand on the doorknob. Ollie was right, but there was nothing they could or should do about it. "It's none of our business. Move it."

Ollie reached for Rosswell's hand and stopped him from opening the door. "You're wrong. And Frizz is wrong. Something's bad wrong with the sheriff."

Rosswell jerked to attention. "Why do you say that?"

"Take a gander at this." Ollie kneeled next to Frizz's desk and jiggled the bottom drawer's lock open with a pick. Rosswell didn't ask where Ollie had learned lock picking or latched on to the tools to carry it out. Ollie pulled open the drawer. A strongbox rested inside. Likewise, the lock on the box was no match for him. He popped it open. The men stared at the contents.

"Holy crap," Rosswell said.

"Yeah. Twenty-five thousand dollars."

Chapter Twenty-eight
Saturday afternoon

As of that moment, Rosswell was officially a felon.

After standing dumbfounded in Frizz's office for what seemed a couple of eternities, they both wiped their fingerprints from the box and drawer, and Ollie relocked them. They sauntered to the dispatcher's area, hoping that Nadine hadn't noticed their absence or, if she had, that she hadn't put any significance on it. Rosswell assured himself that he and Ollie were quite sneaky. Further, there was little likelihood that Nadine would mention that he and Ollie had been skulking about in headquarters, committing a felony. Everything was cool.

Nadine threw down her pencil and jumped to her feet. "What were y'all doing back there?"

"Nadine," Rosswell said, "we need to discuss your garden."

Rosswell had always wondered where the title for that song came from. Now he knew. As if he'd stuck a spigot in her carotid artery, turning it on full force to drain all her blood, she turned a whiter shade of pale.

She said, "What garden?"

Ollie said, "Exactly."

Nadine squinted her eyes, then they flew wide open. "Oh, right." Fetching her pencil from the floor, she sat. "What garden? You must've been discussing a nonexistent garden and it was none of my business."

Rosswell said, "What's none of your business?"

"Everything is none of my business." Her face grew even whiter. "I mean, nothing is my business. Whatever. I'm shut. Mum's the word."

Rosswell said, "You are correct. Absolutely correct." He reminded himself to add blackmailing to his list of felonies. "Nadine," Rosswell continued, "Ollie and I are stepping outside to get a breath of fresh air. We'll be right by the front door. If the phone rings, holler at me. If Candy wants something, holler at me."

"You got it," she said.

Rosswell emphasized, "Don't answer the phone. Or the radio. Or talk to Candy."

Nadine nodded. "You got it."

Ollie helped himself to a bottled water from the sheriff's fridge. Rosswell did the same.

The hog rally, with its booming music and alcohol-fueled laughter, made the courthouse square sound like Bourbon Street during Mardi Gras. After checking that no one was in earshot, in case things might quiet down enough for them to be heard, Ollie and Rosswell discussed the matter.

Rosswell said, "Where the hell did Frizz get that kind of cash?" It was a rhetorical question. He hoped like hell that Ollie didn't really know the answer.

"And why?"

Rosswell ventured a guess. "Someone's paying him off for something."

"Frizz? Maybe he's not pure as a driven blizzard, but he's not that bent. Think of another reason."

A man and woman staggered past them, oblivious to a couple of ragamuffin guys chatting. Or so Rosswell hoped.

Rosswell offered a reasonable, yet sickening, explanation. "He's been skimming off drug busts. Dope dealers keep a lot of money around. They dislike banks. Frizz busts a doper, sticks a hundred dollar bill in the stash under his desk, and the rest goes in the evidence locker."

Ollie whipped out a couple of paper towels from his back pocket. He poured half the water on the towels and wiped his face and bald head.

"Sounds logical," Ollie said. "I know what I'm going to do about this."

"What?"

"Nothing."

Rosswell sipped his water. Doing so made him realize how thirsty he was. He drank half the bottle in two gulps and poured some on his face. Ollie handed him a paper towel, and he rubbed vigorously at the mess.

"Sometimes, Ollie, I really wish you were not so fricking curious about everything. You didn't find anything else in there you're not telling me about, did you?"

"Nope. The cash stash was the first thing I found. I stopped there and fetched you."

Rosswell believed him. If he'd found anything more interesting than a pile of cash, he would've told Rosswell. That's the amount of faith he had in Ollie Groton. *You need to have a pinch of faith in your snitch, else why have a snitch at all? I mean, research assistant.*

Rosswell said, "From now on, don't do any exploring unless I ask you."

"Okay, Judge."

"Here's the dilemma as I see it. We think Frizz has money that's not his."

"No. *We* don't think any such thing."

This conversation, as most of the talks Rosswell had with Ollie, headed downhill towards a lake, to crash and sink out of sight. Rosswell chugged the rest of his water and threw the empty into a trashcan.

"Ollie, why would Frizz keep all that dough locked up in his office if it wasn't legally his?"

"Are you saying that, if it was legally his, he'd leave it lying out in the open?"

Rosswell hated it when Ollie used the hammer of logic to smash the finely wrought vase holding his theories into a powder that blew away with the wind.

"Ollie, get to the point."

"Frizz and his wife are having—how do the counselors say it these days? Marital issues. In other words, their marriage sucks."

One of the advantages of posing as a listening post for every snippet of news that raced through town was that no one discriminated in what he or she spilled. A red dog in the road? Significance was attached and it was discussed to death. A sore tooth? The story got told. Adultery? The news spread like an August prairie fire in Oklahoma. A flat tire on the way home from a drunken orgy? The tale grew and grew. And, if Frizz and his wife were having problems, then Ollie would hear the gory details, true or not.

Rosswell asked a question that he knew the answer to. "And you know this how?"

Ollie said, "You think I sit in Merc's all day contemplating my navel? People tell me stuff. Close to a hundred percent of it is unadulterated bullshit."

"Close to a hundred percent?"

"There's a little dab that's probably true. Once you hear something from five or six different people at different times, you start to wonder."

"And you heard that Frizz and his wife were having troubles? Say, now there's something new. A married couple having problems. Never heard of that happening before."

Ollie said, "Not just problems. Mrs. Dodson likes the casinos. And on her way to the casino, she buys clothes, jewelry, whatever she can lay her hands on."

Rosswell made a snipping motion with his fingers. "Cut up the credit cards. Problem solved."

"You've never been married. You don't realize how easy it is for a woman to get a credit card if she's got a spouse who's working at a steady job. Or vice versa. I could give you a long list of spendthrifts in this county who teeter on the verge of bankruptcy on a daily basis."

"I don't care about them. I want to know about Frizz."

Ollie pointed skyward. "The worst thing."

Chapter Twenty-nine
Saturday afternoon, continued

The worst thing? That could mean only one thing. Rosswell said,
"She's going to kill him?"

"He's going to lose his house."

There could be worse things than losing your house. Ollie exag-
gerated on occasion, and this was one of those occasions. People live
through foreclosures. Folks don't live through murder, which is a worse
thing than foreclosure.

Rosswell said, "What a god-awful mess. How did that happen?"

"His wife spent several house payments on the roulette wheel."

Mosquitoes buzzed around Rosswell's head while he tried reasoning
out this mess. Frizz's wife out of control? This kind of news wouldn't
have been secret for long. One of the bloodsuckers landed on his arm
only to suffer the wrath of his hand, smearing its body all over his
skin. Where had he been? How had he missed hearing about Frizz's
problem? Wouldn't Tina have told him something that significant? But
that's why he hired Ollie, to collect info that he'd missed. As best he
could, he wiped off the bloody mess.

Rosswell said, "And Frizz stole money to cover the mortgage? I
don't believe that."

"The money is still there. He hasn't spent it."

"Or he hasn't spent this stash. How long does it take for him to collect that much money? Maybe he's already used stolen money from an
earlier stash to pay the bank."

"I don't know," Ollie said. "I also don't know if he stole the money. All I know is what we saw. And I also know I'm staying out of it. If you want to have a chat with Frizz about his finances, you go right ahead."

A few of the fairgoers walking by inspected Rosswell and Ollie up and down. Rosswell suspected that after noting how dirty they were, maybe the nice folks had mistaken them for gravediggers.

At this point, there was absolutely no evidence indicating that Frizz had done anything wrong. Rosswell said, "The money is locked inside headquarters inside the sheriff's station. Frizz didn't steal the money. He's got it in the evidence locker in his office."

"So you say."

They stood there in silence, taking in the Hogfest people enjoying the day. The noise of the fairgoers had lowered to the level of a small riot.

"Ollie, you don't have one single drop of evidence to show that Frizz stole that money."

"If his house doesn't go on the auction block, then we'll know the missed payments got made. We'll also know where he got the money. He sure doesn't have it anywhere else."

Ollie's statements rocketed to the stratosphere of fantasy. Rosswell asked himself how Ollie could've known the state of Frizz's finances. Frizz could've left his checkbook lying around in headquarters, but even that wouldn't give a full measure of Frizz's financial health. Ollie had merely winged a guess. That, Rosswell concluded, was the answer.

"You don't know how much money Frizz has," Rosswell said. "Your speculation is rampant."

"Yes, it is. It's also correct."

"And you're basing it on the gossip you picked up at Merc's."

"You and I have an agreement. I tell you everything and you don't ask where I got the info."

"I didn't ask."

"Yes, you did."

Nadine said, "Y'all don't know the whole story."

Ollie and Rosswell both whirled around, confronting Nadine. Neither of them uttered a word. She beat them to the punch.

Nadine said, "Before you ask, I heard everything. Y'all would make lousy spies."

Rosswell said, "And you know the whole story?"

"Whole and entire."

Ollie said, "Spill it."

"I'm not telling you two jokers anything. You'd have it spread all over Bollinger County before sunset."

Rosswell spoke to Nadine without obvious begging or pleading. Or tried to. "The three of us could have a lot to lose if we screw around with Frizz and his personal problems." Labeling the situation delicate would've been a gross understatement.

"Stealing," Ollie said, "is not a personal issue. It's a crime." He squeaked. "Judge."

"Yeah," said Nadine. "What we've done or haven't done won't give Frizz a free get-out-of-jail card."

Although Rosswell doubted that Ollie or Nadine would bring up Frizz's possible crimes in public, it was obvious that they were both fishing for something.

There were too many people on the square. It wouldn't do for the trio to be discussing their criminal leanings while standing in the middle of a street fair. Someone might hear them.

Rosswell said, "Let's get inside." Once back in the sheriff's station, he faced the two and flat-out asked them, "What do you want?"

Ollie said, "I'd prefer never to see the inside of a jail cell the rest of my life."

Nadine said, "I've never seen the inside of a cell and I don't want to. Ever."

"Then what's the deal?" Rosswell asked.

Nadine said, "Ollie, you go first."

Ollie said, "I've kept my mouth shut up until now. You go first."

Nadine drew in a deep breath, wiped some of the crud from her face, and said, "Frizz and I are lovers."

In order to keep his knees from crumbling and tossing him to the floor, Rosswell leaned against the counter. Nadine was right. He'd have made a lousy spy. Frizz was no angel, and Rosswell had never thought the sheriff was a candidate for sainthood. In fact, if it got out that he and Nadine were screwing their brains out, no one in the county would've cared come election time. Maybe fifty or sixty years ago it would've made a difference, but adultery was too common these days. Common evil loses its shock value.

Rosswell said, "Save me one illusion."

Nadine said, "Which one?"

"Frizz didn't know about your dope dealing." Rosswell held his breath, waiting for the answer.

"He did not."

Nadine was lying. Frizz had called the three of them two drunks and a doper. The sheriff knew about her doping and probably her dealing. Frizz wanted to protect his honey.

Ollie said, "I could've told you that. Your garden was one of the best kept secrets around. I never heard a whiff of anything connecting you with dope."

Nadine said, "The news media likes to portray dope dealers as stupid and violent. Most of the time, that's true. With me, I'm smart enough to keep my business dealings low key."

Rosswell said, "Business dealings? I thought you said the dope was for medicinal uses. Or recreational uses."

Nadine said, "You need a business to get your product into the market stream."

I don't trust you, Nadine. You're too damned glib.

Rosswell mulled over Frizz's anger at being left in the dark by Purvis and Johnny Dan. Frizz's rage may've been partially fueled by the sheriff's realization at how easy it was to keep a dope dealer secret. If the sheriff could keep Nadine's dope operation secret, then Purvis and Johnny Dan could've kept Eddie Joe's doping secret.

"And now," Rosswell said, "you want me to assure you that you'll never be prosecuted for dope dealing the rest of your life? No deal."

"No," she said. "I want you to forget what I've done up to now. If you catch me doing something in the future, then I'll face the music."

Rosswell said, "I'm not giving you any kind of guarantee."

Ollie said, "We already said we never saw anything." He touched their written statements. "I didn't put a single word in mine about pot."

"Nor I," Rosswell said.

"That's all I ask," Nadine said.

Rosswell turned to Ollie. "What do you want?"

"You got me into this mess by showing me a weird ring with a Latin inscription. That's my own stupidity. I don't want anything."

"You're not stupid," Rosswell said. "But you're both lying."

Nadine said, "Why would I lie to you?"

Ollie said, "Judge, I haven't lied to you."

"One last thing." Nadine's eyes shined. Rosswell knew she was on the verge of crying. After all this and she was just now crying? "I've got a bad feeling. Someone I know should've been calling me but hasn't."

Ollie said, "Happens to the best of us."

Rosswell made the slice across the throat gesture again. "Nadine saved your life. Quit with the crap giving."

Ollie said to Nadine, "One of your friends dumped you. What's that got to do with anything?"

"No one dumped me," Nadine said. "My friend is gone. An unexplained absence."

Rosswell said, "What's his name?"

Nadine said. "Do you have photos of the bodies?"

"You think your friend was one of the murder victims?" Rosswell retrieved his camera from Vicky. "They're in here. They're not pretty."

"I just need to check," Nadine said.

"Repulsive," Ollie said. "You don't want to look at them."

Nadine rubbed her face with her hands. Dirt and ashes sifted to the floor. "Was she wearing a dress?"

"She?" Rosswell said.

"The female corpse. Was she wearing a dress?"

Ollie said, "You know who it is, don't you?"

Rosswell said, "She was wearing a yellow sundress and red high heels."

Nadine whispered, "Babe."

Rosswell said, "Babe?"

"Yes," said Nadine. "We had a business relationship but we were also friends. Her close friends called her Babe. "

Ollie said, "What do you mean everyone called her Babe? I've never heard of anyone around here named Babe."

"I didn't say everyone called her Babe," Nadine said. "Only her intimate friends knew that nickname. Let me see the picture."

Rosswell clicked to a shot of the corpse and showed it to Nadine. "What did everyone else call her?"

Nadine took a deep breath. "It's her." She hitched a sob, deep in her chest.

Ollie said, "What's her name?"

"Ambrosia Forcade."

Chapter Thirty
Saturday afternoon, continued

Sitting alone in headquarters, Rosswell fumed in both sadness and disgust at Nadine and Ollie.

When Nadine had identified Ambrosia, Rosswell said, "Ollie told me that according to her secretary, Ambrosia's in North Carolina at some kind of legal seminar."

"No, she's not," Nadine said. "Her body's either stuck on the deadfall or she got swept away to God knows where." She shuddered.

"Thanks, Nadine. I'll tell Frizz." They'd both been playing Rosswell, angling for some kind of promise that he couldn't give them. "Now leave, the both of you," he'd ordered them, but not in a stern voice.

Ollie handed Rosswell his statement and a huge report he'd finished earlier. "After I clean up, I'm heading to Merc's. Happy reading."

Rosswell said, "I thought you wanted to go to the emergency room."

"I'm checking into a motel," Nadine said. "I haven't been this dirty since I was a kid."

Rosswell said, "Oh, you're feeling a lot better?"

Ollie said, "We're leaving."

"Great," Rosswell said, "as long as you both keep out of trouble."

Nadine left first. Rosswell caught Ollie by the sleeve and pulled him back into the station.

"Ollie, I don't believe for one minute that Nadine is clear of these murders. We still don't know how many murderers there were. I can see a scenario where Candy and Nadine were the killers."

"Nadine seemed awfully upset about Ambrosia."

"*Seemed*. Nadine is in sales. She's got to be a good actress. There could've been a falling out among local dope pushers. It's been known to happen."

"I'll keep snooping."

After Ollie left, Rosswell rustled up a pot of coffee made as strong as he could get it. He poured a cup, adding sugar to the steaming liquid until it became syrupy. After lightly salting it, he gathered up both statements and Ollie's report, sucked in a few mouthfuls of the sainted brew, and read the statements through. Twice. He didn't want any weird stuff in there. Neither statement contained anything about Nadine's dope pushing. Rosswell hadn't included it either. The words on the crinkly yellow paper showed him that at least all three had agreed on lying by omission.

Rosswell peeked in on Candy. She'd turned on her side, her mouth open slightly, a gentle snoring noise emanating from her nose. Exhaustion had overtaken her. Rip-roaring around in the woods, shooting at the trio, then escaping, left her beyond tired.

Although she'd tried killing three people that day, her face appeared almost angelic. Hell of an actress.

Around two o'clock, Purvis and Frizz bounded through the door.

Rosswell asked, "Did you find anything on the deadfall?"

"It was the male," Frizz said. He was soaked from his hat to his boots. "From what Johnny Dan and Purvis tell me, I'm betting it's Eddie Joe Deckard. Neal's doing the autopsy."

Purvis, also sopping wet from head to toe, said, "We'll know for sure after the autopsy."

Yes, that's generally the result of an autopsy. After an autopsy, you know more than before you started it.

Rosswell said, "I know who the female was."

Purvis and Frizz crowded near to Rosswell, dripping nasty river water on his head.

Frizz said, "Judge, I'm real close to throwing your ass in jail for all the trouble you've caused me. Stop stalling and tell me."

Rosswell told them everything that Nadine had said. Then he added, "Now think about it. There's no way to tell if she's telling the truth until we find the body. Ambrosia could be hiding out in Mexico for all we know."

"We," said Frizz. "You keep saying 'we' like you're included. You're not included."

Rosswell eyed Purvis but spoke to Frizz. "Sheriff, I need to ask you something important."

Taking the hint, Purvis said, "I'm leaving." His shoes squished when he left the station.

Through the front window of the sheriff's station, Rosswell and Frizz watched Purvis, Scooby peeking out of his shirt, climb on to the motorcycle.

Rosswell asked, "How did he keep that little bitty dog from drowning when he was prowling around the deadfall?"

"That's not important."

"That's not what I wanted to ask."

Frizz said, "What do you want?"

"Two things. First, check out these statements. If you don't like them, I'll get Nadine and Ollie back in here to write them to your satisfaction."

"They're gone?" Frizz viewed the office as if he had just then noticed that Rosswell was the only one around the dispatcher's desk.

"They outlived their usefulness."

"Starting to piss you off?"

"You could say that."

Frizz perused both statements, undoubtedly searching for any mention by Nadine of her dope growing operation. When he finished his study, he said, "Y'all were behind the door at the top of the steps the whole time?" Knowing Frizz, Rosswell would bet that he had the statements memorized.

"Yep." A lie.

"You didn't go down in the basement?"

"Nope." Another lie. "We stayed at the top of the steps the whole time." A third lie.

"Even though someone was shooting at you, you stayed behind the door at the top of the steps?"

"That's what I said."

"What kept the bullets from going through the door?"

"It was a fire door. It was thick enough to stop bullets. It's in the statement."

"You're alive even though somebody with an AK-47 was blasting you, with only a door standing between you and the shooter?"

"I'm here to testify that's what happened. It was a heavy metal door. Bulletproof."

Frizz stapled each of the statements and placed them in a folder.

"You're a lousy liar." He wrote on the tab of the file folder *DUMBARTON NADINE.*

"What're you saying?"

"An investigator from the fire marshal's office is headed to Nadine's right now. There's no way that the fire destroyed all the evidence of her dope growing."

"Dope growing?" Rosswell tried sounding astounded. However, as Rosswell thought, Frizz wasn't fooled. Why Nadine had tried to convince Rosswell that Frizz didn't know about her doping was a puzzle. Except that maybe it was as simple as her wanting to protect him. He wanted to protect her. The feeling was mutual, which isn't at all unusual between lovers.

"Can it," Frizz said. "The fire marshal will see what's left of a hydroponic garden, not to mention the heavy-duty doors and windows which were bulletproof. He's going to want to know why her house was equipped with something like that."

Busted.

"Nadine saved three lives. Mine, hers, and Ollie's. I don't give a crap if she was cooking meth. If it hadn't been for her, then we all three would be dead."

"I've noticed something about you." Frizz pulled off his wet boots and removed his socks. "People with killing on their minds follow you around. If you hadn't gone out there, nobody would've been shooting at her."

"And she'd still have her dope garden."

Frizz pulled the wet shirt out of his pants and took off his sodden hat. "What was the other thing you needed to know?"

"Do you believe Nadine about the second body? The female?"

"You've lied to me but you'll get no lies from me on that one. I don't know. It's odd that no one's been reported missing around here, yet not so odd. The woman could've been from California or New York for all I know. There are a million missing people in this country. We may never know who she is."

"That doesn't answer the question."

"I'll check out Ambrosia's house and all her acquaintances. Even if a hundred percent of them say they don't know anything, that doesn't mean that she's the body."

"Ollie and I could do some more snooping."

"Rosswell, do me a favor."

"What's that?"

"Go home. Rest up. Your wound hasn't healed, what with you running all over the county stirring up shit."

"We've had this conversation before and, while I appreciate your concern, I've got lots to do."

"I don't want anything to happen to you." Frizz winked at Rosswell. "I wouldn't know what to do with all the peace and quiet if you weren't around."

"Then that's what I'll do. Go see Tina and then straight home to bed."

Once more, Rosswell hated himself for lying to the sheriff.

Frizz said, "As I said earlier, you're a lousy liar."

"Are you revoking my deputy's commission?"

Frizz only laughed.

Rosswell headed for the door. "Check on Candy. She snores a lot."

Chapter Thirty-one
Saturday afternoon, continued

There was no question that one other person besides the fire marshal was bound to show up where Rosswell was going, that he was sure of. All he had to do was wait at Nadine's house.

After he'd left Frizz, he stayed by Tina's side for a couple of hours. She was awake, although still groggy. Rosswell had difficulty believing that any anesthesia affected a healthy person the way it had Tina. While in her room, he'd tried calling several doctors, including Hakim Al Serafi. No doctor kept office hours on Saturdays. Or Sundays. He'd start calling Monday morning. Although Tina's doctor at Saint Luke's had assured him that she was suffering from exhaustion, the bullet grazing her, and a reaction to the anesthesia, Rosswell wasn't mollified. He wanted Tina healthy and happy so they could snuggle in their special place. The Southern Hotel.

At Nadine's house, the smoking ruins prompted him to do his own investigation before the investigator arrived. What did Rosswell know about investigating fires? Nothing. When he got there, the volunteer fire department wasn't on the scene. The fire had probably been de-clared out and safe, or whatever firefighters say when they've decided they've done all they can do.

When the fire marshal was set to arrive, Rosswell didn't know. He needed to work fast.

Am I going to destroy evidence that Nadine's garden grew illegal weeds?

No traffic moved on the road running in front of her house. No birds sang in the scorched trees around the place. A large white oak on the backside of her property was burnt to the point of death. All of the ornamental shrubs and flowers planted around her house were fried. The smells were horrible. The marijuana aroma hung in the still air. The incinerated plastic and fertilizer gave off an acrid scent. The wood, glass, steel, and whatever else was in the house sent off an odor reminding Rosswell of other house fires he'd smelled.

With his back to the road, he surveyed the destruction at the front of her house. He kicked at a black lump of something lying where her front door once stood. When he picked it up, the lump felt warm. The house was a pile of charred rubble. He couldn't tell one piece of crap from another. The smell of gasoline still pervaded the air and the ruins of the house.

There'd be no doubt how the fire started. Yet Frizz was right. The fire marshal would spot the dope set-up the instant he drove up. This wasn't the marshal's first roundup.

Destroy evidence? Rosswell couldn't even tell what in that mess was evidence.

Wasn't it about time for the only person besides Nadine who knew anything about this operation to show up? Rosswell had mulled over everything he'd heard up to this point and sifted through the information, especially Ollie's report. Only one person could be connected to Nadine.

"Good afternoon, Judge." The voice came from behind Rosswell, on the road.

Of course. No surprises. Rosswell was correct. A pat to the .38 special in his pocket made him brave. "Good afternoon. I've been expecting you." Turning around would've done no good, so he remained staring into the burned mess. And, as he also had thought, no car drove up to deposit the visitor. He'd hiked a good distance, Rosswell suspected. His approach had been silent.

A tall man with close-cropped bright red hair joined Rosswell at his side. Nathaniel Dahlbert.

"Judge, how did you know I'd be out here?"

"How many clues do you want?"

Nathaniel chuckled. "Let's see . . . four."

"Too easy. Number one, you're filthy rich. Before I met you, I would've said that anyone who spends over a couple of hundred dollars on a tea service has more money than brains. But you have brains.

That's number two. If you've got a lot of money tied up in porcelain, then I know you have a lot of money tied up in silver, gold, antiques, other things that can't be traced easily. Excellent planning by a brainy man."

Rosswell took a moment to recollect what was in Ollie's report. "Oh, yes. That book selling business you have is worth a million dollars profit per year, although it's not from selling books. You're selling a lot more than books. Number three is where you get the dope you sell. Our friend Nadine supplied some of it. I'll admit I don't know your other sources. It was easy after I had all the info to realize that Nadine was one of your major sources for pot."

"I asked for four clues. You gave me only three."

"Number four is a stretch, I admit, but you have a hotline phone somewhere in your house. I heard it ringing the second time I was there. It doesn't have an answering machine hooked to it."

"Owning a phone without an answering machine isn't against the law."

"Agreed. But why have a phone in a back room instead of your living room where you conducted business?"

"You're a suspicious person."

"Suspicious and skeptical. When I heard that phone ring, I wondered why you didn't buy a disposable cellphone at Walmart. Simple. You need a credit card to buy one of those. Sure, the phone company has info on you they got when you installed your landline, but that was a chance you'd have to take. The only calls would be local and the phone company doesn't keep records of local calls on landlines like they do on cellphones."

Nathaniel offered his hand to Rosswell. "Congratulations." They shook.

"Admirable business organization you have, Nathan. That is, if your name really is Nathan Dahlbert. I haven't been able to nail down your identity. Give me time."

"Nathan? I don't like that nickname. Nathaniel is my name." He waggled a forefinger at Rosswell. "Besides, a man needs a few secrets."

"Your distraction was only momentary."

"Distraction? What was the distraction?"

"There's no Masonic breakaway group who added the initials EJD to the Latin motto on the ring I found. Fortunately, I recognized that as a lousy story and didn't pursue it." Ollie's report had been thorough on that point.

"True. Eddie Joe Deckard is the only one I know with those initials. He was a scoundrel of the highest order."

The irony of a man who used an Internet book company as a cover to sell dope calling a fellow doper a *scoundrel of the highest order* verged on the ridiculous. There was no time for Rosswell to call him on it. It was an argument he could have with Nathaniel later. Other things had priority.

Rosswell hadn't brought any water. The heat of the day sapped him of the last bit of energy he had. The wound to his arm was healing but it still hurt. His whole body, sad to say, hadn't healed either. Fatigue was a constant worry. Those problems were ones he wouldn't share with Nathaniel. However, falling over in a faint with Nathaniel standing next to him could be a death sentence.

Rosswell pointed to the house and spoke the obvious. "Nadine's out of business. At least for a long time. She spent a lot of money on this house that she'll never get back from her insurance."

"True. But there are a thousand Nadines in Missouri. I'll find other helpers."

No, you won't, Rosswell promised himself. He'd take Nathaniel off the street no matter what it took. Alas. There was that little matter of evidence. Something he didn't have on the book seller. Yet.

Rosswell said, "Let me guess one more thing."

"Guess away."

"Your house, including your computer and paper records, doesn't have a speck of incriminating evidence."

"You are absolutely correct. If you'd like to have your sheriff search the place, you won't even need a search warrant. I'll give you consent. Right here. Right now."

"Why are you out here?"

Nathaniel stepped across what used to be the threshold. "You tell me first." He bent to examine something that appeared to be a doorknob.

"I'm looking for evidence."

Nathaniel straightened, then turned to the woods surrounding the house. "Evidence of what?" He shaded his eyes and surveyed the trees.

"I won't know until I find it."

"I'm also looking for evidence." Rosswell watched as Nathaniel traipsed through the outer edges of the ruins of the house. Nathaniel kept his head down, seeming to calculate each step, careful to make certain that he didn't fall over something. At one point, he stopped and stared for a long time at something in the ruins. What he looked at Rosswell couldn't tell.

Rosswell said, "Why haven't you absconded? You should be running away. From what I know about you, the FBI will hunt you down wherever you go."

"Perhaps."

"Until then, we'll work together?"

"The enemy of my enemy is my friend."

They shook hands again.

"Who's your enemy?" Rosswell asked.

"Let's look around."

They had just started searching for evidence when Candy found them.

Chapter Thirty-two
Saturday afternoon, continued

Baggy blue jeans. Gray sweatshirt. Her hair tucked under a John Deere cap. Dirty blonde hair. Big sunglasses. Big bracelets. Standing in the middle of the road about a hundred feet from them, not even trying to hide. She moved up and then back several times.

She's dancing! Candy's cracked completely.

Candy had somehow escaped from jail, changed her appearance yet again, and cradled her AK-47.

And she was pissed.

How did she escape? Why wasn't Frizz out here? Surely the sheriff would realize that she would return to the scene of her many crimes. Cocking his ear, Rosswell listened for sirens. Nothing but a gentle breeze blowing through the trees.

She's shot Frizz. He's lying dead at headquarters.

Rosswell pulled the pistol from his pocket and aimed it at her head. "Candy, drop that gun."

A blast from the rifle sent Nathaniel and Rosswell scurrying behind Vicky, as if a puny Volkswagen could stop bullets from an AK-47.

I don't think she saw my pistol!

Nathaniel said, "Who the hell is that?"

"Candy Lavaliere. She's a murderer."

"You're correct on that score."

"Candy!" Rosswell screamed at her. "Put down the rifle!"

Rosswell hit the ground, scooted around the back end of Vicky to get into position. More shots rang out, a few ripping through Vicky. If Candy kept that up, he'd have to kill her for sure. No one messed with his car and lived to tell the tale.

Nathaniel said, "Call the sheriff."

"No service."

Nathaniel checked his own phone. Rosswell guessed that Nathaniel didn't believe him.

More shots.

"Candy," Rosswell yelled, "stop shooting. Everyone and their brother is looking for you. You have no way out." Rosswell prayed that was true.

Silence for a moment then more shots.

Rosswell watched as Nathaniel scooted next to him. Nathaniel squinted at Candy and grunted. "That's not a woman."

"What?"

"I'm telling you that the person who's firing that gun at us is not a woman."

"That's Candy Lavaliere. I've known her for years. You don't even know her. She's got some masculine traits, maybe, but she's a woman. Hell, I suspect she and Ollie are lovers. You're fricking crazy."

"Women generally have wider pelvises than men. That's why they sway their hips."

Nathaniel had gone around the bend. Candy was trying to kill them and he lectured Rosswell about female anatomy, giving him facts he already knew. Rosswell had seen stress under gunfire many times. Men sometimes go crazy when someone's trying to kill them. And now Nathaniel was comparing the way males and females walked.

"Rosswell, come out here, you prick," the shooter yelled.

Rosswell said, "What the crap?"

Unless she'd downed a dose of testosterone while in the jail, that voice didn't belong to Candy or any other woman Rosswell knew. It was a deep bass voice of a man. And it was a man he knew. But he couldn't place a name with the voice. Not right then.

"I told you," Nathaniel said. "It's a man."

"No crap."

"Who is it?"

"I know him, but I can't place the voice right now."

"Let me try."

Rosswell said, "Try to place his voice?"

"No. Let me see if I can talk him down."

"Have at it."

Nathaniel scooted a foot or so towards the road, but Rosswell doubted that the bad guy could see him clearly enough to take a kill shot. The shooter knew that spraying them and everything around them with bullets would do the job as effectively as one shot to the head. The guy didn't need good aim. All he needed was a lot of bullets.

"Hey, out there," Nathaniel said.

No answer.

Nathaniel waited a few more seconds, then said, "Let's talk."

No answer.

Rosswell said, "I don't think this is working. I'm going to shoot him."

"Wait," Nathaniel said to Rosswell, then hollered to the shooter, "Talk to me, man."

No answer.

"That does it," Rosswell said, squirming into a sitting position behind Vicky. It was a stable position that would allow him accuracy.

The guy said, "What do you want?"

Rosswell then recognized the voice. "It's Johnny Dan Dumey."

He's been stalking me. The glint of light I saw at the park when we got the tire impressions were from binoculars. Shooting at Tina and me. The woman in the crowd that Hermie's son saw. The knife under my couch. All of it was Johnny Dan Dumey.

"Tell me about him."

Rosswell wasn't about to give up one criminal to another. He'd have to settle for something that would give Nathaniel something to chew on but nothing he could use if they lived through the firefight.

Maybe Nathaniel will do something really stupid out here that he could be arrested for. The two birds with one stone ploy.

Rosswell said, "I don't know him that well. He's an auto mechanic, and his daddy, Elmer, is in a nursing home."

"Good stuff."

"What are you, some kind of hostage negotiator?"

"I'm quite well read." Nathaniel nodded toward the man trying to kill them. "No practical experience, but that seems of little consequence now."

"Ollie will be sorry he missed out."

Johnny Dan yelled, "I said, what the hell do you want?"

Nathaniel cupped his hands around his mouth and said, "Johnny Dan, how's Elmer doing? How's your dad?"

Johnny Dan still hadn't sought cover. Probably because he didn't re-alize that Rosswell was armed. Then again, if he didn't think either one of them had a gun, why didn't Johnny Dan charge and blow their heads off? Something was wrong with the boy's brain, but what bothered him was way beyond Rosswell's knowledge.

In answer to Nathaniel's question, Johnny Dan shot a volley over their heads. "Get out here where I can see you. Who the hell are you?"

"Nathaniel Dahlbert."

"What kind of car do you drive?"

"Infiniti."

"How old?" Johnny Dan asked.

"Brand new."

"Is it silver?"

"Yes. You know it?"

"I've seen you driving around town a lot. You're going to have a problem with that clutch slave assembly. I can hear it going out."

If Rod Serling had appeared announcing the beginning of a *Twilight Zone* episode, Rosswell wouldn't have been more surprised. A madman trying to kill them was giving Nathaniel a little last minute advice about a bad clutch on his car.

Nathaniel said in a low voice, "I've got him talking about irrelevant matters. That's good."

Rosswell whispered, "Keep going."

Nathaniel said to Johnny Dan, "Maybe you could take a look at it."

Johnny Dan said, "You're going to be dead. You won't need a clutch."

Nathaniel said, "Johnny Dan, there are some more things we ought to talk about. Come over here and let's talk. Man to man."

The idea of Johnny Dan waltzing over for a visit while he was toting his AK-47 didn't appear to be a real good idea. However, Ross-well had to admit that as long as Nathaniel had Johnny Dan talking, he wasn't shooting.

Johnny Dan said, "Y'all got any guns?"

"No."

Rosswell was proud of Nathaniel's instant lie.

Johnny Dan strutted up and down the road, never letting his eyes leave what little he could see of them. Hoping they were hidden behind his precious Vicky to the point where Johnny Dan couldn't see them well enough to shoot them didn't bring Rosswell comfort. Parked between them and death was—Rosswell hated to think of her this way—nothing but a hunk of German tin, but Vicky could be sacrificed if she kept them from getting killed.

"He's only got thirty rounds per magazine," Rosswell said to Nathaniel. "I'm hoping he's running out of ammunition."

Nathaniel yelled to Johnny Dan, "Throw down your gun and we'll talk."

Johnny Dan laughed loudly. "That's a good 'un. I'm going to use that." He slung his rifle over his shoulder, posturing like a soldier of fortune. Even though he was disguised as a woman, the sneer was all male.

"Your method isn't working," Rosswell said to Nathaniel. "Let me try something." He nodded. Rosswell stood. "Johnny Dan, come over here and talk to us."

The instant he saw Rosswell, Johnny Dan drew the rifle off his shoulder and slapped it into firing position, but before he could pull the trigger, Rosswell shot him between the eyes. What happened next played out in slowmo, like the movies. Johnny Dan dropped the rifle, raised both hands, and fell backward into the road. It didn't take a second but seemed like it took ten minutes.

In the stillness that followed, Rosswell said, "You saw him aiming for us, didn't you?"

Nathaniel didn't answer.

Rosswell said, "It was clearly self defense."

Nathaniel still didn't answer.

Rosswell said, "He was going to shoot first."

Rosswell turned and Nathaniel had disappeared.

Chapter Thirty-three
Saturday afternoon into Saturday night

People either died or vanished when Rosswell was around. It was beginning to hurt his feelings.

But he had a bigger problem on his hands. He had a dead bad guy lying in the road and no way to call the cops.

"Nathaniel," he called. In the distance, he thought he heard a car start and then drive away from his location. Probably a brand new Infiniti with a clutch going bad. He doubted that he'd ever see Nathaniel Dahlbert again.

He'd have to drive into town and fetch the law. That's the decision he made.

And immediately after he made the decision, he smelled why it would never happen. Vicky leaked gasoline. If she were going to explode from a stray spark swirling around, he didn't want to be near her.

Still pointing his gun at Johnny Dan like the cops do on television, Rosswell approached him with slow yet deliberate steps. The hole in his head told Rosswell that he'd never move on his own again, yet Rosswell couldn't afford any risks. When he reached Johnny Dan's rifle, he kicked it off the road, far out of his reach.

Then he stood over the corpse and stared.

Rosswell didn't like killing people.

He already knew that Neal and Frizz would chew his ass good if he messed up the scene, although he felt an urge to cover Johnny Dan's body out of respect for the dead.

What should he do? Stand there until the mailman or one of the neighbors drove by? No phone. No car. And yelling wouldn't do any good.

The fire marshal's investigator drove up, parking his car far enough from Johnny Dan's body to avoid contaminating the crime scene. A rumpled uniform that transformed into the man sent from Jefferson City eased out of a state-issued car, an unmarked maroon sedan with black-wall tires plain enough to be conspicuous. There may as well have been COP CAR painted on the side in bright orange letters.

The marshal held a silver Colt .45 at his side, ready if Rosswell raised his pistol.

After the marshal glanced from side to side, he said, "You alone?"

"Yep."

The man matched Rosswell's short stature, but topped him by at least forty pounds. The investigator's thinning, straight black hair unbalanced his shiny mustache, onyx, curled, and heavy. How Rosswell envied those handlebars.

The man said, "Are you peaceable?"

"Yep." Rosswell knew enough not to spook a cop who'd arrived on a scene where a fresh body lay in the road. Especially if the cop had a big gun.

Rosswell watched him dip a wad of chewing tobacco out of an open pouch on his car's dash, then squirrel it in a ruddy cheek, all the while holding his pistol. If there's a habit nastier than chewing an expensive weed that burns your mouth, stains your teeth a dead brown color, gives you the breath of a charnel house, causes your stomach to ache, and makes you hawk slimy gobs of greasy crap, Rosswell had yet to discover it. Who kissed this man? Hadn't the man read the warning on the tobacco pouch: THIS PRODUCT IS NOT A SAFE ALTER-NATIVE TO CIGARETTES?

As if on cue, the investigator spit a brown stream and wiped his chin. *Abominable.* Rosswell tracked the gelatinous lump the man had ejaculated from between his grimy teeth as it landed inches from Rosswell's feet. He scowled at the filthy gob, vowing to watch where he stepped from that moment on.

"Jim Bill Evans," he said. "I'm with the Department of Public Safety. Fire Marshal's office."

"Rosswell Carew." He doubted that Jim Bill Evans would be im-pressed that he was a judge.

Jim Bill's tongue worked the weed wad around until it collected in his lower lip, and he spit again. "Mr. Carew, looks like there's been a killing."

"Yep. I killed the guy."

Jim Bill spit again. "You best be handing that gun over to me. Butt first." Rosswell complied. Jim Bill handcuffed Rosswell behind his back. "Now you can get in my car. You're under arrest."

###

Rosswell rubbed his wrists, urging the blood to circulate, after Jim Bill removed the handcuffs.

Frizz and Neal had arrived shortly after the investigator summoned them by radio.

Neal said, "Here's Ross and here's another body."

Frizz told Jim Bill, "He's our judge."

"We've met," Jim Bill said, probably wondering why a judge would go around killing people in public.

Frizz said, "Take his cuffs off."

Rosswell said, "Frizz, I take it you've released Candy again."

"Not yet."

Rosswell said, "Johnny Dan's the murderer."

"I've got to agree with you on that one," Neal said. "Where's your camera?"

"It's in my car but Vicky's leaking gasoline. I'm not sure I should go over there."

Jim Bill appraised the VW and the gasoline dripping from it. "Let's roll it into the road to let the gas soak in the road."

Rosswell said, "Isn't that dangerous?"

Jim Bill said, "Yes."

###

Vicky had been towed into town without incident and Rosswell sat in headquarters with Frizz.

The door was shut.

After a million questions from Frizz, Rosswell said, "Are you through?"

"Until I think of something else to ask."

"You and me . . . we need to have a serious talk."

"That's what we've been doing."

"It's about the money." Rosswell stood and walked behind Frizz's desk, where he pointed to the drawer holding the strongbox. "I need to know why you have a box full of cash."

"How do you know what's in there? This drawer is locked." Frizz pulled on the drawer to demonstrate.

"Ollie picked the drawer then picked the strong box. After we looked, he locked them again."

"Ollie? Hell of a research assistant working for you. I should arrest his ass."

"Let's deal. You tell me why you have the cash and I won't tell anyone, and I won't tell you how I know."

"About what? How much do you know already?" Frizz unlocked the drawer.

"You and Nadine are lovers and your wife is a gambler out of control."

Frizz plunked the box on top of his desk. "Twenty-five thousand dollars. Not a penny less. I've been collecting it for six years. A skim here, a skim there. It adds up."

"How much did you spend?"

"I haven't spent one hot penny."

"Then, legally, you've done nothing wrong. You're the sheriff. You snatched cash as evidence. You have evidence locked in your office. You did what you're supposed to do."

Frizz laughed. "Right. And how do I apportion all that money to however many cases over the last six years? I need to resign. The state needs to investigate me. I need to go to jail."

"Unadulterated bullshit."

"Are you threatening me with Ollie phrases?"

"How many cash stashes do you have in the evidence locker?"

Frizz said, "None."

"Okay, then here's what we do. From now until you get rid of the pile in your strongbox, you slip in a couple of hundred every time you make a legal bust. No one will know but you and me."

"That leaves my wife and Nadine."

"You're on your own there."

"I'll do what everyone else does. Bankruptcy and divorce."

"I'm going home to clean up. Then I'm going to see Tina."

"The evil nurse may try to arrest you."

"I can deal with her."

Chapter Thirty-four
Saturday night

Rosswell, clean and shiny after his shower at home, answered his cellphone.

Without greeting, Frizz said, "I found Ambrosia Forcade's white Cadillac."

"Where?"

"In Johnny Dan's shop, under a tarp. Neal is processing the scene."

"Now what are your odds on it being Babe?"

"Judge, I know how to handle it. I can find Ambrosia or Babe or whatever the hell she's calling herself."

The phone went dead.

Rosswell fetched the letter Tina had written him.

It was late and Tina would be asleep. He'd decided to go to her room, sneaking past the nurse guarding the door if necessary, and sit by her bedside. There he would open the letter and read it. What a spot of calm in an ocean of problems. He sitting by his beloved reading what had to be a love letter. That is, if it wasn't a get-lost letter.

At the hospital, the door to Tina's room at the end of the hallway was open, but inside it was dark.

Junior Fleming stood at Priscilla's desk, chatting, laughing. Apparently he didn't find her quite the ugly stick anymore.

A dark room was a good sign. Tina slept, he assured himself. She needed rest. Tina hated resting, but that was the major thing she needed. He would sit by her bed and watch her sleep.

Tina was not in the room. Rosswell walked to the nurse's station.

"Junior," Rosswell said, "where's Tina? Where's the deputy?"

Junior turned to face Rosswell. "Tina's in there, sleeping." He pointed to the dark room. "The deputy went to supper."

Rosswell went back in the room, knocked on the bathroom door. No response. He opened the door. The bathroom was dark and unoccupied.

"Crap," he said under his breath. Tina was out gallivanting in the halls, visiting who knew who. She loved talking to people, and she'd perked up enough to be bored, and boredom had finally overcome her. He'd give her a good lecture which, of course, she'd ignore.

Rosswell stuck his head out the door to her room. Peered up and down the hall. No one in sight but Junior and Priscilla.

"Junior, she's not here."

The cop bolted for the room and turned on all the lights and checked the bathroom. He radioed security. "I'm on it, Judge." Junior left, apparently to search the whole hospital by himself.

Roswell began walking the corridors. After half an hour, Rosswell returned to her room. Still no Tina. The bed was mussed as if she'd just gotten out of it. Nothing appeared to be missing. Except Tina.

A security guard approached him. "Are you Judge Carew?"

"Yes," Rosswell said to the young man he'd never seen before. "But something's bad wrong. Do you know where Tina Parkmore is?" He pointed to her room.

"Let me check," the man said, hunching over a computer. "Says here she's still a patient."

Priscilla frowned. "She's not in her room. The judge has been looking all over for her and so has Junior."

Rosswell said, "Where else would she be this time of night?"

The security guard said, "I've called the sheriff. He's on his way. I'll be searching the grounds."

The nurse strode to Tina's room and did a search of her own.

Doesn't she think that Junior, the security guard, and I could find one woman in a hospital room?

"Not here," the nurse said. She dialed a number and spoke to someone, then said to Rosswell, "My supervisor will be right here."

The supervisor was Benita Smothers.

"Ross," she said. "How are you making it? You healing okay?"

Rosswell gritted his teeth. Then he said, "Yeah, I'm doing fine, but Tina Parkmore is not in her room."

Benita also searched the room. "Doesn't look like she took anything so I doubt that she left the hospital. I need to call security."

Priscilla informed her that security and Junior were already searching for Tina.

Benita hung her head and tapped her foot. A thinking position, Rosswell assumed. "Call the sheriff."

"They've already done that," Rosswell said. "Benita, please step in here and talk to me."

After Rosswell had shut the door to the room, he said, "Have you ever seen anyone have a reaction to anesthesia like Tina had? Ever?"

Benita said, "You really should be asking the doctor—"

"I'm asking you."

Benita rubbed her hands together rapidly. "I'm not supposed to give my medical opinion about things. Generally speaking."

"I asked you one simple question."

Benita folded her arms across her chest. "Judge Carew, you didn't hear this from me."

"Hear what?"

"Something was wrong with that girl. Tina. Something was bad wrong and it wasn't from the anesthesia. At least not at first. I tried to tell the doctor, but he said she was mentally and physically exhausted, that she'd been grazed with a bullet, shock, blood loss, allergy to the anesthesia, on and on."

"Are you saying somebody could've been doping her?"

"That's exactly what I'm saying."

###

An hour later, Frizz made the decision at the sheriff's station. "Tina's missing, foul play suspected."

"Frizz," Rosswell said, "there's no signs of a struggle."

"We've ferreted the hospital top to bottom. She's not at her house. She's not at your house. She's not at anyone's house. She's gone. Her car's gone. No one she knows has any idea where she is. That's not like Tina. She wouldn't leave willingly without telling someone." Frizz wiped his face with his handkerchief. "She's gone."

"Doesn't the hospital have surveillance tapes?"

"Rosswell, that's the first thing I asked for. They're on the way."

Purvis Rabil shot through the door. "Sheriff, something mighty strange just happened out at the park."

Frizz said, "Tell me before I arrest you again."

The big man looked from Frizz to Rosswell, then back again. "I saw something that may have to do with Miss Tina."

Rosswell grabbed both of the flaps of Purvis's vest. Scooby, obviously scared, yipped. "Where the hell did you see this?"

"Like I said," Purvis answered, "at the park. It was dark but someone drove up to the bank of the river in a car that looked like hers. They got out and jumped in the river. The car's still there."

Chapter Thirty-five
After the memorial service

Rosswell attended the memorial mass for Tina. He owed that much to Father Mike, Frizz, and, of course, Tina. Yet Rosswell knew something that none of those other people would admit. Tina was alive. Why was everyone in a rush to put her in her grave?

Tina was gone, he admitted that. The who, how, when, and why she'd disappeared, he couldn't even begin to guess.

But not dead. He wouldn't—couldn't—accept that. And he had physical proof.

Rosswell had spent hours reviewing the surveillance videotapes the hospital turned over to Frizz. First, Rosswell watched the tapes covering 12 hours before he got there and then 12 hours after. Then 24 hours before and after. Then 36.

On one grainy black-and-white tape, he saw a tall man with close-cropped curly hair pushing a laundry cart into the parking lot. Of course, the cameras didn't cover the area where the man had parked his vehicle. The man—Rosswell was convinced it was Nathaniel Dahlbert—had kidnapped Tina. Why, Rosswell couldn't fathom. The FBI, the Missouri Highway Patrol, Frizz, and hell, yes, even Junior Fleming had scoured the whole area. Nothing.

Still, that was physical proof. If Nathaniel had wanted her dead, he would've killed her in her bed. Therefore, she was alive. And it was imperative in Rosswell's mind that Nathaniel must have received help from someone inside the hospital. But again, the who, how, when, and why eluded him.

Rosswell wandered from the church and stood in the sunshine. Several people shook his hand and muttered platitudes. The scent of the incense and flowers in the church lingered in his nose. Sweat began rolling down his face.

I need to ask Father Mike for an exorcism. A demon possessed me, and that's why I'm wearing a black, three piece suit on a sunny, hot, and humid day.

"Rosswell," Purvis said from behind him.

Rosswell gasped when he turned around. "You're wearing a suit!"

Purvis said, "I couldn't bring myself to shave."

"Thanks for reporting what you saw. And thanks for coming back for the service."

"I'm sorry things didn't turn out the way you wanted."

Frizz joined them. "Purvis, you did what you could. No one could've identified somebody that far away in the dark."

Rosswell said, "It wasn't Tina."

Purvis nodded. "If it wasn't Tina, then who stole her car? And why did the thief jump in the river?"

Frizz said, "Let's step over here where we can talk privately."

The three men walked to the side of the large brick church where they stood in the shade of a tall cedar tree. A mockingbird, high on the roof of the church, began its repertoire of songs.

"This isn't for public consumption, hear?" Purvis and Rosswell murmured their agreement. "We found Johnny Dan's ledger in his garage. Had tons of transactions listed, but no names. He used a code of some kind. He scrawled at the bottom of one page he was going to kill someone."

"Who?" Rosswell asked.

Frizz said, "Johnny Dan called him Toothpick Chief."

Rosswell nodded. "Ribs Freshwater."

Frizz said, "That was my first guess."

Purvis said, "Who's he?"

Frizz said, "He's a tall, skinny, Native American who, by the way, has disappeared."

No one spoke for a long time.

Rosswell said, "I . . . uh . . . kind of checked up on Nathaniel Dahlbert. His house is clean and empty. Must've had one hell of a moving crew to come in at night."

"We were there way before you were, Judge," Frizz said. "We couldn't find clue one. I wouldn't be surprised if Ribs and Nathaniel are together, somewhere on the run. I've sent out a persons of interest bulletin on them both."

Rosswell didn't ask and Purvis probably didn't know enough to ask what the fire marshal's investigator had turned up after sifting through Nadine's house. Rosswell suspected that the investigator had built a bombproof case against her. That could demolish Frizz if it ever got out that he was protecting a dope pusher. Rosswell had also heard through Ollie that Frizz had hired two lawyers: One for divorce and one for bankruptcy.

Purvis said, "What about DNA, Frizz? You got any tests back?"

"Neal's taking care of that. He ran a profile on the male corpse that he matched to a sample in Eddie Joe's car. Also matched up to the knife I found under the judge's couch. Johnny Dan must've slipped in and planted it." Frizz removed his hat and wiped his head with his handkerchief. "Obviously we don't have the female corpse, but we have a sample from Ambrosia's toothbrush and comb from her house. In case she ever shows up."

Purvis shook his head. "Look on the bright side. You've made some progress."

Frizz said, "Progress. Yeah, progress." He fanned himself with his hat.

Purvis screwed up his face, or at least the part of it that Rosswell could see. "Candy?"

"A weird girl," Frizz said. "It seems that the younger generation is getting weirder instead of smarter."

Purvis said, "Why did Candy confess to the murders?"

Frizz cleared his throat. "There's a lot of . . . activity going on around here." He cleared his throat again. "If we can put any stock on what Candy told us, Johnny Dan was screwing Mabel."

Purvis said, "That's no surprise, is it?"

"None at all," Frizz said. "According to Candy, Johnny Dan was also doing her until Ollie interfered. Then Ribs Freshwater started chasing Candy and apparently came out on top—so to speak. Ribs was well on his way to winning Candy all for himself. But Johnny Dan still lusted after Candy even though he was going with Mabel."

Purvis said, "I missed something. How would all that make Candy want to confess?"

"My guess," Frizz said, "is that Candy somehow suspected Johnny Dan of the murders. Truth be known, he'd probably knocked her around some. She knew he was violent. If Candy confessed, she'd take the heat off him and then Johnny Dan would take the heat off Ribs, who was her true love."

Rosswell said, "I don't believe a syllable that Candy has uttered. There's not a smidgen of evidence that Johnny Dan smacked on Candy."

That is, if Ollie's telling me the truth about his investigation of what Candy did and didn't do.

Purvis stroked his beard for a few minutes, apparently trying to digest the soap opera without a scorecard. "Mabel screwed Johnny Dan who screwed Candy who then screwed Mabel's father. Perverted. That doesn't make sense."

Frizz said, "A lot of this doesn't make sense. But Candy's a couple of beads short of a rosary. She's liable to think or do anything."

Rosswell recalled a slightly different version of the Candy story, one supplied by her shortly before the memorial service. She'd called Rosswell over to her golf cart.

"Johnny Dan made me confess," she said in a voice so low that Rosswell had to strain to hear it.

"How did he do that?"

Candy began crying. "He caught me talking to Elbert."

"Elbert? Who's that?"

Candy sniffled. "You remember when I got first place in the pie baking contest at the county fair last year? And the year before that?"

"Uh . . . no. I don't really keep up—"

"Elbert gave me those prizes. 'Cause I talked to him. Some. Not much. Just some."

Rosswell completed the thought for her. "Johnny Dan said if you didn't confess to the murders, he was going to kill Ribs and probably Ollie, too, then tell everyone you . . . I guess the term is . . . uh . . . cheated . . . to get the prizes for both years. Am I right?"

"Yes. If that got out, I'd never be able to show my face in Bollinger County again. Judge Carew, please don't tell anyone."

"Never in a million years."

Now, with Frizz and Purvis standing before him, he didn't burden them with Candy's scandalous yet unverifiable story. He'd promised. Instead, Rosswell said, "I killed the murderer."

Rosswell needed to have another chat with Father Mike about that.

###

That night at Picnic Area 3 of Foggy Top State Park, Rosswell leaned against his black pickup truck under a full moon in a cloudless sky. The temperature had gone down to around 80 degrees but the humidity stayed high.

He pulled the envelope from his back pocket, opened it, withdrew Tina's letter, and re-read for—what?—the thousandth time?

Dear Rosswell, I love you so much. When I wake up in the morning, you're the first thing I think of. When I go to sleep at night, you're the last thing I think of. You're on my mind every hour of every day. I want to know you and love you the rest of our lives. I've got something really important to tell you. I'm so happy to tell you. And I want you to be happy, too. I'm pregnant.

When you finish reading this letter, come to me and hold me and never let me go.

I love you always,

Tina

Rosswell folded the letter, replaced it in the envelope, and slid it into his breast pocket.

He drove for town, regretting that he'd killed the best mechanic for miles around. Vicky needed repairs. Lots of them and soon. She was fixing to carry him on a journey. He was going to find Tina. Wherever she was. Where was he going to go? He didn't know.

When he parked at his house, his phone beeped. *MISSED CALL*. It was from a payphone in Ste. Genevieve, Missouri. How cruel, thought Rosswell, to get a call from the town where their special place was. Tina and Rosswell had spent a weekend in the old French town at the Southern Hotel. His phone beeped again. *VOICEMAIL*. He clicked on it.

Tina spoke to him.

"Rosswell, come get me. I'm—"

The message stopped.

Rosswell didn't take time to pack.

The End